Emily Gould is a writer and publisher and the co-founder of Emily Books. She also runs a blog at emilymagazine.com. With Zareen Jaffery, she co-wrote a YA novel, *Hex Education*. She is the author of an acclaimed collection of essays, *And the Heart Says Whatever*, and *Friendship* is her debut adult novel.

'An irreverent, witty and sometimes uncomfortably familiar tale of two female friends living in New York City. We can't get enough' *Vogue*

'A great summer read ... An interesting novel for anyone who is staring down the barrel of the "turning 30" gun' *Grazia*

'Beneath Gould's breezy aperçus on millennials and social media there lurks a sharp study of female friendship' *Observer*

'Gould describes with acerbic clarity the difficulty of finding your way through unfulfilling work, rising rents and underwhelming sex' *Independent*

'Amy and Bev's conversations have a real ring of unsanitised truth (this is how you talk to your best friend), but it's the varying thoughts on growing older that really chime' *Emerald Street* (Stylist online)

'Gould recreates with wit and insight the New York I know: a place full of fame and money that's not yours, where friends become family, and life's big questions stay unanswered for a long time' Chad Harbach, author of *The Art of Fielding*

'[A] sharply observed first novel ... it points to Ms. Gould's abilities as a keen-eyed noticer and her knack for nailing down her ravenous observations with energy and flair' *New York Times*

'Life is messy and life in New York is messy and expensive. Ms. Gould writes about maturity and money, among many other things, in a thoughtful and hilarious way' *Wall Street Journal*

'*Friendship* has that same magical universality-in-specificity that makes us care about the local politics of *Middlemarch* or Clarissa Dalloway's floral arrangements. In tiny brushstrokes, Gould captures the small weirdnesses of being alive, of sitting in an interview and being suddenly and unaccountably struck with a desire to bite through the rim of a teacup. It's enough to make your heart sing' *NPR*

'A wry, sharply observed coming-of-age story for the post-recession era' *People*

'Razor-sharp humour and observations about life ... Perfect summer reading' *Kirkus Review*

'Gould's novel is admirably, readably realistic – she knows these girls and the world they live in (including the omnipresence of technology and the way that it pervades relationships) ... Gould nails the complex blend of love, loyalty, and resentment that binds female friends. It is worth reading for the richness of its details ... and it offers new insight into the experience of young women' *Publishers Weekly*

'A savvy first novel that, in piercing prose, zeroes in on modern ennui and the catalysts that force even the most apathetic out of their complacency' *Booklist*

'Truth-teller Emily Gould hurls her heart and mind into this hilarious, bittersweet tale' Jami Attenberg, author of *The Middlesteins*

'*Friendship*'s characters are brave, smart, wounded, stupid, petty and wise, like most of the people I know and love' Sam Lipsyte, author of *The Ask*

'A moving, focused, highly readable, very funny novel. Intimate and insightful' Tao Lin, author of *Taipei*

FRIENDSHIP

Emily Gould

virago

VIRAGO

First published in Great Britain in 2014 by Virago Press
This paperback edition published in 2015 by Virago Press

1 3 5 7 9 10 8 6 4 2

All characters and events in this publication, other than those clearly in the public domain, are fictitious and any resemblance to real persons, living or dead, is purely coincidental.

A CIP catalogue record for this book is available from the British Library.

ISBN 978-0-349-00441-9

Typeset in Caslon by M Rules
Printed and bound in Great Britain by
Clays Ltd, St Ives plc

Papers used by Virago are from well-managed forests and other responsible sources.

Virago Press
An imprint of
Little, Brown Book Group
Carmelite House
50 Victoria Embankment
London EC4Y 0DZ

An Hachette UK Company
www.hachette.co.uk

www.virago.co.uk

To R.C.

I knew, sitting there, that I might be a real nihilist, that it wasn't always just a hip pose. That I drifted and quit because nothing meant anything, no one choice was really better. That I was, in a way, too free, or that this kind of freedom wasn't actually real – I was free to choose '*whatever*' because it didn't really matter. But that this, too, was because of something I chose – I had somehow chosen to have nothing matter . . . The point was that, through making this choice, I didn't matter, either. I didn't stand for anything. If I wanted to matter – even just to myself – I would have to be less free, by deciding to choose in some kind of definite way. Even if it was nothing more than an act of will.

— DAVID FOSTER WALLACE, *The Pale King*

Can I handle the seasons of my life?

— STEVIE NICKS, 'Landslide'

1

The temp agency's application was only four pages long, but somehow Bev hadn't managed to fill it out. She'd told herself that she would do it on the subway on the morning of the interview, but then the train was so crowded that it was impossible even to reach into her bag to get the form. Also, J. R. Pinkman was in her subway car, waving to her from his own packed corner. She smiled – it was nice to see someone she knew, in this context, to be reminded of who she was underneath her costume. 'Dress corporately,' the woman at the temp agency had told her in an email, and now she was riding the B train at 8:30 a.m. in a taupe trench coat over a jacket and skirt that were slightly different shades of black. But while it was good to catch a glimpse of a familiar face, she didn't want to actually *talk* to J.R. She wanted to grab a seat when the train let half its passengers off at Grand Street and then use the remaining ten minutes of the commute to fill out her form. She waved back at him, but dropped her gaze and dipped her head down, conveying preoccupied busyness and giving him tacit permission to do the same.

The train stopped at Grand Street, and J.R. bumped and pushed down the length of car between himself and Bev. They'd worked together at Warwicke Smythe, a literary agency, and Bev had even maybe had a slight crush on him when she'd first met him. But in this morning subway light no one looked too great. J.R. was also carrying several dingy tote bags, presumably containing several different shitty manuscripts, in addition to the one in his hand.

'Where are you headed?' he asked, gesturing at Bev's outfit.

'I'm temping,' she said. It felt good to admit it and then, in the silence that followed, less good to have done so.

'I thought you were in grad school!'

'I was, for a year.' She smile-winced. 'It, uh, it just started seeming like this huge waste of money. But now I have to start paying back the huge amount of money I already wasted.' She pointed at the manuscript he was holding, desperate to redirect the conversation and to remind him (and herself) that she'd left the literary agency for a good reason. 'Reading anything good?'

J.R. shook the sheaf of printed-out pages in his hand. 'Ha, are you kidding? It's just more of Warwicke's memoirs.' J.R. was one of a team of assistants employed mostly to type up and copyedit their ancient boss's never-to-be-published memoirs, and also to roll him to the restroom every half hour or so. 'You must be so thrilled that you don't have to think about any of this bullshit anymore.'

'Ha, yeah. Thrilled. Unemployment is thrilling.'

The train shuddered to a halt at Broadway-Lafayette. 'Well, tell everyone I say hi!' Bev said as J.R. gathered his tote bags and prepared to disembark.

'I will. I'll make an announcement about it in the morning meeting,' he shouted over the mechanized command to stand clear of the closing doors.

'Don't tell them I'm temping!' she called after him as he left the train, but he didn't turn around and Bev wasn't sure whether he'd heard her.

She climbed up out of the subway into Bryant Park five minutes before the interview was supposed to start and looked around for a spot where she could huddle and fill out the application. The first raindrops of a sudden storm were falling just as she got aboveground, and her taupe trench coat immediately developed ugly dark blotches. She was going to have to buy one of those street vendor umbrellas. They cost only five dollars, but they were pretty much worthless, so it always seemed like a shame, and five dollars represented a depressingly large percentage of Bev's current net worth. Ducking under an overhang by the library steps, she checked the ledge at her elbow for pigeon poop before putting the form down on it. The standard stuff – references, employment history – she completed quickly, then found herself unexpectedly stymied, with only a minute left, by a question on the last page.

'What are your grandest aspirations?'

There were spaces for three grand aspirations, each space about half a line long. Not even long enough for a full sentence. Bev glanced at her watch, then spent an infinite frozen moment watching a pair of finches hopping around in the grass, yelling their little heads off over a scrap of chain-café cookie. The last time she'd confronted this stupid question had probably been in high school, or in church as a teenager. She imagined teen Bev filling in the blanks with zero hesitation: *1. Serve God. 2. Marry a good Christian. 3. Raise children in the ways of the Lord.* Had she believed these were her true goals, even then? By freshman year of college, the grand aspirations would already have shifted to *1. Read every book. 2. Live as far away from the Midwest as possible. 3. Never turn down an opportunity to get shitfaced.*

But what were her grandest aspirations now, and more important, what could she pretend they were so that the last page of this godforsaken form wouldn't be empty? She peeked at her cracked old iPhone to make sure her watch was correct, saw the time, and then hurriedly began to write. The truth, as usual, came to her more easily than fiction.

'1. Achieve financial stability' was real, if obvious.

'2. Find community' was vague, but who cared, and

'3. Feel like I'm playing an important role in life' was maybe too weird, but it was the first thing that popped into her head, and better than a blank line.

Ten minutes later she was sitting across a small table from a sweet-faced woman in a miniature windowless room with blank walls. It looked like an interrogation room. Bev resisted the temptation to make a joke about requesting that her lawyer be present. The application was on the table between them, and the woman flipped through it. She nodded, nodded, nodded, then wrinkled her forehead.

'There's a little gap in employment here, Beverly. Can I ask why?'

'Oh, yes, sorry. I didn't know how to indicate what happened there.'

The interviewer made a little mm-hmm noise, tilted her chin up, and widened her eyes, as though she were generously trying to keep an open mind.

'When I left the publishing house, it was because I moved to Madison to be with my boyfriend, who was going to law school there. I lived there for a year, and I had a service job, working in a wine bar. I didn't think it was worth mentioning, and I don't have the information for the manager or anything.'

'But then you moved back here and worked at the literary agency?'

'Yes, three years ago.'

'And then you quit working at the agency to go to graduate school.'

'I started a master's program. I decided that particular program wasn't for me, and I might, uh, apply to other programs. At some point.'

The woman grimaced, so quickly Bev almost didn't notice. She was wearing a mall-jewelry necklace made of oversize knobs of fake silver and gold, in which Bev could see a distorted reflection of her own face. 'So is your boyfriend all done with law school now?'

'I assume so. We broke up, and I moved back to New York. I mean, I obviously wish I'd never quit my job and moved to be with him, but what can you do?'

'I'm really sorry, I didn't mean to bring up a touchy subject.

And of course that's not germane to the interview. I think we should probably say you took a year off to travel – how's that?'

'Sure.'

'And you're a writer?'

'Yup!'

'That's so cool! So what kind of stuff do you write?'

Temp agency applications. 'Oh, everything. I mean, all kinds of stuff. I'm working on some stories right now that are sort of . . . memoiristic?'

'I think that's so interesting! Where would I have seen your work? I love memoirs! Right now my book club is reading *Eat, Pray, Love.* I love the author. She's so . . . *gutsy*, you know? Just leaving her whole life behind and traveling alone for a year.'

'Yes, she was very gutsy.'

'What you did was sort of like that!'

'Sort of!' Bev felt an involuntary tightness in the back of her throat, as though she might start crying. She willed it away with a brisk shake of her head that she hoped was subtle. 'So what kinds of placements, I mean, with my qualifications . . . what are you thinking? My friend who referred me to your agency said that potentially you could find me an admin assistant placement . . . I have lots of experience being someone's assistant, as you can see . . . '

The interviewer's eyes skimmed over the résumé again and then, unsubtly, over Bev, taking in the scuffed pumps, the mismatched blacks, the spill of corn silk-colored hair that Bev had hurriedly tried to corral with a chip clip because she couldn't find a hair elastic. Bev had a natural, farmgirlish loveliness, but she had never been able to pull off what fashion magazines called a 'polished' look, maybe because that look required either preternatural self-grooming talents or having been born rich.

'Well, a lot of those positions are in finance and law, and with your ... qualifications it seems like you'd be better suited to publishing. I don't have anything in publishing available at the moment, but we could wait a few weeks and see if anything came up?'

'Oh. Okay. Well, um, do you have anything that isn't admin? I would be happy to do other kinds of projects. The thing is, I'd just like to get started as soon as possible.'

The interviewer flipped cursorily through her binder, but then something caught her by surprise and she stopped. 'Oh! Wait. There is this. Commercial real estate company. They're putting together sales report packets and need help collating the reports for distribution to their shareholders; they don't want to outsource it to a document prep service because the material is confidential. What do you think? You'd also be filling in for a receptionist, but the work is mostly collating and binding. Maybe some light phones. Your own desk and everything.'

'That sounds perfect!' Bev said. All words spoken in this room were so disassociated from meaning, she thought, then reminded herself not to be a snob. This temp job wasn't an option she could take or leave. It was the difference between eating and not.

'Great! You could start tomorrow, actually, if you liked. Oh, and it's ten fifty an hour. So I'll just get you a packet with your contract and some stubs for your hours, and we'll be in business!'

'Wonderful!' said Bev. Ten fifty – minus the taxes they'd

withhold, minus the hour-long lunch that would be deducted even if she spent it at her desk. If she could somehow work at this temp placement for the next twenty years and not spend any money on food or rent, she would be able to pay back her student loans by the time she was seventy-five.

2

Initially, Amy's job at Yidster had been proposed as a three-month gig. She would sweep in, the plan went, and 'reimagine' their blog, then move onward and upward to some more compelling opportunity. This was right after she'd had her one great job, the job that had made her, momentarily, famous, or at least notorious; now that she was neither, it mattered less which one it had been.

Three years in, she still half imagined her no-longer-new job as temporary: she had no desk ornaments, had resisted even the temptation to claim a dedicated coffee mug. But on some level she realized that she wasn't going anywhere, not in this economy. She sometimes looked for other jobs, halfheartedly. Partly she was insulted that other jobs hadn't sought her out. But there was also something comfortable and comforting about Yidster; its cheery, clean office with big windows overlooking the Manhattan Bridge made her feel, each morning, that something might be accomplished there. It didn't matter, in those morning moments, exactly what that something might be. Yidster's DUMBO location was perfect, too. Of course the third-most-popular online destination for cultural coverage with a modern Jewish angle was located not quite in Manhattan, but *almost*.

Yidster provided health coverage, a decent salary, and free coffee, in addition to the perk – well, it was sort of a perk – of frequent lunch meetings at nice restaurants with their founder-benefactors, Jonathan and Shoshanna Geltfarb. The brother and sister team were heirs to a hosiery fortune (faded lettering on the side of a Hester Street tenement still proclaimed 'A lady who knows / wears Geltfarb hose') that had been compounded many times over by the savvy non-hosiery investments of Jonathan and Shoshanna's father, Mr. Geltfarb. Now, though, the Geltfarb gelt was being steadily depleted by Yidster, but Amy wasn't too worried about that. Or maybe that was the chief source of her worry – that the Geltfarbs would *never* run out of money and she would be stuck at Yidster forever.

The founders had many evolving and contradictory ideas about the website's mission. They would meet with the Yidster editorial staff – which consisted entirely of Amy, two other staff bloggers named Lizzie and Jackie, and their managing editor, a combative Israeli expat named Avi – at Vinegar Hill House or the River Café and discuss ideas over very expensive food. Then the staff would go back to the office and tentatively begin to implement the ideas, stalling on the important stuff as they waited for the inevitable email from Jonathan and Shoshanna saying they'd changed their minds, that more concepting was necessary, more reimagining, more going back to the drawing board.

All the strategizing and pivoting meant that Amy sat down at her desk every day and did, basically, nothing. She responded to several dozen all-caps urgent emails about MAKE HEDS MORE SEO and TEASE JUMPS HARDER and various other meaninglessnesses from Avi, who sat five feet to her left when he wasn't taking one of a million daily smoke breaks, and she assigned Lizzie and Jackie to write a series of filler blog posts about the issues of the day, 'with a modern Jewish angle.' This meant skimming her RSS feeds and picking a few posts from other blogs for Lizzie and Jackie to, er, reimagine. Then the rest of the day was hers to waste.

This day, she'd unlocked the Yidster office door at 9:30, about an hour before anyone else typically rolled in. She'd nearly sprinted past the security desk, as usual, rushing toward the moment when she'd log in to the Yidster CMS with a sense of great urgency – not because she was eager to get to work, but because she was eager to get through her fifteen minutes of work and then get on with her life. Who knew where the day would take her? Maybe a caffeinated morning of recreational rage spent in comments sections, vicariously enjoying controversies about music and art and politics and feminism, putting in her two cents on Twitter where appropriate, then checking back to see whether anyone had responded to her responses. Then lunch, then an afternoon of online window-shopping and Wikipedia rabbit holes and listening to productivity-enhancing playlists on her headphones and Gchatting with Bev. In theory, this was the time she had for her supposed *real* work – the time for her to open one of the files with names like bookproposal8.docx and specpilotREAL.pdf that littered her desktop like so many five-inch knitting projects. But there was something about the office – something in the air, maybe (wi-fi, for one thing). By 6:30 she would feel sleepy and dazed as she stood up to leave – worn-out, as though she'd been working hard.

But not today, she realized as soon as the office door swung open. There, at the conference table to the right of the foosball table, were Jonathan and Shoshanna and Avi, peering intently into a laptop. Getting closer, she saw that the screen was open to StatCounter. Jonathan and Shoshanna looked very grave. They were dressed impeccably, as usual, and Shoshanna smelled amazing – her glossy ringlets and creamy skin radiating something somehow simultaneously ripe and chilled, like an expensive melon on display at a gourmet grocery store. Shoshanna waved her hand, and Amy went and sat down next to them.

'We've been brainstorming about what to do about these stats,' Avi said eventually, as Jonathan and Shoshanna continued to frown at the screen.

'Oh. Of course, the stats.' Amy wondered when she'd last logged in to StatCounter (several months prior), and whether they could tell at a glance that this was the case. Probably not; she suspected that the idea of 'stats' had just been explained to Jonathan and Shoshanna, maybe by a segment on the *Today* show or by some nail-salon magazine.

'We were thinking, what do people love on the Internet – like, what are our most popular posts? And we realized – duh! Video!' Shoshanna's beauty disappeared the minute she opened her mouth; all that glowing skin and shimmering hair couldn't compensate for the kind of voice you immediately associate with someone calling from the temple sisterhood to remind you it's your turn to plate the *oneg* after Shabbat service.

'We, um, we've never posted original videos, though,' Amy said. 'The popular video posts are all just embedded YouTube videos of, like, Amy Winehouse.'

'Let's not get bogged down in technicalities, Amy,' said Jonathan. He was often opposed to 'technicalities.'

'We think we should start shooting video, like, today! And editing it and posting it. Today. Little video segments about pop culture, or maybe comedy. You know, a comic take on the issues of the day.'

Amy had skimmed the front page of the *Times* during her commute. 'Like … a little video of me talking about the latest Hezbollah bombing?'

Jonathan scowled. 'Nothing about Israel, Amy, you know that. Dad would freak.'

Avi fumbled in his pocket, pulled out a Marlboro Red, and shoved it behind his ear, maybe unaware that he already had a cigarette shoved behind his other ear. He drummed his fingers on the table. 'Have you two thought about a budget for these videos?' he asked. 'We can figure out what we need to do, but no one on staff is an expert video editor. And I don't know about Amy as an on-screen presence. No offense, Amy.'

'None taken.' *Douchebag.*

'No, Amy is *perfect*,' said Shoshanna. 'She's got that realness. She's authentic. I don't want someone super media trained. We can just go in the conference room and do one right now. What do we need, a camera? Just, like, send an intern to B&H and get a camera. Or you can even just use a phone, right?'

'I don't . . . uh. What am I going to talk about?' Amy asked.

Jonathan and Shoshanna glanced at each other. Clearly they hadn't considered this. When Jonathan responded, he spoke slowly, as if he were deciding what to say as he said each word (which he was). 'How about . . . we pick a topic . . . and you can just kind of ad-lib about it . . . and then we'll edit it to be really funny and cool. We'll call it . . . the Daily Yid Vid!'

'Yideo!' shrieked Shoshanna.

'Vyideo,' murmured Amy.

'The Daily Vyid.' Jonathan's pronouncements had an air of finality; it was a talent that probably came with always having been rich enough that no one ever disagreed with you.

'Okay, done! Settled! We will absolutely get right on that!' announced Avi, twitching and scrabbling behind his ear. 'I'll walk you guys downstairs and we can hash out the rest of the details.' He stared meaningfully at Amy. 'Amy, you'll get busy working out logistics. Drop everything and focus on this.'

'What about Morning Yidbits? What about, um, the rest of the site?'

'We'll get around to it,' he said, almost running toward the door, Jonathan and Shoshanna following close behind him. As soon as they were out of earshot, Amy said '*Ughhh*' and stomped over to her desk.

She had finally sucked her way to the icky cordial at the

center of her candy-sweet job. Writing the occasional bylined post was one thing – there was enough of her on the Internet already that a few YidRants weren't going to affect her future in serious journalism if she ever got her act together and decided to have one. But was she really now going to humiliate herself in a way that might go viral, leaving her stupid facial expressions gif'd and reblogged across the Internet for days?

It could never be as bad as her last job, she thought, then hurried to tap her knuckles superstitiously against the wooden frame of the foosball table behind her. Still, why couldn't Lizzie or Jackie do it instead, or even twitchy Avi? Being pretty, or whatever Amy was from the right angle, had always struck her as overrated: an invitation to a lame party you never wanted to go to in the first place but somehow didn't quite want to leave once you got there.

Alone in the empty office, she wandered over to the window. Midmorning haze obscured the details of the skyline and the bridge. It was so overcast that she could see her reflection in the window, and experimentally, she began to speak, holding her own gaze as she did so, as though the window were a camera lens.

'Hello, this is Amy Schein,' she said slowly, admiring the way her lips parted to reveal her orthodontured teeth. The front two were bigger in a way that had always struck her as sexy. Her mouth was her best feature; for years she'd had a little photo of her own lips as her AIM avatar. Higher up, though, were some problem areas: her nose, slightly too long and broad, and her eyebrows, straight across, like one stroke of a paintbrush, no matter how expensively she had them groomed. Worse, though, was the way they *moved.* 'And you're watching Jew Vids,' she said to the imaginary camera. 'I mean, Yid Vids. Vyideos.' The brows waggled upward uncontrollably, and her eyes darted from side to side even as she willed them to focus on one spot. Her eyes were another problem area, giant and deep set in their sockets in a way that precluded the wearing of any eye makeup; even the merest mascara smear made her look ten years older at best, domestically abused at worst. She turned away from the window, disgusted, then snuck a last look back as the office door opened to admit little frizzle-haired Jackie, who gave her a were-you-just-talking-to-yourself look before she slipped on her headphones and began her own day of faffing around online.

Amy sat down at her desk too, but instead of researching how quickly a camera could be messengered over from B&H (they had no interns; Avi tended to repel interns in ways Amy didn't want to spend too much time thinking about), Amy got out her phone and texted Bev.

'YT?' It was their shorthand for 'you there?' and the answer was nearly always yes. Amy and Bev tended to stay in constant text or Gchat communication through the day; if a 'YT' went unanswered for more than a few minutes, the person on the other end was presumed to be asleep, on the subway, in a movie, or being held captive.

'At temp agency, just finished Excel competence test. have achieved rank of Excel "Int-Expert."'

'Congratulations! Let's pick out medals.'

'Well, it automatically prints out a certificate for you on the dot matrix printer, so depressing.'

Amy looked out past the foosball table and took a deep breath to calm herself, then realized she could still smell Shoshanna's perfume, and she breathed more shallowly again. She wished Bev would hurry up and get a temp job so she could be bored at a desk somewhere else in the city, able to Gchat with Amy all day again the way they'd done when they first met. She missed those days, at the dawn of their friendship, when they'd worked as assistants at the same staid corporate publishing house and chat was still new enough that their bosses thought they were busily typing something related to their jobs. Amy decided to dig through her Gmail and find funny tidbits from conversations they'd had in 2005 and send them to Bev to cheer her up and encourage her. That would be a good activity for the rest of the morning.

Amy left the office at midday and walked to her favorite lunch spot in the neighborhood, a sushi bar whose exterior was so inauspicious almost no one ever joined her at its counter. Though she never took a chance on the plastic-wrapped, distressingly static contents of Sushi Zen's raw fish display case, she was partial to its footbath-size bowls of soba noodles. She put in her order and was happily anticipating the comfort of slurping down all those carbs when her phone vibrated with news of an incoming call. It was her mother.

She hit 'silence' because if she hit 'ignore,' her mother would know she was screening. Then she watched the silent screen light up a second time. On the outside chance that her mother's persistence indicated that something terrible had happened, Amy picked up the phone, already suspecting that she had once more been outmaneuvered.

'Hi, sweetie. Are you busy? Is this a good time?'

Amy inhaled. *No, no, no, no, no, no, no*. 'Sure.'

'Okay. I just wanted to go over the plans for Rosh Hashanah. Did you already make travel arrangements? Because if you didn't, I just wanted you to know that your father and I discussed it, and we'd be willing to pay for half of your train ticket, or all of the nicer bus. I know tickets are expensive, especially when you wait until the last minute to book your trip.'

'Wow, thank you ... that's really generous of you guys,' Amy said, permitting herself to make an exaggerated eye-rolling facial expression as a reward for keeping any hint of sarcasm out of her voice.

'I just wanted you to think about it. I happened to glance at your bank balance recently, and it seems like you might not be able to afford the trip on your own, the way things are going for you.'

Amy's mom had set up Amy's bank account to be linked to hers ten years earlier, and Amy hadn't ever figured out how to unlink it, even though obviously this was a little bit like not being able to figure out how to snip a bedraggled, half-rotten umbilical cord that had somehow snaked its way up I-95 all the way from the D.C. suburbs to New York. But the moments when it occurred to Amy to unlink the accounts never seemed to coincide with moments when it seemed as if it would be okay to give up the hundred-percent overdraft protection that the link offered, probably because the latter kind of moments had never occurred. Her decent salary was no match for her tendency to spend every penny she earned and then some. But in spite of her profligacy, she never seemed to have anything to show for her debt: she lost cashmere sweaters, wore down the heels of designer boots and left them in the closet unrepaired, threw away bank statements unopened, lazily paid the ATM fee rather than walking the extra few blocks to her own bank, and consistently paid only the minimum balance on the credit card she'd used to purchase the lost sweaters and ruined boots. Without any of the fun of having a gambling problem or a drug habit, she'd still managed to find a way to keep herself living paycheck to paycheck. Being reminded of this made her uncomfortable, and feeling uncomfortable made her want to stop on the way home from work at a gourmet grocery store and spend eleven dollars on a two-ounce jar of pine nuts.

'I really couldn't accept help from you guys. You know how I feel about that,' Amy said, smiling as she talked so there would be a smile in her voice, aware that anyone who happened to glance at the resulting rictus would think she was insane.

'You didn't always feel that way! But okay, if that's how you feel now. Just please know that it's not a big deal for us. We'd like to help.'

Then why did you offer to pay for only part of *the ticket?* 'What would happen if you were authentically yourself with your mother?' the therapist Amy couldn't really afford had once asked her. Amy had been tempted to tell her therapist that she couldn't risk being any more 'authentically herself' than she already was in any context of her life, but she hadn't felt like going down that road, so she'd just said 'I don't know' and stopped seeing the therapist soon afterward, mostly because she'd bounced a check to her and didn't want to spend another two hundred dollars in order to have a protracted therapeutic conversation about why she'd bounced a check.

'And I'm grateful, but it's not necessary, because . . . and I'm sorry, I was going to call today to tell you I just really can't get away from work. I don't have any more vacation days left this year, and I'd be taking unpaid leave. I can't afford to do that right now. Well, as you can see! I'm sorry. I should have planned it better, but all those weddings this summer . . .'

Silence on the line. Amy's noodles arrived. The waitress beamed proudly as she set the bowl down in front of Amy and handed her chopsticks, miming a sweet, protective 'eat it fast before it gets cold' gesture in a way that someone, probably not Amy, might have described as 'maternal.'

'Amy, this is very disappointing.'

Amy forced herself to finish her mouthful before responding. 'You know, I'm also disappointed! But this is what I have to do. I hope you can understand.'

'Of course *I* understand, but you know how hard it is to explain this kind of thing to your grandmother. I hope you'll give her a call and tell her you'll miss seeing her. And don't mention that your work won't give you the time off – I don't think she'll understand why a supposedly Jewish workplace wouldn't let you miss work on a Jewish holiday.'

'Is it really so hard to understand?' Amy said, finally – inevitably – losing her patience. 'If I ran a business, I also wouldn't give my employees endless unpaid time off! I was out basically all of June, depleting the last of the ozone layer by flying to the stupidly lavish celebrations that my least ambitious friends arranged to try to convince themselves and their families that their lives have meaning! That's not *my fault.* I don't have *any control* over that!'

'I'm sure you have more control than you think,' said Amy's mother, using the tone of voice she probably took with difficult teenagers in her social work practice.

The noodles were cold when Amy finally managed to end the call. When the waitress came to take away the half-eaten bowl a few minutes later, she gave Amy a look of disappointment.

Amy paid her bill, overtipping as usual, then gathered her things and started walking back to the office. On the way, she passed the homeless man who begged all day outside Peas and Pickles, the twenty-four-hour Korean greengrocer with gourmet pretensions that had sprung up to cater to the employees of businesses like Yidster. She passed him several times a day and never made eye contact; he was the pushy and unpredictable type of panhandler who'd take any attention as an excuse to follow someone partway down the block, repeating his request in a singsong voice while all the pedestrians who'd eluded him tried not to stare at the person who'd been singled out. Just saying 'Sorry, I can't' was sometimes enough to provoke him, so Amy didn't. But for whatever reason he chose her anyway, walking alongside her as she pretended to ignore him.

'Girl, I know you got money. Help me get something to eat,' he said, shaking a stained coffee cup in her direction. In situations like this, Amy had seen her mom stop and have a twenty-minute conversation, inquiring about shelters and halfway houses, asking the right questions, the ones that revealed the heartbreaking truth underneath someone's practiced sob story. Amy did not have twenty minutes, or one minute, or even one more second. She wanted to check her email, badly. She reached for her phone but then stopped herself, not wanting to look like or to be a horrible person.

Halfway down the block the man seemed to hit some sort of invisible barrier that tethered him to the territory around Peas and Pickles, and he turned back. Amy picked up her pace but was still within earshot as he shouted to his next target, who'd apparently ponied up: 'Oh, thank you, ma'am, God bless you, you're so generous, not like some stuck-up bitches who think they're the only person in the world.'

3

The most disgusting of all the many disgusting things associated with fertility and conception, Sally reflected, was how totally vile all the euphemisms were. It had been bad enough when she was in the beginning stages of telling people that she and Jason were 'trying.' What could be more antithetical to the effortless dissolution of self that sex had always promised than 'trying'? The word inevitably called up images of grunting, effortful slog-fucks, like the scene in *Election* when Ferris Bueller has to imagine his sexy pupil goading him on in order to ejaculate inside of his pathetic wife. Their 'trying' wasn't like that, though it was true that it sometimes took more coaxing to get Jason's dick hard than it used to. But that was to be expected. Sally's private parts also felt a little psyched out by this point. After decades of having joyously consequenceless sex – well, it had been mostly joyous, and never, ultimately, consequential – she couldn't ever quite shake the creepy awareness that this perfunctory three-minute ritual before sleep or that unexpectedly rough and exciting surprise in the shower might be the moment that would change her life forever. Or might not. It was just weird. Everything *meant* something now. What had once been stains on the sheets were now transformed into zillions of little part-babies. How had she never noticed before how bizarre that was? All that jizz over the years. Gallons of it. She felt like a mass murderer. A cannibal.

Anyway, 'trying.' But trying was only the tip of the iceberg.

She leafed through the magazines on the glass-topped cube next to the fancy UES gyno's waiting room couch. They weren't bad – *Surface*, *V*, *W*, *Town & Country* (which still existed, oddly. But rich people would always want to read about other rich people's horses, she supposed). And then there it was, on the bottom of the pile, the inevitable issue of *Plum*, the magazine for mature mothers. '*Plum*, something highly prized,' was the cover line. It was a reminder of how many women were in her exact same leaky boat – enough women to sustain a magazine, even in the post-print era – which wasn't exactly reassuring. *Plum* always had a celebrity mom on the cover, typically the star of a TV show Sally had never seen. This month's mom looked way old, though very botoxed – a redhead, they never aged well. Her toddler twins had red hair, too. If they'd been conceived with donor eggs, the donor had been well chosen. God, she'd probably *auditioned*.

Plum had plenty of ads to keep it thick, a sign of stubborn health, increasingly rare in the print magazine world. Sally's husband was a magazine person, so she was sensitized to this stuff. They still had friends who worked at these places, or what was left of them, producing *con*tent for their websites and tablet apps. She'd been jealous of them once, but now she wasn't, really. She had left that world of competitive consumption and networking and status jockeying behind when she moved upstate.

'Sally Katzen?'

'Yes!' she almost shouted, as if this were the counter of Veniero's bakery and they'd called her number and they'd move on to the next customer if she didn't make her presence known right away. She smiled vaguely in the beckoning nurse's direction and followed her down the hallway to be weighed and blood pressured, then took the little cup into the bathroom and peed in it. Crouching over the bowl, she felt creaky, undignified. Her aim was off, and warm pee trickled over her fingertips. For a moment, rage flickered through her tensed body. How often in the average man's life was he asked to pee into a cup, not counting road trips? Probably fewer times than she'd done it just in the last year.

She barely bothered to glance in the mirror as she screwed the cap onto her pee jar and washed her hands with the smelly antibacterial soap. She'd been told often enough that she looked sad, even when she wasn't. Catcallers had always tended to yell 'Smile!'; there was just something gloomy about the downturn of her mouth and the size of her eyes. And today it was worse because she actually *was* sad. She looked distraught. The doctor would probably offer her tissues.

She left the warm cup on the ledge and followed the nurse

down the hallway to the examination room, where she disrobed quickly, again not really looking in the mirror, not bothering to assess her own nakedness before tying on the plastic-and-paper gown. If today didn't bring good news, Jason would probably try to talk her into some form of pseudo-medical intervention she hadn't tried yet: acupuncture, hydrotherapy, giving up some delicious type of food or beverage. Jason was committed to the idea of having a baby. He talked about the baby all the time, as though the baby existed somewhere already and was just waiting for them to claim it as their rightful property: a prize in a machine, the kind you reach for over and over again with a mechanical claw. Sally wanted a baby too, but more than a boring *baby* she wanted a *child*: she wanted to see the world fresh through a new person's eyes. It was a pretty standard reason for wanting a kid, but who cared: it was her reason. Jason's reasons, though they'd never actually talked about them, were probably slightly different. In those weird conversations about 'the baby,' he slipped sometimes and called the baby 'he.' No matter how much he professed his distance from his parents' culture and values, she still suspected that he wanted a son. It was not PC, but it was kind of cute. Like a king wanting an heir.

Lite FM was blaring over the office PA system, an overproduced song about heartbreak and loss. 'I'll die without you . . . my life means nothing without you,' a woman's voice keened, endowing each word with ten extra syllables to show off her vocal range. For no specific reason, and for every reason, Sally decided at that moment that no matter what the doctor said today, she was done with this place and all the places like it that she'd been to over the last two years. She would smile and nod through one last examination, one last lightning-speed lecture about the state of her insides, and then she would be free forever. She never wanted to see an issue of *Plum* again, even on a newsstand. If having biological children was so important to Jason, he could donate sperm. Sally would meanwhile try to convince him that there were other ways to become parents, or something like parents: adoptive parents, foster parents, some innovative variation on the theme of parenting that she'd invent herself, the way she'd invented everything else about her life. She just didn't care enough about perpetuating her genes to keep putting herself in this pathetic, clichéd situation. She had better things to do, she suspected, and she needed to busy herself figuring out what they were.

4

The placement the temp agency had found for Bev was in the East Sixties. She sat at the reception desk and stared at the phone, willing it not to ring, and for the most part it obeyed her. Once in a while, though, it rebelled.

Bev had been trained hurriedly in how to operate the multiline phone's giant keypad, and even though the woman who'd explained it to her had made it seem easy to put people on hold and then redirect their calls, it somehow wasn't proving easy at all. 'You just hung up on me,' said a grown-up frat boy in a tone of bored irritation, and Bev apologized sincerely. She *was* sorry. Boy, was she ever sorry. She was filled to the brim with regret, and even though this regret wasn't specific to the dropped call, it was kind of nice to be able to tell someone how very sorry she felt.

After the morning flurry of phone calls died down, it was time for Bev to start collating, which meant standing in the break room and spiral-binding packets of information about different buildings that were for sale. This was pleasant, repetitive work, and once she got the hang of it, Bev began to almost enjoy it. Certainly she was enjoying being away from the phone, with its aura of menace.

The only bad thing about standing in the break room was that other people came into the room too, and some of them seemed to feel it necessary to acknowledge her in some way. 'How's it going?' they asked as they reached into the fridge for bottled water, Diet Snapple, and string cheese (all of which Bev was in charge of restocking when they ran low, a duty that had been explained to her with grave seriousness during her first hour in the office). After experimenting with a too-blasé 'It's going' and a very slightly sarcastic 'Awesome!' Bev had mostly settled on a cheery, noncommittal 'So far, so good.'

'How's it going?' asked a swarthy, shortish guy in a pink shirt. Bev dimly remembered having been introduced to him during the perfunctory tour around the office she'd been given first thing that morning. Though she couldn't say for sure, she thought maybe it was the guy to whom she had apologized earlier for dropping his call. She decided to think of him as 'Steve.'

'So far, so good!' Bev said.

Steve lingered in the break room, and Bev realized he was filling a paper cup from the hot water dispenser. Was he actually going to stand there, a foot behind her turned back, while his tea steeped? He was, of course.

'So, have you been temping long?'

Temp here often? 'No. Actually this is my first time temping in a while. I mean, since right after I graduated from college.'

'So you just graduated?' Steve was stirring his tea, only half listening.

In spite of herself, Bev was flattered, and she should have just said yes and let the conversation end there – except it wouldn't have, probably; it would have continued on into the realms of 'from where' and 'with a degree in what,' and Bev would have had to make up all kinds of lies on the spot, which she was terrible at doing. So she told the truth. 'No. I'm just doing this for the moment.'

'What do you really do?'

'Oh, all kinds of stuff.' The silence expanded and became awkward, and Bev suddenly sensed that Steve was imagining something illicit, so she hastened to say, 'I was in grad school for writing. I want to be a writer. I mean I am one, I guess.'

'That's so great! I mean, I just push numbers around all day.'

'Well, there's a lot to be said for that!'

'I guess. It's boring as hell,' said Steve. 'So, what's the ultimate goal?'

'What?'

'Your ultimate goal. What is it?'

Bev turned the crank of the binding machine. She'd made it at least a decade without being asked this question, and now twice in one week? Existential angst was far, far above her pay grade. The binding machine crunched through a sheaf of papers with a satisfying loud noise. Her *ultimate goal. You're looking at it!* she was tempted to say.

'Um, I dunno. Write a book, I guess.'

'Whoa, you're writing a book? That's awesome!'

'Ha-ha, nooo, I didn't say that. God, these days I can barely *read* a book. Much less write one.' This wasn't strictly true – Bev was always reading at least three books at any given time – but it was something to say.

'*Dude*, I'm relieved to hear you say that. I keep trying to read this book Bill – you know, Bill, the CEO? – recommended to us. *Outliners* or something? And I just cannot fucking concentrate on it for the life of me. Excuse my French. It's like, at the end of the day, how are you supposed to sit down and read a *book*?' Steve looked overjoyed as he said all this, and Bev realized that this conversation was probably the highlight of his day, then realized it was almost certainly the highlight of hers. She felt embarrassed for both of them.

'Maybe it's the book, not you,' she said.

'You're probably right. But, sorry, we were talking about the book you're going to write.'

'Ha, no, that's boring. Hey, so – what's *your* ultimate goal?'

'Ha-ha. Uh, that's kind of personal,' Steve said. He twiddled the stirrer stick in his Styrofoam teacup. 'Damn, you know? I should get back to my desk. Speaking of goals. See you later, Beth.'

He left the break room. Bev slid a spiral clip onto the back of the machine and slipped the stack of papers into its grip, then crunched it closed again. She had a momentary flash of wanting to smash something made of flesh, her own hand or someone else's. Crunching the papers satisfied the urge, almost. The edges of the packet were a little bit ragged, and she spent some time smoothing them until they were perfect.

Toward the end of the day Steve came over and stood by her desk. There was a bowl of gum and candy there that Bev had been told to continually replenish. Steve was pretending to be sifting through it, but really he was waiting for her to acknowledge his presence. She kept her eyes trained on the screen, as though there were something important to see there, for as long as she plausibly could, but eventually she looked up.

'Are we out of your favorite flavor? I can order some more.'

'Could you? That'd be great. Bubblemint. Thanks, Beth.'

'It's Bev.'

'Oh, fuck me. I mean, heh! Oh man. Please don't sue.'

Bev bit her inner cheek to quash her automatic impulse to simultaneously gratify and tacitly excuse him by laughing. 'No worries. Anything else I can help you with right now?'

Steve furrowed his brow. 'I think we got off on the wrong foot. Let me make it up to you.' With a practiced gesture, he held out his hand to her; a business card protruded from between his pointer and middle fingers, and because there was no other possible course of action, Bev reached out her hand. She snatched the card quickly so that no one would witness the handoff.

Steve smiled. 'Okay then. See ya. Bev.'

'See ya,' she said, already turning back to her screen. Then the phone rang, and she answered and transferred the call with a practiced gesture, feeling the tiny thrill of having learned a tiny skill. She didn't do anything with the card until she could see via her peripheral vision that no one was anywhere near her desk, and then she took out her phone and entered the numbers into it, saving the contact as 'Steve' because she'd never remember, otherwise, whose number it was. (Steve's actual name was Matt, but who cared.) She ran a ragged fingernail over the embossed words 'Executive Vice President' before crumpling the heavy little square of paper and slipping it into the trash can under her desk next to a pair of someone else's comfortable slip-on flats.

5

Standing on the sidewalk outside and looking up at the brownstone where she lived still gave Amy a frisson of pleasure, even though it didn't belong to her and none of the little details that made it so nice – the window boxes, the clean-swept stoop – were any of her doing.

She'd never understood what some people found appealing about the boxy concrete high-rises going up all over Brooklyn, with their office-parkish floor-to-ceiling windows and their sad, skinny balconies just big enough to balance a bike. This building had history and character and old, wide floorboards. It also had mice and bad plumbing and was pervaded constantly by the smell of her landlord's Black and Milds, but those things were a small price to pay for charm. The light that poured in through its thick windows was honeyed and fiery at sunset; her block had been planned at a time when builders still paid attention to such details as the angle of sunlight. No glassy high-rises cut off this flow of light – yet. Eventually they would, but Amy would probably have to move out before then. The rent had increased by almost half during her tenancy because the boxy buildings were making her once-liminal neighborhood newly desirable, and now the rent was cripplingly, insanely high, almost twice what someone with Amy's salary could realistically afford. Other people might have let this bare fact penetrate their minds and affect their decisions, but Amy had so far refused to allow it to do so.

'Hello?' she called as she opened the door to her apartment, in case Sam had spent the day there. But there was no answer, and Amy felt a pang of mild disappointment. It was nice to come home to Sam; on the days he didn't have to teach at the art college, he usually spent the whole day sketching at her kitchen table. It seemed like a waste of the rent on his studio, but Amy wasn't in a position to criticize. She looked forward to seeing his day's doodles; she liked to imagine the paintings they would become.

Sam's thing was painting ordinary objects in unstinting detail. He wasn't a star, but he had fans and a gallery and seemed to be gaining traction in the fluctuating, irrational art market. An eighteen-foot rendering of Amy's KitchenAid stand mixer had sold at auction last year for the price of a small luxury car; he'd given most of the money to his parents, who'd emigrated from Moscow when he was seven and gone from being professors to operating a small, bad restaurant in Sheepshead Bay. Some people might have taken a small part of that check and used it to buy new shoes, but Sam didn't see any problem with his old ones. Maybe when they got a hole, he said, then he'd consider it, but they'd served him so well for four years that replacing them seemed disloyal, insulting. Amy had rolled her eyes and dropped the subject. She could stand to be a bit more like Sam, of course. She hoped they might eventually find a happy medium, mutually rubbing off on each other.

He'd left a note, as usual, on the kitchen table: a deft little sketch of Amy's cat, Waffles, with a cartoon text bubble coming out of his cat mouth. 'Buy me more cat food, Amy!' cartoon Waffles was saying. Real Waffles snaked around Amy's ankles, then made an attempt to climb her left calf. She told him to chill out and went to the cupboard, but Sam was right; she was completely out of cat food.

It was annoying to have to go right back out; she'd already taken off her shoes and everything, was thinking through the steps of the dinner she'd planned and hungry for its results, but Waffles would only get more annoying the longer he had to wait for his dinner. She lay down on the floor for a moment and played with him, stroking his seal-sleek back and letting him climb over her legs. He headbutted her face affectionately, as insistently needy as a dog. Waffles loved or at least depended on Amy, which for cats probably amounted to the same thing. For her part, Amy loved Waffles with a passionate ferocity that she felt a little bit guilty about not being able to feel, most of the time, for humans. It probably helped that he was constantly doing cute shit and couldn't speak.

She slipped her shoes back on and was unlocking the front door, still preoccupied with thoughts of dinner, when she noticed the certified letter lying just inside the door on the welcome mat. Her landlord had slipped it under the front door sometime after she'd arrived home.

This kind of weirdness was par for the course; even though Amy was one of the building's two tenants, her landlord, whom she saw almost daily, pruning his roses or sweeping the same square foot of concrete front yard repeatedly, had a habit of behaving like the distant administrator of a vast and impersonal business enterprise. And maybe the tactic was designed to take the sting out of moments like this one – the letter, addressed to 'all tenants of 99 Emerson Apartment 2,' rather than to Amy, announced another rent increase 'effective immediately.'

'Well, that's just *illegal*,' Amy grumbled aloud. She had no idea whether it actually was. She crumpled the letter and shoved it into the catchall drawer in the kitchen under a layer of plastic utensils and rubber bands, then paused, removed the letter, uncrumpled it, and put it on the kitchen table where Sam would see it. She'd been living in the apartment for five years. She should think about moving out, or at the very least emptily threaten to move out so Mr. Horton would reconsider the increase. She and Sam had been dating for about half of that time. Maybe they should move in together; maybe the letter was a sign.

Amy clomped down the stairs, hoping Mr. Horton was home and would be irritated; then, halfway down, she remembered that she should try to stay on his good side until she was sure she couldn't get out of the rent hike, so she tiptoed down the remaining steps and past the parlor-floor entrance. But she wasn't quiet enough.

'Miss Schein. How are you today,' Mr. Horton said.

'I'm fine, Mr. Horton, but I'm just wondering . . . about the letter?'

'Please respond in writing if you intend to re-sign your lease at the new rent.'

'But I don't think . . . I mean, I'm not sure you're allowed to just raise the rent like that?'

Mr. Horton raised one graying eyebrow. 'Please address any questions you may have to my lawyer.'

'Look, Mr. Horton, I've been here five years – I'm right above you, I'm a good tenant, I'm sure you don't want to have to go looking for another. The only people who are going to be able to afford to live here at that rent are college kids whose parents are paying, or couples.'

'That rent is what the apartment is worth in today's marketplace. Please let me know promptly if you intend to leave.' He smiled without moving any of his facial muscles besides the ones that lifted the corners of his mouth; really it was more of a flinch. 'Have a pleasant evening.'

Amy opened her mouth, but before she could say anything, he'd closed his door.

During the entire trip to get cat food Amy was consumed with blind rage, which abated only somewhat when she realized that the pet food store was right next to the nice wine shop and it would be silly if she didn't take the opportunity to go in and get a bottle of something. The cute label that leaped out at her was on a nineteen-dollar bottle, a little bit more than she usually liked to spend, but it had been a hard day and she deserved a treat. She opened the wine as soon as she got home, and by the time Sam walked in the door, just as Amy was putting the plates of pasta on the table, she'd already had a couple of glasses. Maybe three glasses.

'Hi, baby! What's that green stuff?' Sam unshouldered his

heavy gym bag and pressed his sweaty face to Amy's for a salty kiss. 'Mmm, you taste like booze. I'm just going to hop in the shower.'

'Baby, something terrible happened!'

'Oh, no! What?'

Amy opened her mouth but then realized she didn't know how she wanted to talk to Sam about the rent increase – whether she was launching a campaign to move in together, or asking for advice about how to manipulate Mr. Horton, or just looking for sympathy. 'Oh, just some stuff. Nothing really *terrible* terrible. I'll tell you when you're out of the shower.'

He let her kiss him again before he closed the bathroom door. She put the letter back in the drawer; then she sat at the table playing with her phone and drinking another glass of wine and eating just a couple of bites of pasta so they'd be able to eat at the same time.

Ten minutes later Sam came out of the bathroom with one of her towels around his waist, and as he walked to the bedroom to get dressed – several of her dresser drawers were full of his clothes – she took the opportunity to covertly admire his muscular back. They'd met when Amy had been assigned by Yidster to cover – 'from a Jewish angle,' presumably – an exhibit he was part of, and they had been effortlessly together more or less since going home together that night. At first she thought he was a little old for her – thirty-five to her twenty-seven – but two and a half years later the difference seemed negligible. In ordinary time, two and a half years of dating wasn't all that much, but in New York time it was lots of time, especially as you neared thirty.

Was that what was nagging at Amy, the idea that she and Sam should get engaged and married because she was getting old? It wasn't that, exactly. If she really thought things were going somewhere with Sam, she wouldn't mind getting old. They would get old together. It was just that Sam seemed so . . . neutral, somehow. He would get up early and stay up late for weeks in advance of a small show somewhere, but he couldn't ever seem to make plans with her more than a few hours ahead of time, nor could he ever be convinced to dip into scheduled work time to have any kind of unplanned fun. She'd thought artists were supposed to be spontaneous! It was as if he had some kind of phobia. Was it Amy-phobia? More likely it was some phobia of the future, of preparing for the future. And why should he prepare for the future? Everything he wanted was already here.

She kept watching him, trying not to be creepy about it but enjoying the sight of his wet, naked body as he pulled his clothes on. She would have loved to just run in and pull him down onto the bed, but his antipathy toward spontaneity extended even to sex. He doled out sex as a reward for good behavior; sex was for the end of the day, after you'd washed all the dishes and spent a final hour tying up the loose ends in your in-box and finally the lights were off and you could relax. The idea of interrupting this order of operations made no sense to him. This attitude was understandable, on the one hand, and on the other hand totally maddening. He seemed to exist to refute all those women's magazine tips about Surprise Him! and Spicing Things Up. On the other hand, it was a pleasant contrast to all the other guys Amy had ever been with, whose perpetual availability had inevitably made them seem, like any perpetually available thing, less valuable – i.e., the way Amy probably seemed to Sam.

Later, after dinner and dishes and email and sex, Amy and Sam were just drifting off to sleep when she became aware of a distant high-pitched electronic peeping. It came at regular intervals, spaced just far enough apart that it would seem to have stopped, and then it would come again: *peeeep*.

'What is that?' Sam asked.

'Oh, it's the smoke alarm in the other room. I think the battery is dying.'

They were both on the verge of dozing off, Amy extra drowsy and lazy from the wine. But the peeping continued, seeming to get louder now that it had been noticed, as though it were going to enjoy putting on a little show.

'Do you want to, like, do something about it?' Amy asked eventually. Sam had fallen asleep completely, and he mumbled 'What?' in Russian, as he typically did when roused.

'Well, I'm going to do something about it!' Amy said, throwing off the covers, feeling a little upset.

'Baby, just close the door. We'll deal with it in the morning.'

'Are you nuts? It's so annoying. I'll deal with it now.' She was already dragging a chair from the kitchen table, positioning it under the alarm. She scanned the room for implements she could use to pry it off the ceiling, and when her eye lit on a hammer, she grabbed it.

'Amy, be careful. Jesus. Are you drunk?'

She didn't answer. She swung the hammer at the side of

the alarm, probably a little bit harder than was strictly necessary. It clung to the ceiling resolutely, she whacked it again, and this time it clattered to the floor, where it began to bleat out a loud, panicky cry. She jumped down off the chair and pried open its stomach, and it gave one last sad bloop as it disgorged its batteries. As she stood over it, feeling victorious, she became aware that Sam was standing next to her. He kicked the alarm gently, and half of it clunked over and scattered onto the floorboards in plastic shards; Amy's hammering had shattered the case.

'Amy, you didn't need to *break* it. Your landlord will make you pay for the new one.'

'It wouldn't shut up!'

Amy grinned at Sam, feeling an absurd sense of triumph. He turned away and got back into bed. He was already half asleep as she joined him.

'You really didn't have to do that,' he murmured when he felt her curl herself into his back.

'I definitely did. What was your plan – ignore it?'

'I would have closed the door. It would have died out eventually.'

'That's, like, your thing, that you don't take action unless or until you actually have to,' Amy said.

Sam sighed. 'Okay, Amy, that's my thing. Any guesses about what your thing is?'

She tried to come up with an answer, but as her brain spun out possibilities, they got muddled up with the beginning of dreams, and eventually she was sucked under by a warm tide of sleep.

6

'So then I was like, "that's like your whole *thing*," but he just rolled over and fell asleep. I'm sorry, I don't know why I'm subjecting you to this.'

Bev was partly listening to Amy talk, partly being very aware of the time. She'd looked at Google Maps to see exactly how many more minutes she had before the subway came. They kept going back to this inefficient coffee shop because it was locally owned and they would have felt guilty going to the Starbucks that had opened two doors down, but it had been half an hour since she'd placed her to-go breakfast sandwich order and she was starting to regret being so idealistic about breakfast. The girl who'd trained Bev at her temp assignment had emphasized promptness as much as she could without being downright insulting: 'Basically, the phone starts ringing at nine, and if there's no one here to answer it right then, it just, like, starts to create this image that's not very professional, and so if that happens, it's almost like there was no point? In hiring, um, a temporary staffer?' she'd said, clenching her teeth as she smiled. Bev had smiled too, saying, 'I'm a real morning person.'

Amy hadn't ordered a sandwich, and anyway it didn't matter – Bev was sure she could arrive at Yidster at noon, if she wanted, or just not show up at all and tell her bizarrely indulgent bosses she was working from home and she'd probably still keep getting paychecks. Bev knew that sometimes Amy actually *forgot to deposit* her paychecks. Once, Bev had noticed a paycheck that sat on Amy's coffee table for an entire week, unavoidable in Bev's peripheral vision as they watched TV. Bev had never in her life let a check go undeposited for more than twenty-four hours.

'So what do you think I should do?'

'About which, the apartment or the Yid Vids?'

Amy frowned into her coffee cup. 'Whatever. Either.'

'Uh, I'm not really qualified to give relationship advice. I don't know. You love Sam, and he totally makes you happy. And you're not disgusting or creepy or nerve-racking to be around when you're together. So I personally would be fine with it if you moved in with him, with the caveat that I am supposed to remind you that you promised yourself you'd never move in with anyone again unless you were – I think what you said was, "related by blood or marriage."'

Amy rolled her eyes. 'I said that?' She snorted. 'I must have had more money then.'

'You did. It was when you had your old job.'

'Ugh. Which brings us to the second question. Can I really let Yidster make me do something so degrading?'

Now Bev rolled her eyes. 'You do realize I'm about to

spend my day collating and binding, right? And trying to remember the name of the company where I'm working so I answer the phone correctly? I'm not really in the mood to hear about how you find making Internet-televised chitchat about some Jewish celebrity's nose job *degrading*.'

'It's not that I find it degrading,' said Amy. 'I misspoke. I more find it, um, humiliating. It's different.'

'Ha!'

Bev took a deep sip of coffee. 'I'm going to go and ask what happened to my sandwich. I have to be on the subway platform exactly eleven minutes from now, so I'm getting a little bit nervous.'

'Are those Google predictions real? Do they work? They do, don't they. Okay, cool, another thing I have to start paying attention to so that my life can be fully efficient and optimized.'

'I have no idea why you think of every app you put on your phone as this enormous new burden,' Bev said just as the countergirl called her name. She felt a surge of relief as soon as she knew she wouldn't be late for work, and as she scurried over to the counter to pick up her sandwich, she felt a burst of affection for Amy. Silly Amy, who couldn't figure out how to operate her own expensive phone.

When Bev came back, Amy was busily scrolling through the functions of her new app. 'Bev! It tells you exactly when the train is going to come!'

'I know! Oh – and really quick before I have to go, I wanted to ask if you could go out of town this weekend.'

'This weekend? I would love to, jeez. Where are we going?'

'J. R. Pinkman – do you remember him, from my old job? – was supposed to house-sit for this couple who have a house upstate, but he had to bail at the last minute, and he thought of me, I guess, because we ran into each other recently. They need someone to, like, water their organic kale. We can rent a car near the train station in Rhinecliff. They seem neurotic but nice; before I even said yes, the woman sent a multi-paragraph email about the inner workings of their house. It looks gorgeous.'

'Will it depress me because it represents a future I'll never attain?'

'Uh, probably. Does that mean you don't want to go? Look, I'll forward you all the emails and stuff, and you can peruse them at your leisure and decide. I told her I'd let her know today. Does that sound good?'

'I don't know. I might be too busy at work to think about this stuff,' Amy said.

'Oh, okay. Well then, I can . . . '

'Kidding! Duh. Of course. Let's go!'

7

Bev drove so infrequently that the mechanics of driving occupied a lot of her brain when she did it. Even after she and Amy got to the mostly two-lane part of the drive from the car rental place near the train station in Rhinecliff to Margaretville, she found herself clutching the wheel slightly. To Amy, who had never learned to drive, Bev's focus on the road probably registered as pensiveness, to the extent that it registered at all. She'd even asked whether Bev was okay. Bev had grunted something noncommittal, and ever since then Amy had no trouble filling the intra-car silence with a steady stream of observations about landmarks they were passing or things about the area she remembered from the Woodstock wedding she'd once attended or things that had recently annoyed her ('Don't you hate it when someone RSVPs no to a Facebook event on its wall with some comment about the fun thing they're doing instead? "Wish I could make it, but I'll be in Africa for the next six months."

Fuck those dickwads!'), initiating a conversational volley that tended to peter out after a few halfhearted return serves from Bev.

But Amy seemed content to continue lobbing her thoughts into a void, and the resulting white noise was pleasant to Bev, even relaxing: she could feel it starting to gradually unmelt the frozen-feeling areas around her trapezius. For the rest of the weekend she didn't have to impress Amy or even seem normal around her – Amy already knew what she was really like.

She darted her head over her shoulder again, slowing down to keep several car lengths between the car in front of her and the car she was driving. Bev had stored all the contents of Sally's emails about the care and maintenance of the house and its surrounding organic garden in her brain under a tab marked 'nuisances that are worth it.' She liked to imagine her consciousness laid out like a browser window. The open tab right now was 'driving,' and she could click over from it intermittently to sample the other tabs' contents.

There was always one tab that she kept trying to close, but it persisted in remaining open on her mind screen. It was maybe more like a pop-up window – the 'Had That Year of Grad School Been Worth It?' window. It could be disabled, sometimes, but only with five or more drinks. Just the jingle of change in a pocket or the one-dollar toll to get over the Rhinecliff Bridge was enough to remind Bev of the thirty thousand unrecoupable dollars, plus interest, that she owed.

By dropping out, she had also forfeited the right to tell people at parties that she was in grad school. Had a year of easier party interactions with strangers been worth thirty thousand dollars? She knew what her parents would say to that, or rather, what both of them would think and what her father would be delegated to say. *Be your own person, Beverly. Who cares what those numbskulls think? You know who you are.* And Bev did know who she was, actually. Her parents didn't, though, and hadn't for years. At the end of every phone call they still asked whether she was planning on going to church that weekend.

'Oh, it's that statue of a bear! I know where we are now,' said Amy.

Bev, who had known where they were for the duration of the drive, smiled. 'Yay, right? We're almost there!'

She half swiveled to the right to exchange a smile with Amy, but Amy seemed troubled.

'Uh, I hate to ask,' Amy said. 'I can keep holding it till we get there if it's, like, twenty minutes . . .'

'It's more like half an hour. I could use a coffee. There's a place coming up – I figured we'd make a pit stop there.'

Amy smiled and sat back, then reached toward the cup holder. 'Might as well fill my bladder to capacity, then,' she said, taking a glug from the bottle of Poland Spring water she'd bought forty-five seconds before their train's scheduled departure.

When they got to Catskill Coffee, though, there was a sign posted above the register: NO PUBLIC BATHROOMS. Bev wordlessly grabbed a paper cup and began filling it from the thermos on the counter that had a sign indicating it was the strongest brew, and then she watched with half her attention as Amy approached the cashier. He was sweaty, red-cheeked, hemp-necklaced, maybe in his second year at Bard.

'Hey, I'm so sorry to bother you,' Amy began.

The boy turned his stoned gaze toward her. 'Yeah?'

Bev could never pinpoint exactly how Amy went about doing what she did next. It was like watching a nature show about an animal that can strategically change color. Amy certainly hadn't gone to any trouble today to avoid looking dowdy: her thick brown hair was pulled back in a haphazard lump, and she was wearing a grease-stained sweatshirt that emphasized her broad shoulders. But as Bev watched, she somehow turned the entire Bat Signal beam of her personality on the cashier. Her tone was confiding and personal, as though her need to pee was an inside joke only she and the boy shared. He said something noncommittal, but in a friendly tone of voice, and Amy laughed, color rising to her cheeks. Emboldened, he made a real joke, and Amy cracked up with total abandon. She was still laughing as he reached for the key to the bathroom.

As she waited for Amy to finish peeing, Bev leaned against the counter and sipped her coffee. She could have been a shadow or a ghost or a breeze, for all the attention the cashier paid her, and as usual, she both relished and resented her ability to will herself invisible. She was physically unimposing, that was part of it, tidy and petite but also self-contained. Amy entered a room and diffused little particles of Amy into every corner of it. Bev was solid.

She knew it was selfish, but she was glad Amy had failed to become an actual celebrity, though it had briefly seemed as though she might be on the cusp of doing so. When they first became friends they'd been assistants at the publishing house, jobs they'd quit almost simultaneously – Bev for a stupid reason she couldn't usually bear to think about and Amy because she'd somehow snagged a high-profile job at a locally prominent gossip blog mocking New York City's rich, powerful, corrupt, ridiculous elite. But Amy had made the mistake of mocking the wrong rich, powerful person, and the person, who was friends with the blog's owner – a rich, powerful, corrupt, ridiculous person himself – had intervened. The owner had instructed Amy to post a retraction and apology, which she'd refused to do, mistaking her own stubbornness for some kind of principled stance worth fighting for. The owner retaliated by firing her in a way that made it seem as though she'd either misunderstood some basic concept or made the whole thing up. Amy had gone from being a rising star to being an untouchable in a matter of days. If it had happened a few years later, Amy – and Bev, for that matter – would have known what everyone who's lived in New York for more than five years knows: that such shamings were inevitable and could always be overcome just by waiting for enough time to pass until someone else's more recent shaming eclipsed your own in everyone's ADD-addled memory. Amy also thought she'd stood up for something important, when basically she had stood up for her right to be mean on the Internet. She assumed that being fired in such a public way meant that she'd be blacklisted, and because she believed this, she effectively was: she stopped going to parties, so people stopped inviting her; she didn't apply for good jobs, so she didn't get them.

Amy's life was okay now – stable, certainly better materially than Bev's – but everything about it was curtailed, a diminished version of what might have been. In drunken, vulnerable moments, Amy sometimes talked to Bev about her 'comeback,' which was eternally just around the corner. These were the only times when Bev felt pity for Amy, whereas Amy, Bev assumed, felt pity for Bev a lot of the time.

The rest of the time, Bev felt her affection for Amy mingle with a comfortable, manageable level of envy, for the small but dedicated blog audience Amy took for granted, for the thoughtless way Amy spent money that was literally impossible for Bev, and for having the ability to make the essentials of life – money, attention, keys to the bathroom – come to her without her making what seemed like much of an effort. For the millionth time, Bev reached inside herself and turned the envy off completely, as easily as twisting a tap shut.

Bev could decide to put up with Amy because she'd often been the recipient of that Bat Signal beam herself. That was the thing about Amy; she said and did the exact right thing at the exact right time just as often as she said and did the exact wrong thing at the exact wrong time. When Amy gave Bev a compliment, Bev knew that she meant it because she was thoroughly, hopelessly incapable of lying or even being less than honest: she was the person who, when you asked if your new haircut was bad, would tell you it was, whereas everyone else would allow you to delude yourself. When Amy had told Bev that she thought Bev was a good writer and should see how far she could take her talents, Bev had known that she'd meant it. She had been the first and so far the only person to see Bev's potential.

Amy came out of the bathroom smiling; she tossed the

keys back to the cashier with a big, cheesy wink, then half skipped toward Bev and grabbed her hand, pulling her to the car. 'I can't wait for our fun weekend getaway to start! We're going to drink a lot and eat so much food and go to bed early!' she trilled, swinging Bev's arm as they walked out to the car. A surge of love for Amy welled up in Bev. Of course she loved Amy; they were allies in a world full of idiots and enemies. She couldn't afford to harbor resentment toward her even for a second. And besides, she had something that Amy, despite her stable and basically okay-seeming life, would never get to have again: the potential to make a good first impression on the world. When the time was right, Bev knew, she'd will herself un-invisible. She just had to figure out exactly how to do it.

8

When Bev first started making friendship advances toward Amy, she was so dogged that Amy thought Bev might want to sleep with her.

Bev wanted *something*, that much was clear. She had been hired at the office where Amy worked a year after Amy started there. Amy had the best prospects for advancement in the editorial department, and all the other assistants knew it. She was the protégée of an editor who was on a hot streak; his books were bestsellers, and his anointed former assistants had all gone on to great things – i.e., they had become full editors before their thirtieth birthdays, which in book publishing was the greatest thing anyone could realistically hope for.

Bev was meek and put-upon; her office clothes were poly-blend jackets and skirts from the part of H&M where you went when, broke, you still had to try to dress for the job you wanted. Amy wore Marc by Marc Jacobs blouses (so coveted, in the early aughts) with short sleeves that showed her tattoos. She'd been Bev exactly one year earlier, and for this reason she avoided her as much as possible.

Bev either didn't notice or did notice and still blithely persisted in her attempts to cultivate Amy's friendship. 'Hey,' she said one day while waiting outside Amy's boss's office for his signature on a form attached to a clipboard – Amy's boss was, as usual, on the phone – 'You seem like you might like Sleater-Kinney. I have an extra ticket to the show at Roseland on Thursday. Do you want to go?'

'Um, I have to check,' said Amy, thinking fast. 'My boyfriend and I might be doing something that night.' This was unlikely; Amy's boyfriend at the time was a pot-dealing sometimes musician, and the things they did together didn't tend to require advance planning, because they mostly involved sitting on the couch, smoking joints, and watching pirated DVDs.

'Relax, Amy, I'm not gay,' Bev said, and Amy looked up from her screen, where she'd been pretending to check her Outlook calendar. She was shocked by Bev's perceptiveness. 'I just like Sleater-Kinney. It's possible to like them and be heterosexual. It's not like I invited you to go see Tegan and Sara.'

In spite of herself, in spite of her overwhelming desire to maintain her place in the office hierarchy, Amy laughed. 'Okay. Well, but I hope we can still go to the Michigan Womyn's Music Festival together,' she said, and Bev cracked up. They kept making jokes, eventually devolving into one of those punchy overcaffeinated office gigglefests, until the marketing director, who *was* gay, came out of her office and shot them a dirty look that was kind of a joke but was still mortifying, and then a second later Amy's boss came to the door of his office and, without really looking at either of them, made it clear that he needed Amy to do something other than sit on her ass and chat with Bev. Bev, for her part, grabbed the clipboard off the edge of Amy's cube and rushed into his office, hurriedly explaining its importance. After he'd signed it, Bev scurried back out of his office, but not before depositing the Sleater-Kinney ticket, which she'd had in her blazer pocket the whole time, in Amy's in-box, as if it were just another interoffice form or letter to file.

Roseland was packed with girls in their twenties who were wearing comfortable shoes and no makeup, and Amy felt better than she had in ages. Next to her, Bev pogoed around to the music unself-consciously, singing along with the band. Amy also wanted to do these things, but she'd had only one plastic cup of light beer and there was still an outside chance that Bev might take the opportunity of any display of Amy's vulnerability to sabotage her in the office somehow, and also she never danced. She stood silently watching the band, feeling the music reverberating up through the floorboards and into her tensed legs. A terrible gulf of experience existed between the Amy who'd seen this band as a teenager and the Amy who now spent her days filing things and dropping clipboards into in-boxes and killing time on the Internet. Bev turned to her, brushing sweaty hair out of her face, and yelled that she had found out in advance what kind of beer the venue sold and had brought some in her tote bag. Did Amy want one? Amy did, and soon after she drank it, she started bending one knee and then the other in a kind of rhythm. By the time the band played its final encore (an inspired cover of CCR's 'Fortunate Son'), you might have even said she was dancing.

In the weeks that followed the Sleater-Kinney show, Amy and Bev started taking their lunches together in the park across from their office building, where previously Amy had eaten her lunch alone while reading submissions. Amy offered to read the proposals that Bev championed in ed meetings and gave her tactical advice about how to appease her boss. Bev took Amy to cheap bars in her deep-Brooklyn neighborhood and listened to Amy complain about her pot-head boyfriend. Their friendship officially transcended the workday, surprising them both.

That summer, Amy and her pothead boyfriend finally broke up, undramatically for the most part, except that Amy had to find a new place to live in a hurry. Luckily for her, her alpha-bitch maneuvering at the publishing house had paid off in the form of a promotion, which enabled her to convince herself that she could afford to live alone. She'd had to clean out her retirement account to afford the first and last month's rent plus security deposit, but the sacrifice seemed necessary. It felt psychologically important – after all those years of pre-mature cohabitation and sedated early evenings eating chicken curry on the couch – to find out what she was like when left entirely to her own devices.

But on the first night in her apartment under the BQE,

after the movers left and the energy of packing and carrying and unpacking drained from her limbic system, she surprised herself by not being ready to revel in solitude just yet. She sat at the kitchen table, hungry but too exhausted to figure out how to get food, drinking a dented bottle of Poland Spring water she'd been nursing all day in the July heat. She watched the daylight fade outside her uncurtained windows. A creak in the floorboards above made her jump. She realized that without being aware of it, she'd always assumed that she was safe when her ex-boyfriend was there, which made no sense to her conscious mind; if someone had broken into their apartment, he probably would have offered the intruder a bong hit and played him some prog rock. But still, up until this moment in her life, Amy had been going around assuming that her safety was at least partially someone else's responsibility. But it never really had been, and now it was impossible to pretend otherwise. She was completely alone.

It was nine o'clock. Without quite realizing what she was doing, she dialed Bev's number. They weren't yet the kind of friends who called each other out of the blue for no reason, so Amy was relieved when Bev picked up.

'Hi! How did the move go? You must be exhausted.'

'Oh, the movers did most of it. I just carried the little stuff, the breakable stuff. The real nightmare is unpacking, of course.'

'Want me to come over and help?'

'No! I mean, don't help. I don't want to do any more tonight, and I wouldn't inflict that on you. But do come over! I mean, if you want.'

Fifteen minutes later, Bev was standing at Amy's door with

a bottle of wine and a paper bag full of take-out sushi. 'I had just ordered this, but I always order enough for two people,' she explained. Her hair was in shiny plaits, making her look even more innocent than usual, like a milkmaid on an antique can label. Amy felt a pang of gratitude so extreme that tears briefly, unnoticeably came to her eyes.

They ate the sushi and drank the wine on a little ledge of roof they could crawl to from Amy's fire escape, which the broker who'd shown Amy the apartment had described as a 'deck.' Rotting fallen leaves clotted one corner and made the hot summer air smell more like the woods and less like car exhaust. They balanced the plastic trays of spicy tuna rolls on their laps and looked out at the cars on the BQE and, beyond that, the storage warehouses, the Navy Yard, and, across the East River, Manhattan, just visible between the nearby buildings, skyscrapers with all their lights on, wastefully twinkling.

Soon the sushi was gone and they were on their third plastic cups of wine. Amy felt almost too tired to talk, so she listened to Bev, who was telling her about the latest terrible thing her boss had done:

'It wasn't even that she claimed credit for my work. I mean, that's what I'm there for, I'm her assistant. It was that she wanted me to continue the fiction when we weren't even in the meeting anymore, when we were just alone in her office. She wanted me to congratulate her on the great idea she'd had for the subtitle! If I felt like being really self-destructive, I'd have called her out on it, but it's just not worth it. She'd just pretend she had no idea what I was talking about, and then she'd be angry at me for a week and take it out on me by deliberately leaving me off some crucial scheduling email, then having a screaming fit when she arrived at the wrong restaurant to have lunch with Marcia Gay Harden or whatever C-lister she's currently courting.'

'I think you should call her out on it, regardless of the consequences. If you don't assert yourself, if you just keep being the world's best assistant, you'll never get promoted,' Amy said.

'If my boss despises me, I'll never get promoted.'

'Ahh, a catch-twenty-two.'

Bev pulled out a pack of Camel Lights, Amy's favorite brand of cigarettes. Neither of them really smoked, but when Bev pretend smoked, she bought Parliaments. The Camels were another kind gesture on her part, like the wine and the sushi. They lit cigarettes and smoked with exaggerated seriousness, enjoying the ritual of the burst of flame, the first puff of smoke dissipating into the night air.

'I have something I need to ask you, and I'm afraid it'll be awkward,' Bev said, speaking quickly. They were still facing the highway, not looking at each other, but Amy snuck a glance at Bev's face. Bev seemed tense but resolute.

'Okay, what is it?'

'Well, you know, growing up where I did, I was often considered kind of an odd duck. I mean, I wasn't a total social reject. I always had a couple of people to, like, eat lunch with in the cafeteria, but I definitely never had a best friend, and I'm not sure how it works.'

'How what works?'

'Like, becoming best friends. Do you have to say something, confirming that you're best friends?'

'Are you asking me whether we're best friends?'

'Well, yeah. I assume you've had a best friend before, so you know, generally, how it goes.'

Amy thought about it for a second. 'I've had close friends, for sure. But mostly I've had boyfriends. You always think they're your best friend, but that's obviously bullshit.'

'Yeah. If you're having sex with someone, they're not your best friend.'

Their cigarettes were almost done; Amy poured a little bit of wine into one of the empty plastic soy sauce cups and stubbed hers out in this makeshift ashtray so as not to further befoul her new deck. 'Is this ... are we having the DTR conversation?'

'The ... wait, let me guess what it stands for. Determining ... No. Defining? Defining The Relationship?'

'Yeah!' said Amy.

'Yeah, we are. Sorry, I just ... Look, it's okay if you don't feel the same way. But you're my best friend. And I guess I just wanted you to know that. No pressure! Ha!'

Bev's tone was casual, but when Amy stole another glance in her direction, she looked pained.

'Bev, of course you're my best friend. It wouldn't have occurred to me to say anything, but you are, for sure. I'd be lost without you. Like tonight, for example. I would have died of starvation, or gotten a second wind and tried to unpack boxes and then died of exhaustion. Or I would have gotten paranoid and barricaded the door with my one stick of furniture. Before you came over, I was feeling so unsafe here. Not for any good reason, but just because I felt alone. And now that you've been here, even when you go home, I won't feel that way. I feel safe now because I know someone knows where I am and gives a fuck.'

'And it won't change when you get a new boyfriend?'

'No. Will it change when you get a boyfriend?'

'No, and anyway, it's impossible to imagine that happening.'

Amy shook the wine bottle, determined that there was still a little bit left, and divided it equally between their glasses. 'Well, we're still relatively young, you know? I'm sure all kinds of unimaginable things will happen.'

9

Several years full of unimaginable things later, Bev and Amy were lazing around in a borrowed beautiful house. They woke up late, and when they began to feel bored, around noon, they went out for lunch and a hike in Balsam Lake Mountain Wild Forest.

They started at the visitors' center, where Bev talked to the park ranger about which would be the best hike for them considering their fitness level and the amount of time they had and which of the park's attractions they would most like to see from the scenic overlooks. The park ranger and Bev instantaneously discovered that they were both fluent speakers of the language of useful people who are accustomed to communicating a lot of information simply and effectively to strangers. Amy had known this language at one point but had mostly forgotten it, in the same way she had forgotten her high school French.

Bev and the forest ranger looked at maps, and Amy stayed

out of their way, wandering around in the visitors' center, examining a slightly threadbare taxidermied owl, a chart that explained what the national park had looked like three thousand years ago, and some rusty pieces of metal that, at some impossible-to-imagine time in the past, had been the height of technology. Reading the word 'technology' caused Amy to realize that she had left her iPhone in the car. She itched for it, just slightly.

When they reached the mouth of the trail, they paused as Bev squinted at the map. 'So we kind of loop around the park; it goes next to the road for a little while, and then it's a pretty steep climb up to the top of this hill. That guy called it a mountain, but he was being kind of generous, I think. The elevation gain is only five hundred feet. And then it goes back and around behind the visitors' center. Anyway, it's much shorter on the way down,' Bev said, basically to herself.

'Cool, that sounds great.'

And they set off, with Bev in front.

At first Amy tried to make conversation, but then – a little belatedly – she sensed that Bev wasn't super interested in talking and might want to be alone with her thoughts and/or nature, so she shut up.

Bev's shoulders were strong and white in her tank top, and she walked quickly, with dutiful purpose, hitting the ground hard with every step. This was how she always walked. In a small shared living space it tended to seem like stomping, but on a hike it was appropriate. She seemed as if she knew where she was going, always, regardless of whether she did.

Twenty minutes later they were at the top of the hill. They peered out over miles of wooded landscape; the leaves were at the height of their greenness, some just starting to dry out or turn red at the edges. Down below was a river, and in the middle of the river there was some sort of wooden structure that had been overwhelmed by the water, maybe carried downstream. Butterflies flew all around them as they stood there resting before starting back down the hill. Amy supposed this was fun. Bev, at least, seemed to be having fun, in her determined way.

As they walked downhill, careful with every step not to slip on the rocks and twist their ankles, Amy's thoughts finally drifted into a contented, daydreamy rhythm. For the first time in a long time she did not think about sex or a grudge or try to tease out a solution to a problem. They passed a tree that had been sliced in half by a thunderbolt. The brown leaves of the charred dead half were curling on the ground.

'Probably that thunderstorm on Friday,' Bev said.

'No way. Look how brown the leaves are. It's definitely been down for longer than that,' Amy said. 'Um. Obviously I know this due to being a forensic . . . botanist.'

Bev laughed, sincerely, and Amy loved her for it.

As they walked on in silence, Amy thought about trees. All this slow-motion life was happening constantly inside their trunks. A miraculous confluence of circumstances had led to these trees – of all the tiny seedlings that took root in the forest every year – growing up to be the ones that didn't get eaten or trampled or killed by disease or lack of sunlight or uprooted to make way for a new path or crushed by an adult tree that had been hit by lightning. Tree infant mortality had to be something staggeringly close to one hundred percent, and then teenage trees probably faced a whole new set of problems.

How powerless the trees were! They got to make only one decision, and then they had to reap its consequences for their entire lives. On the plus side, though, they were relieved of the burden of having to make any further decisions. There was that to be said for being a tree.

When they got back to the house, it was already the low-blood-sugar shank of the day. Bev went out to do all the garden tasks while Amy sluggishly started washing and chopping vegetables for their dinner. She sang along to radio pop from Bev's iTunes as she tore up lettuce. Bev came in from the yard, they consulted about the meal, and then she went back outside to light the grill. Amy took a cup of tea out to the living room and sat there with a book, unengrossed, looking up every few minutes and noticing something new about the room each time.

Beneath the cow-skin rug, there were dark and light types of wood inlaid in a geometric pattern in the floor. The chair opposite her was made of birch twigs but still looked comfortable. The curtains were made of a clean, worn-thin type of white cloth that looked like an apron someone might be wearing in a black-and-white photograph. Amy felt uncomfortable in the room, as if she were a misplaced detail amid all that precise beauty. The house she'd grown up in had been pleasant but unstylish: there had been furniture, of course, but almost none of it was beautiful or old or handmade. There was one glass-fronted cabinet that had been in her mother's family for years, but its beauty was spoiled by the paperback books on its shelves, with their unattractive clashing spines: Civil War histories and Carl Hiaasen thrillers and joke books, the sources of young Amy's haphazard early education. She remembered most vividly an early edition of *Our Bodies, Ourselves*, a paperback of *The Prince* with her mom's college notes in the margins, and a book called *How to Talk So Kids Will Listen and Listen So Kids Will Talk*.

A couple in a photograph on a low shelf caught Amy's eye suddenly. It wasn't a snapshot – there would never be such a gauche thing as a snapshot in a house like this one – but a posed informal portrait, the kind you'd see in an art or fashion magazine. The man was slight and Asian and almost shorter than the woman, who wore a pearl-gray dress with a wide sash at the waist. She looked sad, somehow, even though she was beaming.

These were the house's owners. Amy picked up the photo and studied it for more clues. Was this from their wedding? How old had they been? They looked older than Amy, but not by much.

Amy was jealous of people who got married, even though she wasn't sure she wanted to get married. It wasn't the party or the presents or the patently unrealistic promise of eternal love she craved, not at all. Well, maybe it was the party, slightly. It was more – well, it was a lot of things. For one thing, people who got married seemed to be granted special exemption from the otherwise ironclad law that after you stopped being a child, you had to give up your belief in magic. The spells and talismans of marriage – the vows, the rings, the veil – retained their mythic power, over Amy at least. It was maddening. But she couldn't stop herself from caring, from being curious and jealous and moved when she saw these symbols, no matter how much she agreed with the pundits who attacked the institution on pragmatic and feminist and philosophical grounds, and no matter how many novels she read about the inevitable end of love.

Sam had been married once, in his early twenties, and that seemed to have sufficed for him.

Bev stomped inside and saw Amy holding the photo. There was a smudge of gray charcoal dust across her sweaty forehead. She looked over Amy's shoulder at the photo. 'Our hosts,' Bev said. 'Is that from their wedding? She looks miserable.'

'I bet a lot of people are miserable at their weddings. Think of that pressure for one day to be perfect. I would have nonstop stress diarrhea.'

'I'd make sure you took some of my Klonopin.'

'A cocktail of Klonopin and Imodium. Perfect.'

'Glad that's settled.'

They stared at the photo for another moment, then went to set the table with the beautiful hand-thrown plates and Riedel stemless wineglasses and heavy square-handled cutlery that had probably been given to the couple in the photo as wedding presents.

Later, ensconced in her cozy bedroom under vintage quilts in an antique bed, Amy took a chance on the flickering cell service and called Sam. He was still at the studio.

'The signal sucks out here. We have to be prepared to be cut off at any time, so you can't say anything important,' Amy warned him.

'Okay, baby. Are you having a fun time? Waffles and I miss you very much. Waffles is expressing his sadness, actually, by licking my feet all the time. I don't understand why he does this, baby. I think you aren't a very good cat disciplinarian.'

'Don't blame me for Waffles's behavioral problems. I didn't have him in his formative years. What are you working on?'

'That big Cuisinart. Painting the part now where you can see that the plastic is kind of smeary and grubby.'

'Did you eat dinner?'

'I had some chicken and broccoli. I'm turning into a health nut. Baby! What happened on the Internet today?'

He asked her this almost every day, like a parent asking a child 'How was school?' And like a child telling a parent how school had been, she usually said something boring and non-committal. How were you supposed to describe the millions of things that had happened? And all those micro events were so inconsequential on their own but so compelling in the moment. All of them were tricking you into thinking they might eventually add up to something, and maybe they would.

'Not a lot. I mean I wasn't online a lot today,' she said. 'We're in the country, you know. We hiked and stuff. We saw scenic vistas. The people who live in this house are weird; everything is arranged in this really anal way. They live here year-round – which I can't even imagine how someone would be able to stand to do that. It's so quiet here, and like ten people live in this town. I guess they go into the city pretty often. Anyway, tomorrow we're going to—' And then she looked at the phone and realized he hadn't heard any of it because they'd been cut off. She thought of calling back, but a wave of sleepiness overtook her and she texted 'Cut off! I miss you' before rolling over and turning out the light. She was lightly asleep when her phone lit up with a reply. 'I miss you too baby. I kiss you. Goodnight.' She wished he'd said 'I love you,' but it wasn't really a thing they did.

10

There was a big, muddy footprint in the middle of the patch of watermelons, and the kale had been picked unevenly – its mature outer leaves left alone, its tender inner leaves ripped out too roughly, leaving ragged edges. The house sitters had also left a load of laundry in the washing machine, which, if Sally and Jason's flight had been delayed or something, would have moldered there for a day before anyone could have transferred it to the dryer. But other than that, Sally had to admit to herself that she was impressed by how well the pair of girls had taken care of things. She walked around the yard and then reentered through the basement, taking pleasure in surveying her domain. She liked letting people stay in her house when she wasn't there – aside from the minor inconvenience and grossness (their skin flakes in her guest room mattresses, the hair too dark to be hers and too long to be Jason's in the shower drain). Her house was too beautiful not to share. She hoped the girls who'd stayed there had been impressed and jealous.

She was down in the basement laundry room, loading their sheets into the dryer so that she could put her London clothes in the wash, when she heard the doorbell ring and hurried upstairs to answer it.

'I'm so sorry, but I forgot my computer charger, and I just googled them, and did you have any idea how much they cost? They cost like ninety dollars!' said the person at the door. She was taller than Sally and wearing a hooded sweatshirt. Sally peered at the girl on the steps behind her, who was smaller, with limp blond hair. The tall girl hazarded a smile. 'I'm sorry. We're the ... we were here this weekend? Amy and Bev?'

'Hi!' said Sally. 'Sorry it took me a minute to put it together! I'm so jet-lagged. Please come on in. Do you know where you left it?'

'I think it's either in the dining room or the office,' said Amy, stepping past Sally, scanning the room for her lost charger. Sally stood back and let her enter. It was odd to watch a stranger move around in your house as though she lived there. The other girl hung back. Sally motioned for her to step all the way in and then shut the front door behind them.

'I'm so sorry you had to come all the way back here. Are you going to miss your train back to the city?'

'No. We can't miss it, because it's the last one tonight, and some of us will get fired if we don't show up to our jobs at nine a.m. tomorrow, so we are definitely not going to miss it,' said the second girl, talking directly to her friend, basically treating Sally like an interfering parent.

'Oh my god, Bev, I am so sorry, okay? I said I was sorry. If I can't find it in five minutes, I'll just buy a new one.'

'Ugh, I'm not mad at you. I'm mad at me for having this stupid temp job,' Bev said. She joined Amy in rummaging around under the glass-topped dining room table, looking in the corners of the room.

'No, it's fine, be mad at me! I'm mad at me!' Amy said.

Bev cracked a smile. 'Fine, I'm mad.' She looked at Sally. 'I am so sorry to invade like this, but I'm just going to head up to the study. Is that okay?'

'Sure. I mean, I think Jason might be in there, though,' Sally said, but Bev was already on her way up the stairs, taking them two at a time. Seconds later, she was running back down the stairs. *'I found it!'* she shrieked.

'My hero!' Amy said, and as Sally watched, they embraced each other without a hint of self-consciousness. 'Okay, it's five fifty-four. Can we do it? Can you drive superfast?'

'I think so.' The girls were almost out the door before either of them seemed to remember that Sally was standing there.

'Thank you so much for having us, Mrs. ... uh, Ms. Katzen,' Bev said, sounding like a midwesterner. 'I hope you had a nice trip!'

'Please come back anytime,' Sally called after them as they dove into the car.

When she came back into the dining room, Jason was standing on the landing. He seemed amused, if slightly bewildered.

'What was that?'

Sally shrugged. 'I don't know. I kind of enjoyed it, though.'

'Me too,' said Jason.

'Ha, you perv.'

'Not like that, just . . . it's nice to see who's been here, you know? I wonder if they liked it.'

'Of course they liked it,' said Sally, heading to the kitchen to start dinner. 'They probably live in some hovel.'

'Like your old hovel?' When Jason met Sally, she'd lived in 350 square feet above an old pornographic movie theater on Second Avenue. The sad, repetitive porn music had reverberated through her floorboards.

'Nowhere near as glamorous as my old hovel,' Sally told him.

Sometimes Sally wished for her younger self to come and hang out with her, to come over for drinks on the porch, maybe, like any friend might. She could show young Sally her beautiful house and watch her be impressed, and young Sally could tell her some entertaining story about working at a gross titty bar or a used bookstore that was like a cult, some anecdote that old – older – Sally had forgotten, even though she'd experienced it.

This was impossible, of course, because of the laws of space and time. But maybe she could become friends with Bev and Amy. That might be the next best thing.

11

Bev rode her bike to the restaurant where she was meeting Steve, even though she knew it would mess up her hair and make her sweaty. She had also resisted the impulse to dress nicely, had instead worn her worst jeans and a billowy top that had once caused a well-meaning stranger to give up his subway seat because he'd assumed that she was pregnant. She knew it was dumb, that it didn't make any sense to accept Steve's invitation and then do her best to sabotage the date, but it was a way of affirming to herself that she was there only for the meal. Tolerating Steve's company was the price of her dinner. At least sixty dollars, maybe more with lots of drinks, and she certainly planned to order those. It had been so long since she'd had a nice meal in a restaurant with someone else picking up the tab.

And they were no longer coworkers, at least. The new week had brought a new temp assignment: she was answering the phone, which so far had rung once, at the New York corporate headquarters of a small French bank. There was nothing to do, because no one gave her anything to do. Everyone in the office treated her as though she were brain-damaged because she didn't speak French. By 10:00 a.m. she had decided to call Steve, and after they made plans for that evening and hung up, she'd spent at least an hour at her desk examining the restaurant's menu online, thinking about what she would order.

As he walked into the lounge at the front of the restaurant, Steve looked genuinely happy to see her and also, she hated noticing, kind of hot. He looked like he'd come straight from work and he was wearing a nice dark-colored jacket and a button-down shirt. When he leaned in for a polite half-hug hello, she smelled his cedar cologne and felt the heat of his body through the crisp shirt. She regretted her own sweaty rumpledness for a moment, then mentally chided herself for caring.

They were seated quickly. Steve seemed to know the whole staff, glad-handing his way to their table with a series of high fives and smile-nods. They barely had time to exchange 'how was your day' type pleasantries before a waitress came to their table and began listing the specials, using the New York-specific restaurant dialect Bev had almost forgotten: 'I have an appetizer of house-cured gravlax on toast, and that's going to be coming with a house-made ricotta and it's going to be fourteen? And it's really, really super yummy.' The girl smiled impersonally at them. 'I'll give you a minute?'

As she walked away, Bev and Steve both noticed the waitress's butt, clad in high-waisted jeans; the waitress was the rare individual who looked good in them. They turned from the butt back to each other and were unable to avoid acknowledging its perfectness.

'Damn,' said Bev.

'She could serve drinks off that thing! I'm so glad you said something!' Steve said. 'I was like . . . do I say something, or would that be just totally inappropriate and rude?'

'Ha, well, it's an amazing butt,' said Bev.

'I just want to grab it! Don't you just want to reach out and touch it?'

'I . . . uh. I guess.'

'Ha! You're cool, Bev.' Steve smiled. 'You want to do some apps? I'm gonna do the fried artichokes, I think.'

'I think I'm going to . . . uh, the gravlax thing sounded good,' Bev said weakly.

'We're definitely doing a bottle of wine, right?'

'Definitely. Yes. Most definitely.'

The wine didn't arrive right away, and as Bev struggled to make small talk with Steve, she felt her bike sweat curdling into the makings of a panic attack. Why had she agreed to spend the next few hours in the company of someone she didn't like? Was she that hungry? Her scalp prickled, and she could feel a flush creeping up her neck, her milk-pale skin betraying her as usual: a transparent screen her feelings were projected onto from the inside. 'I'm just going to run to the bathroom real quick,' she told Steve.

In the bathroom she scrabbled in her purse for her little pill case, broke a Klonopin in half with her teeth, then, after a split second of consideration, swallowed both halves with a handful of cold water from the sink. She ran cold water over her pulse points and looked herself in the eye, willing herself to feel normal. She took in the details of the bathroom, its studied stylishness: the EMPLOYEES MUST WASH HANDS sign lettered in Helvetica and printed on heavy card stock, the black and white tiles. Noticing details calmed her down as it always did, but the drug hadn't yet kicked in; she dropped to her knees and pressed her forehead to the tile for a moment, breathing deeply. Whenever this happened, she felt something like nausea that wasn't nausea, quite, but it had in common with nausea the feeling of having something inside that needed to be expelled. Bev felt full of something terrible, but she was trapped in the feeling: the something-terrible was part of her, inextricable from the rest of her.

When she stood up again, the tile had made a red mark in the center of her forehead. She hoped Steve would be too busy staring at their waitress's ass to notice. It was a lot more comfortable to feel straightforward contempt for him than to feel anything else.

'Did you fall in? Heh, just kidding, I know there's always an intense line for the bathroom here. You know why?' he lowered his voice to a whisper. ''Cause the whole staff is cokeheads. That's why the food is so good. They have, like, a *laser* focus.'

Their wine had arrived, thank god. Bev drank half of her first glass in a gulp. 'Uh, all staff at all restaurants everywhere are cokeheads,' she said. 'Have you never worked at a restaurant?'

'Nah. I worked construction in college. My dad's an electrician.'

'Oh, cool. My family's also in construction, sort of; my dad runs a small lumberyard.' Bev had not wanted to tell Steve anything about herself, nothing real at least, but she'd been taken aback by his revelation. She had him pegged for a child of privilege, or at least of a general contractor.

Construction and their respective families took them through the first course, which Steve ate with gusto and terrible table manners, which Bev sort of liked because she didn't have to feel self-conscious about her own ungraceful fork maneuvers. She felt comfortable with Steve in general, she realized, and not only because of the wine and the antianxiety medication. He reminded her in some ways of Todd, or at least of how she'd felt around Todd. She thought this, then realized that if she was going to keep acting normal, it was very very important not to think about Todd. Anyway, Todd had had perfect table manners.

'You're quiet all of a sudden. Is everything okay?'

'Oh! Yeah, sorry. Just focusing on the food. To be honest, it's the best meal I've had in a while.' Why. Jesus. It was like neural impulses were just exiting straight through her mouth.

'Right? I told you! To cocaine!' Steve raised his wineglass in a toast. 'Let's get another bottle, right?'

Two bottles of wine and three courses later, Bev was rehearsing a little speech about how she had to get up early and it had been so much fun, but Steve wasn't ready for the fun to end just yet. 'Oh, they have a whole menu of after-dinner drinks! Digestifs! What do you say, Bev? I love cognac and Armagnac and all that shit. Sambuca? Pastis? Anything?'

Bev skimmed the dessert menu the waitress had left on their table, and her eye caught on a rare vintage of Flemish liqueur familiar to her from her stint pouring wine at that pretentious wine bar in Madison. She'd treated herself to many covert sips of the stuff, but never a full glass. And it really would be nice to aid her digestion. She certainly hadn't needed to eat the lobster quenelles *and* a pasta course; a sip of Flement would sluice right through them. Her system was more used to rice and beans and kale, the staples of her low-budget grocery runs.

Moments later, she was raising a snifter of the syrupy liqueur to her lips. It tasted like sun on a field. A sense of well-being radiated throughout her entire digestive tract. It was the sensation, concentrated in a glass, of having enough money to pay for dinner out anytime you wanted.

Steve took an appreciative sip. 'Holy shit. How'd you know about this stuff?'

'Oh, I just – a few years ago I decided I was tired of not ever having any idea what to order, and I took a class.' She was such a better liar when she was drunk! She had also gotten really good, at the wine bar, at the flicking motion that undid the foil overwrap on a bottle top with an efficient single twist of her wrist.

'Damn, Bev. You've got hidden depths.' Steve leaned tipsily toward her. 'I have to get to know you better. Find out allll your secrets.'

Was he fucking kidding with this? At the same time, the cedary smell and the creamy shirt were enticing. The smell and feel of luxury were overwhelming to her hungry senses. She took another honeyed sip. 'Hey, you didn't say where you lived,' she said casually. She could leave her bike locked to a stop sign near the restaurant; no way she was dealing with it right now.

'It's funny, actually, so near here,' Steve said. 'I'd love to show you my place. It's nothing fancy, but I have a huge flat-screen. We could watch *Parks and Rec*, or something.'

'It's already over,' Bev murmured.

'No worries, dude. I DVR'd it.'

12

Amy was tempted to ignore her ringing phone – it wasn't even seven o'clock! – but she saw Bev's name on the display, hit 'talk,' and lay back down in bed with her eyes closed while Bev spoke.

'Have you ever taken the morning-after pill?'

'No, but . . . '

'Do you know anyone who has? I think I might have to take it, but I want to know first whether it's going to ruin my whole day.'

It emerged that Bev had gone on a date with a guy she'd met at one of her temp placements, some suit-wearing dude.

'Gross,' Amy said.

'Fuck you! Judging me when I'm at my weakest!'

'Whatever. You know I think it's disgusting to fuck strangers. Make out with them, by all means, go home with them, I guess, or take them home, but don't actually allow them to insert their body parts into your orifices – that's the first law of self-respect.'

'According to Colette, washing your vagina every night before bed no matter how tired you are is the first law of self-respect.'

'I love that you know that. Did you check the wastebasket and the floor before you left? Maybe there was a condom wrapper.'

'Thanks, Nancy Drew.'

'I'm just trying to be helpful! Also, when is your period due?'

'It's … next week, in theory, or maybe a week and a half from now? I haven't been keeping close track. Probably because I haven't gotten laid in several eons.'

'Oh, well … it seems like you should take it, then, right?'

'I guess? But I'm not even sure that I had sex, and it's forty dollars I definitely can't spare.'

'I'll totally give you the forty dollars. This is important.'

'I'm not taking money from you, Amy. You know I can't do that. I also just don't want to ruin my day. I'm so hungover, I don't want to add mystery ingredients to my body chemistry, and I have to be in Midtown by nine.'

'Okay. Well, I still think you should, but if you're sure you don't need to … But do you promise never to do this again? And get tested ASAP?'

'I definitely won't. Do it again, I mean. Please, you know this is the first time I've maybe had sex in like … uh, I'm not even actually going to do that math, it's too depressing. Do you want to get coffee, as long as we're both up?'

*

They took their coffee to the community garden where Bev had cultivated a little patch of cucumbers. She was a junior member of the garden, so her plot was near the back edge, where rats sometimes chewed through the fence and pillaged the growing vegetables, but otherwise it was nice to have a plot there, a five-by-five square of tangible life accomplishment that Amy admired.

Bev greeted a middle-aged woman who was crouched near the entrance pulling weeds. They walked past Bev's plot, toward the back of the narrow yard, to the ring of benches near the composting toilet. It wasn't clear whether they were really out of the weeder's earshot, but the overgrown rows of plants made the yard feel muffled and private.

They sat there in silence for a moment as Bev sipped her iced coffee.

'Well, you had sex with someone who wasn't Todd! That's good just in and of itself.'

Bev glared at her.

'B, I'm just trying to put a positive spin on the situation. And I mean, maybe you should date this guy! He's probably rich. It's not a bad thing!'

Bev sucked hard on her straw. 'It's definitely a bad thing. You have no idea. He lives in one of those new condos with the floor-to-ceiling windows. I woke up this morning, and the first thing I noticed was his gaming console. He has, like, a PlayStation or something. And zero books. Also I sincerely have no idea whether we did it or, like, what motivated me to go home with him . . .'

'What's the last thing you remember?'

Bev wrinkled her forehead. 'Um, we had finished dinner,

and I was going to make my excuses and leave, but then he was like "One more drink!" and then I guess we were going to go back to his place to watch TV? I remember him telling me how big his TV was.'

Amy giggled. 'And that sealed the deal for you? The size of his . . . TV?'

Bev rummaged in her tote bag and fished out a tissue, and for a second Amy thought Bev was going to start crying, but she was only blowing her nose. Amy didn't want to embarrass her by looking straight at her while she snorted into the tissue, so she looked up into the grapevines, where a bird was trying to grab onto the flimsy vines long enough to pluck a few grapes; it kept losing its footing and flapping wildly a few inches from its target as the overripe grapes scattered onto the ground below.

'Did I tell you I had drinks with Mary last week?' Bev asked after she was done getting all the snot out of her nose. Mary was someone Bev and Amy had both worked with at the job where they'd first met.

'No. How is she? Is she still with that guy?'

'She is. She had, like, unexpected psychological insight into me, I thought.'

'Why, what did she say?'

'She said that it's hard for me to accept that there's anything good about me, so I always hang out with people who never give me any positive feedback.'

Amy drank some of her coffee and tried not to see what Bev had said as an accusation exactly.

'Not . . . "people" so much as "guys." Like Todd. How Todd never said anything nice, like, gave me a compliment or anything, and that somehow made me like him more. Or how when people said something nice about my stories in class, I stopped trusting their opinions.'

'Well, everyone has that, I think. I think that's just part of being human, actually.'

'Is it? I keep meeting humans who seem to just *love* themselves. Like that guy last night. It's weird, it's like ... the more objectively horrible they are, the more likely they are to love themselves.'

'To seem to love themselves.'

'Well, yeah.'

'And are these humans mostly dudes?'

'No, not even. I mean yes, they skew dude. But mostly they're just people who seem to know what their spot in the world is and inhabit it comfortably.'

'Well, get Mary to explain it. I'm at a loss, personally.'

They finished their coffee and a few minutes later agreed to leave the garden. The sun was coming up over the grapevine-covered wall. It seemed destined to be an exceptionally hot day, and Amy tried to imagine what she might do with it. All kinds of things needed to be done, of course, but none of them more than any others. She and Bev turned toward each other to say goodbye. They saw each other so often that they didn't usually hug when parting, but to Amy right then it felt appropriate. It didn't to Bev, though, apparently: she made no move toward Amy. 'I'll see you soon,' she said as she turned away, as though sentencing Amy to some dire fate.

13

The next day, Amy woke up at a normal time. She lay still, waiting for the details of her disturbing dream to come back to her. She'd been in some long hall, some sunny corridor, opening doors one by one and finding unexpected people behind them. Her dreams tended to be full of comically blatant symbols: bags too heavy to carry, secret hidden rooms. This one, she hazily remembered, had culminated at some kind of party where she'd watched from a distance as a blurry man went down on one knee, as in an advertisement or reality show, and proposed to a pretty girl. The diamond ring generated blinding flashes of light, the couple embraced cinematically, and dream-Amy had felt pierced by the ring's rays with cramplike pangs of grief. As she opened her eyes, she thought of explaining this idiotic dream to Sam. Making fun of it. Still dozing, he put a lazy paw on the curve of her hip and pulled her toward him, and she rolled into the warmth generated by his body.

They pried themselves out of bed and Sam got into the shower and Amy went to her kitchen to start the coffee and clean up last night's dishes, but as she sponged the counter and listened to NPR with a quarter of her brain, the brokenhearted feeling generated by the dream persisted. It had nothing to do with logic, nothing to do with her actual life. She stared out the window, looking at the flashes of movement between the leaves of the backyard tree: finches bobbing from branch to branch, shaking off a few mulberries each time they landed. It was already the first week of August, it would be her birthday soon; she would be thirty.

Sam had made a portrait of his ex-wife that Amy thought about sometimes when she thought of getting older. It was painted with thick brushstrokes, and the woman's face was half in shadow, with purple stains under her sad dark eyes. Amy hated to look at the portrait. She avoided the corner of Sam's studio where it hung. She hoped someone would buy it so she'd never have to see it again.

When he got out of the shower, Sam came up behind her at the sink and nuzzled her neck. What a jerk she was to be sad. What did she have to be sad about? She turned and pressed her lips against his and felt the luxury of his soft mouth, a minor treat she could revisit in sense memory for the duration of the day. He pulled away from the kiss before it could get too full of intent.

'What are you doing later?' he asked her.

'Nothing. Why, what are you doing?'

'Mmm, I dunno. I have an interview today for that residency. If it goes well, I thought we could go out to celebrate.'

'What residency?'

'It's that one where a bunch of painters stay in this rich lady's house in rural Spain. She's just this rich lady who loves being surrounded by painters or something. And they give you a studio, and you're in Spain, and then it looks really good on your CV and buyers are impressed. I don't know, I thought it was worth a shot.'

'Geez, how long would you be in Spain for?'

Sam shrugged. He lazily moved a spoon around in his cup, stirring honey into his coffee.

'I don't know. I guess it's flexible. Probably at least a couple of months. You could visit! It would be fun.'

'A couple of *months*?'

'Yeah! What?'

'Two months is a long time! Won't you miss me?'

'Of course I'll miss you! I'll miss you a ton. But you'll send me such great emails. You are the best emailer. I would partly be going away to get your emails.'

'You can stay here and I'll send them anyway, how's that?'

'Oh, baby. Come on. It'll be romantic when you visit me.' He pressed the length of his body against her back again as she scoured a formerly nonstick pan that had lost its nonstick coating. 'And there's no guarantee I'll get it. Let's not have a fight about it until I get it.'

'Huh. Okay, that seems reasonable.'

The drone of the NPR host's voice filtered into their silence for a moment, and Sam petted her hair.

'There's something I've been meaning to tell you, though,' Amy said.

'Uh-oh.'

'Yeah, uh. So Mr. Horton shoved this letter under the door the other day ... he's raising the rent. It's more than I can pay, I think.'

'Oh, so ... Do you want me to chip in a little? I'm here all the time. You're right, it's only fair.'

'Uh, would that mean ... Would you live here? Like, would we live together?'

Sam laughed. 'It can mean whatever you want, baby. I mean, it'll mean I'm paying some of the rent so you can keep your apartment and you won't have to look for a new place and all that nonsense. You don't want to move, do you?'

Amy looked around at the sunny little kitchen, the wide planks of its wood floor, the familiar tree outside the window. It was a best-case-scenario one-bedroom, even if it was basically under the BQE. 'I guess I always thought that if I left this place, it would be because I was moving in with someone.'

'Uh-huh ...'

'But I also thought, like, I wouldn't just *live with* someone. Because then when you break up, the two worst things that can happen to you are happening simultaneously. You're breaking up, and you're looking for an apartment.'

'Well, we won't break up!'

'But does that mean we're going to get married?'

'Amy,' Sam said, taking a quick gulp of coffee. 'Are you proposing to me? That's not very romantic.'

Amy rolled her eyes. 'Sorry. Sorry not to be superromantic all the time, like you, Mr. Fucking Romance.'

'Hey, hey. How did we get here? Look, I'm applying for this thing. If I get it, we'll talk about what that means. If I don't, we'll plan some other things. But there's no point in having this conversation now, right?'

'What does *any* of that *mean*?' said Amy, humiliated to find herself on the verge of tears.

Sam reached up and turned off the radio, shutting *Morning Edition* up in mid-sentence. 'Baby, baby, baby. You're my baby. I couldn't live without you. We'll figure this out. I'm not going anywhere right this minute. And I'm totally willing to chip in on the rent – how much is the increase? I'll just pay whatever the difference is from your old rent. That makes it so there's nothing to decide.'

'If you say so, I guess. We definitely need to talk about this more. But right now I have to go to work.' Amy sniffled. 'At my stupid job. That I hate!' Giving up and succumbing to the tide of irrational sadness that had welled up from her dream life and crossed over into reality, she put her head down on the kitchen counter and allowed herself to sob for a solid minute while Sam stood over her, mussing her hair and whispering to her as if she were a skittish animal. After the minute was up, she went into the bathroom and washed her face, took out and reinserted her contact lenses, applied deodorant and tinted moisturizer. When she came out, Sam was intently sketching the nail clippers, which he'd posed on the back of his coffee cup, and rather than disturb him, she kissed the top of his head and quietly walked out the door.

14

Amy, Jackie, and Lizzie often took their lunch break at the same time. They'd get soup and sandwiches from the French bakery and then go sit and eat them in the park near the water. The wind always whipped off the river, drowning out their scraps of conversation. They'd eat their food with quiet determination and stare out at the water and Manhattan, glad not to be eating pathetically alone but also glad that the wind was so noisy that they didn't have to talk to one another.

Today, though, they crammed down their grilled veggie paninis in record time and turned their backs to the wind so they could hear each other speak.

'I talked to Avi this morning while I was coming back from getting coffee at One Girl and he was on one of his smoke breaks, and he had just gotten off the phone with Jonathan and he seemed really upset,' said Lizzie, fretfully twisting a lock of her thick hair around her finger.

'More upset than usual?' said Jackie. Her engagement ring caught a spark of light coming off the water and gleamed, as did the thick black frames of her glasses. Jackie would be fucked if it turned out that they were all fired. She and her fiancé, Mark, were getting married at the Brooklyn Botanic Garden in June, and theirs would be the kind of wedding where everything from the cake to the table decorations would look handmade and artisanal, as though Jackie and Mark had made them, which would be – Lizzie and Amy knew, because they were often told – superexpensive.

'He was freaking. He may have been smoking two cigarettes at once.'

'I'm surprised he didn't eat them or put them up his nose.'

'Amy, this is serious! I asked him what was wrong, and he was like "You should probably start packing up your desk."'

Amy smirked. 'Come *on*. He always thinks Yidster is about to fold. It's because he was in the Israeli army. And because he worked at so many start-ups that folded. He has PTSD.'

'Well, this time he means it! I asked him what Jonathan said, and it was something about how if the site doesn't start making a profit by the end of the year, their dad is pulling the plug.'

'But we've never made a profit. I don't think we even try to sell ads anymore. We just do that ad swap with Jewbilation and Parentheeb.'

'I know! I'm our ad sales manager!'

'You are? I thought I was,' muttered Lizzie. She absently stroked her iPhone's bedazzled case with one finger, as though tickling a small animal under its chin.

'Oof. I would be so bummed if we all lost our jobs,' said Jackie.

'I kind of would be and kind of wouldn't be,' said Lizzie, turning the phone over and swiping meditatively through her email in-box. 'It might be time for something new anyway. You know? I mean, obviously our jobs here are kind of a joke.'

'I like that about our jobs. Where else am I going to get a job where I can just spend all day on *The Knot*?'

'Just go work at some blog For Women, spend all day on *The Knot*, and write blog posts about your wedding feelings. I'm sure you'd barely notice the difference.'

'That's harsh, Amy.'

'Sorry. Sorry. I guess I'm freaking out a little. I mean, I don't really know where I'm gonna go from here.'

'You've never thought about it?'

'Of course I've *thought* about it.' Her thoughts, though, had never been particularly realistic. They'd been along the lines of, maybe she'd go edit a new site that would be created expressly for her, or she'd write a book or a TV show about something she couldn't quite imagine yet. Herself. Someone slightly more interesting than herself.

They made their way back down the cobblestone street and up the stairs to their office, half expecting to see a dejected Avi carrying boxes down the stairs as they climbed them. But when they got there, he was at his desk, shouting at someone on the phone in Hebrew, which was normal, and they trooped back to their stations around the room as they always did.

They didn't hear anything else about Yidster's supposed demise that day, so it was still possible to dismiss it as just another blip, a rumor that had amounted to nothing. But the next day, Amy got back from a meditative, solitary soba-noodle lunch to find Jonathan and Shoshanna sitting at the conference table.

'Amy. Where are the Vyids?' said Shoshanna immediately, not even bothering with pleasantries. Lizzie and Jackie, who were wearing headphones and pretending not to notice what was happening at the conference table, surreptitiously muted the volume on their respective computers.

'I thought we had moved on,' said Amy weakly.

'Moved on? You were supposed to have ten of them ready for our approval by today!'

Amy felt a stab of genuine rage, similar to the emotion she deliberately provoked in herself by reading *Slate* comments or Styles section profiles of vacuous, rich pseudo-artists, but this was sharper, right in the center of her sternum. 'Was that maybe something you told Avi, or was it in an email? Because – I'm so sorry if I've overlooked something – I just didn't get that assignment, actually?'

Jonathan and Shoshanna exchanged looks, maybe telephathically communicating their commitment to the alternate reality they were busily creating.

'We discussed this in our last meeting. Did you not take notes? We gave you *very specific* instructions. We kept refreshing the site, waiting to see that you'd taken the initiative, but no. I'm just wondering what happened.' Jonathan was employing that maddening strategy of pretending to be confused, not angry.

'I wasn't . . . aware that I'd been given specific instructions. I certainly wasn't given . . . a budget? Equipment?'

Shoshanna turned her silver MacBook Air toward Amy. 'This girl just sits in her bedroom and uses the built-in camera on her laptop, Amy! She got two million hits on this, and it's just a video of her explaining why she chose these specific scents of Yankee Candle!'

Amy watched the video, which was on mute, for a few seconds. She felt as if she, too, were on mute. There just wasn't any possible response. *Trying to make a viral video is the worst idea you've ever had, and you've had nothing but bad ideas – in fact, I work for one* was just the merest beginning of what Amy wanted to say to Shoshanna. There was also *This girl's shirt is very low-cut and she appears to be around fifteen* and *A lot of people are watching this in order to make fun of it, and I suspect there is at least one death threat in the comments*, but Amy wanted to keep her job, at least for another few weeks or months until she could find another one, so she didn't say anything.

They all sat there in silence – Jonathan, Shoshanna, and Amy watching the muted video in the center of the room; Avi, Jackie, and Lizzie sitting at the periphery, pretending to be engrossed in their screens. When the girl finished holding up candles and the video ended, Shoshanna crisply clacked her slim computer shut and stood. 'I can't wait to see what you come up with,' she said, and then she and Jonathan were slithering toward the door.

Amy watched them leave, then stood and walked back to her desk, trying to glimpse her coworkers in her peripheral vision. After she sat, she tried to modulate her typing so it wouldn't appear frenzied as she Gchatted with Lizzie and Jackie.

Amy: you heard all that, right?
Lizzie: duh
Jackie: mmhmm
Amy: Well maybe this will be fun! We can all take turns doing them and
Lizzie: no fucking way
Jackie: yeah, no one told us to do shit. You're on your own here
Lizzie: you're the one with expertise in these matters
Amy: NoOOOOooooo
Lizzie: Oh, come on, it won't be that bad. And like no one will see them
Jackie: no one is even going to watch them
Lizzie: Jinx
Jackie: heh
Amy: ughhhhhhhh
Lizzie: cheer up, dude, you'll do one and then they'll forget all about it
Amy: if you hear of any jobs lmk
Jackie: If I hear of any jobs I am applying for them, bitch
Amy: you two suck

Amy is busy, you may be interrupting.

15

The first time Bev had ever taken a pregnancy test was in her junior year of high school, two weeks after losing her virginity to Trevor Gillespie. Her period wasn't late and Trevor had used a condom, but she'd driven three towns over to buy the test anyway. She was certain that God would punish her for having sex, and for no longer believing in him. Bev had wondered a lot, while she was driving, how it was possible that she thought a God she no longer believed in was still capable of punishing her.

She was sure that with time, she would get out of the habit of feeling guilty about every single thing she did. So recently, though, she and her sisters had been forced to recite memorized verses from Scripture every night at the dinner table. Bits of them still got stuck in her head on repeat, like the boy-band songs that were just beginning to dominate the newly Clear Channel-owned airwaves. But instead of Backstreet's Back or 'As Long as You Love Me,'

Bev's internal monologue chanted at her about virtuous women and pure hearts.

She and Trevor had not lain in sin, exactly. They had remained standing, behind a toolshed, in sin. Probably that was even worse.

Another bad thing: Trevor did not, generally speaking, acknowledge Bev's existence when he encountered her at school. His official girlfriend was a fellow senior, a person with teased bangs and a big gaggle of teased-bang friends. But Trevor had worked for several years after school at Bev's dad's lumberyard, shouldering stacks of two-by-fours and loading them onto trucks, the kind of work her dad had begun to hire more workers to do because he'd lifted those heavy things for so many years now that he couldn't anymore. Trevor and Bev had been acknowledging each other with nods and grunts since she was a seventh grader, and then, when Bev started high school and finally grew breasts, he started occasionally saying full words to her, such as 'Hi' and her name.

At first this attention had led Bev to make the classic mistake of ascribing to Trevor all the virtues of the characters in the books she read, people she found infinitely more interesting than anyone she knew in real life. She hadn't even had what most of the isolated, book-loving heroines of the books had: one good teacher or wise old relative or like-minded confidante. She'd been realistic enough to know, at least, that she couldn't expect Trevor to become her confidant. Maybe, though, she thought, he would become her boyfriend. She excused their initial clandestine make-out session to herself with this hope. It would be worth a little bad behavior if

Trevor would elevate her from 'almost friendless, library-dwelling weirdo' to 'senior's girlfriend.' Not to imply that she had let him kiss and touch her unwillingly, with some mercenary goal in mind. It had been her idea, actually, to ask him to go for a walk to the perimeter of the property with her, and she had spread out her hoodie on the grass and motioned for him to sit.

He'd sat and looked at her with wide-set blue eyes. He smelled sweaty and pleasantly sour, like wood shavings, and dirt ringed his big neck. In a few years he would begin to look like most of the men in Bev's hometown, still thick around the shoulders and arms but with pregnant-looking guts and ham-hock thighs from fast-food lunches and hot-dish dinners. But right then, at eighteen, he was a perfect specimen, if a little Neanderthalish. Bev wanted to see him naked. She imagined him naked and herself fully clothed. In her mind's eye she saw him kneeling in front of her in the cornfield – naked, begging – while she stood over him wielding mysterious, enormous power.

'You know I have a girlfriend,' he said.

'Yeah, but I thought this could be, like, a casual thing. No strings attached, et cetera.'

He'd grinned, showing a broken tooth that hadn't been capped. 'Damn, Beverly, I thought you were some kind of holy virgin! But if you're okay with it . . .'

'I'm okay with it. This is just for fun,' she'd said, and he leaned in and kissed her.

She hadn't been expecting anything, really, so she'd been surprised at both the vehemence of the kiss and its subtlety. Other boys – not that there had been many, just a couple of pro forma Bible camp closet fumblers – had mashed their tongues into her mouth carelessly. Those boys had seemed fundamentally uninterested in kissing, more occupied with semi-covertly rubbing their boners against some part of her – her knee, her hand, the side of her leg, it didn't seem to matter – just like little dogs. Trevor, she realized right away, was different. He had kissed her collaboratively, teasing her, letting her tease him back, having a kind of conversation with her that was much more interesting than anything he'd ever said to her with words. For the remaining moments that she was still capable of conscious thought, she'd thought he would be a good person to have sex with.

But sex, when they tried it a few clandestine-make-out-full weeks later, was almost ruined by Bev's body, which was undermined by guilt in a way that her mind was somehow not. 'It's okay,' she said numerous times, but it wasn't, and for a horrible moment she thought that Trevor had given up. They moved away from each other, breathless, Bev feeling leaden with disappointment. To have gone so far, then failed! It was humiliating, not to mention just as much of a sin as the actual completed act would have been. She'd expected Trevor to shrug back into his pants and jacket as easily as he'd shrugged them off and leave her there and never come back. Instead, he leaned back toward her, kissing her again.

'It's because you're scared,' he'd said quietly. 'What would make you less scared?'

'I don't know. I'm sorry.'

'It's safe. There's nothing to worry about.'

There was so much to worry about, always. She couldn't make her mind shut up.

'I have an idea,' he said, and then he knelt – she was short enough, and he was tall enough, that kneeling had put his face right between her legs – and he pushed her clenched thighs apart with one gentle but peremptory gesture.

'Oh my god, no way,' Bev said, somewhat involuntarily.

'I want to.' His voice somewhat muffled.

'This is not going to make me more relaxed!' Bev could feel herself blushing with horror, humiliation, and shame. There was no possible way for her to enjoy what he was doing, and the idea that *he* might enjoy it was almost frightening. Was he enjoying it? And then somehow the shame became part of what was unignorably becoming fun. She was being so bad! Oh god, she was so dirty and disgusting and bad. Oh.

Later, as the back of her head knocked gently against the toolshed, and her heels – still shod in her Converse sneakers – left the ground slightly with each thrust, Bev had no thoughts, not even about her own badness. And even in the immediate aftermath, when she and Trevor found themselves unable to quite make eye contact – they had left reality together and were now back in it, apart – she had no thoughts save one that repeated over and over: she had to get out of the Midwest, she had to go somewhere where the kind of thing she'd just experienced was accepted, a regular occurrence, popular, possibly a public utility. She had been on the fence about remaining in Minnesota for college. Now she was determined to go as far away as possible, maybe to another country. She could not have cared less about Trevor in that moment. She wanted all of the Trevors, available whenever, forever.

Two weeks later, though, during which Trevor had reverted to his previous monosyllabic relationship with Bev and she had found herself pining stupidly for another kiss or even just a smiling acknowledgment of what they'd done, she'd found herself worrying, and needing to know for sure that at least her life hadn't been ruined. The single-lane road wound around and took forever, but she kept driving until she found a convenience store where no one could possibly know her.

After she bought the test, she'd pulled over into a cornfield and pulled down her jean shorts and peed on it right there, waiting the length of a Dixie Chicks song coming from her car's speakers before checking the results. No one was around for miles, so no one heard her whoop of relief.

The part of the whole experience that she remembered most vividly now, as she awaited the test result in her Brooklyn bathroom, was the packaging of that first test: a picture of a pastel-clad mother with a fluffy blond hairdo, cradling an infant, looking radiant: Madonna and child. The test she was taking now had come in stylish modern packaging. On the stick itself there was no blue or pink line; the test was more high-tech than that, though she still had to check the package insert to confirm that what the digital display meant by ☺ was that she was pregnant.

16

'It seems improbable that this hasn't happened to us before.'

'Us? Are you going to start saying "we're pregnant"?' Bev cringed. 'We're not a couple, Amy.'

'I meant "happened to either of us," but we are a couple, in a way. I mean, we're life partners. All these people' – Amy gestured at the couples walking by them at the outdoor flea market, eating grilled corncobs and tacos, grinning at each other in Ray-Bans – 'are obviously going to break up once their sexual chemistry peters out. But we'll be together forever.'

'I know, but this isn't happening to you. It's not your problem; it's mine.' Bev took a bite of her own grilled corncob, chewed it slowly, then spat it into her napkin. 'Ughhh. I'm so ravenous, but then I put something in my mouth and I feel like I'm gonna puke again.'

'Are you sure you're not just hungover?'

'I thought so at first, but my hangovers don't usually last for a week. And I also typically get them from drinking, not from, like, existing. And I did take a test.'

A nearby baby crowed loudly, as if on cue, and they couldn't stop themselves from turning to look at it. It was a rosy perfect baby from the rosy perfect baby dispensary in central Brooklyn, where rich, responsible thirty-three-year-old women went to be issued babies from some sort of giant bin. This baby was doing a clumsy bouncing-in-place dance while taking the radish slices from its mother's taco and flicking them one by one onto the pavement, narrating its activities with a battery of earsplitting bird noises.

'What a little monster,' Amy said before she could stop herself. She and Bev continued to stare at the radish-flicking baby, transfixed, and then Bev calmly turned her head to the side and vomited a neat mouthful of corn chunks into an empty taco tray. No one even noticed. Amy felt a pang of disgust, or maybe sympathetic nausea. She waited till Bev was done wiping her mouth.

'Um, do you wanna go home?'

'No. I like being around people right now. It makes me feel more normal. I've been holed up in my bedroom for the past few days, turning down temp assignments and watching bad TV on my computer. And reading stuff on the Internet about abortion and eating bland food and vomiting it up.'

'Why didn't you tell me sooner?'

'I guess because having this conversation with you officially makes it into something that's actually happening?'

'Fair enough.' Amy picked up her taco, but her eye caught on the little yellow puddle of frothy corn vomit in Bev's tray and she put it down again. 'So, okay, have you made the appointment yet, after all that online research?'

'Yeah. They said I have to wait another two weeks for there to be enough baby cells for them to vacuum out of my uterus. So, it's two Thursdays from now. Are you, I mean ... '

'No, duh, of course I can come.'

'Phew.'

'Obviously I'm coming, dude! I want to help, I mean, what you said is true, but you shouldn't feel like you're alone dealing with this. I'm right here!' Amy said, remembering with a twinge that she had a lunchtime waxing appointment that Thursday that would be annoying to reschedule. 'So how are you feeling, aside from nauseated and freaked out?'

Bev turned and looked at the taco baby again; it was impossible not to. He had tired of his taco flicking and was now lying, sleepy and docile, in his mother's arms, a look of beatific happiness on his dollish face. The mother was wearing tall Frye boots and at least five hundred dollars' worth of smooth leather jacket, and was talking animatedly to a friend, absently stroking the baby's little topknot of silky hair. Bev was wearing Vans that had once been black and white and were now brownish gray and white. Her own hair looked as if it had either just been washed in the last hour or had not been washed in days.

'Mostly I feel like a total failure. I mean, by the time my mom was my age, she'd had three babies. I look at my life, and it's just completely insane – laughable – to imagine bringing a child into it. Think of a child in my apartment that I share with my disgusting roommates! It's all one big exposed, chewable wire. My baby would grow up eating roaches straight off the floor.'

'Well, I'm sure plenty of babies do,' Amy said, then looked at Bev's face and realized that this wasn't quite the pep talk that was called for. 'Hey, you know, this is so not a big deal. You will totally have a baby later if you want to. Your accidentally getting pregnant right now is not some kind of referendum on the state of your life. It could happen to anyone! And Thursday after next it'll be like it never happened at all.'

'But I'm just saying, like, we're not at an age anymore where abortion is the only rational thing. People we know have babies.'

'No one we're close to. And obviously no one in our, like, tax bracket. I get your thought process here, but just because you're pregnant doesn't mean you have to feel bad about not being ready to have a baby.'

Bev laughed. 'Um, of course it does. How could I possibly avoid thinking that? Wouldn't you think that? I mean, what would you do if this was happening to you?'

Amy had thought about this and knew exactly what she would do. A baby was supposed to be the trophy you received for attaining a perfected, mature life, not another hurdle to surmount on the infinite sprint toward that infinitely receding, possibly nonexistent finish line. 'What you're doing, of course. It would be a no-brainer.'

'It isn't a no-brainer for me.'

'Because of your . . . religion? Or like, not your religion, but how you were raised?'

'No, not even. Not at all. I mean, maybe very subconsciously there's some vestigial hell stuff still in my brain, but it's maybe more that, like ... I don't know, I think I have this idea about adulthood that kids are the only thing that can make you an adult. And I don't imagine that there's ever going to be any other way for me to have a kid than to be surprised and forced into it, as bizarre as that sounds. It's just, like, clearly never going to happen for me any other way.'

'That *does* sound bizarre to me. And of course it could happen another way! You're only thirty!'

Bev sighed. 'I'm sorry. I don't have the energy to keep thinking about this. Don't worry, I'm just explaining my thought process, not saying I want to have a baby.'

'I mean, clearly it would be better to have neither baby nor abortion, but that ship has sailed.'

'It did sail. It go, it gone. Bye-bye.' They smiled at each other wearily. A barbecue-scented breeze washed over the concrete bleachers, and Bev audibly gagged. 'Okay, fine, let's get out of here. I left the house, many bonus points to me for doing that.'

'Many bonus points for telling me.'

'Don't mention it. See you Thursday?'

'It's a date.'

17

The eleven days between Bev's telling Amy she was pregnant and her appointment at Murray Hill Gynecology Partners dragged endlessly. On Monday Bev called in for another temp assignment because otherwise she would be scraping dangerously close to the bottom of her checking account, and she got assigned to the French bank again – which was good, in a way, because they expected so little of her that no one even seemed to notice that she was spending time away from her desk, hunched over a toilet in a stall in the freezing-cold hall bathroom, where luckily no one was ever peeing; they seemed to have no female employees besides the one she was filling in for.

After work on Monday she came straight home, sprinting up the four flights so quickly she almost tripped over the loose tile on the third-floor landing that she'd been nagging the super about for the duration of her tenancy. The landing smelled like moist old newspapers and canned soup, as usual.

As she opened the door, she almost walked straight into one of her two roommates, Sheila, who was on her way out the door; she worked night shifts as an orderly at a psychiatric hospital.

'Are you feeling okay, Bev? You've been sick a lot lately. The bathroom, um, is getting a bit out of hand, sorry to mention it.'

'Oh, yes, sorry! I'm getting over a little stomach flu. I'll do a deep clean tonight. I'm really sorry.'

'I'm glad to hear you're feeling better. I see enough vomit at work, you know? Ha.'

'Ha. Okay. See ya later.'

It was actually rare for her to cross paths with Sheila; Bev usually did errands or saw Amy or Mary after work, but tonight she just wanted to crawl straight into bed. She had to force herself to do a few life-maintenance chores first, though, including cleaning the bathroom. There was also something else she was going to have to get over with eventually that she might as well do right now, so she could stop dreading it. She could even do both things at once, for maximum efficiency and masochism. She put her headphones in and attached them to her phone, dialed, then put on rubber gloves and started filling a mop bucket with hot water and disinfectant.

Steve picked up on the first ring. 'Hey, Beverly! I'm pumped to hear from you. The other night was so fun! You wanna make a plan to hang out again?'

'Uh. Well, I was calling about the other night, actually.' She couldn't keep dread and a little bit of what probably sounded like anger out of her voice. Already she was regretting calling him. But it was the right thing to do, and besides, he could potentially be helpful, financially – it was completely reasonable to expect him to, at least, go halfsies on the abortion. She hoped he'd offer to pay for all of it. He hadn't stinted on drinks or dinner, after all.

'Uh-oh. You sound upset,' Steve hazarded, in a less chill tone of voice.

'Oh, well . . . yeah, I guess I kind of am?'

There was a long pause, and when Steve finally spoke again, his voice was cold. 'You definitely said yes. You clearly wanted it. If you had regrets afterward, that's not my problem. But I definitely didn't do anything wrong, and I hope you're not planning to say otherwise.'

Bev almost dropped the sponge she was using to scrub the toilet. There was no vent or fan in the windowless bathroom, and the smell of the disinfectant, which had been pleasantly bracing at first, was starting to make her head spin now.

'That's not where I was going with that, but, wow. Okay.'

He tried to play it off. 'Oh, you know what I mean. But I'm sorry, you're right, that was a harsh way of putting it. Is everything cool?'

'Well, actually, no. I'm . . . look, I need to have an abortion. The appointment's this week. I was hoping you'd help pay for it.'

'Uh, sorry if this is rude, but isn't there someone you could ask for a loan who you know a little better? We've gone on one date.'

'I'm asking because it's partially your . . . your fault!' Was he really this dense, or was he pretending to be? She tried to remember what he did at the real estate company. Was he a lawyer? She didn't think so.

'How do you know? Where's the evidence?'

There was no way she was going to achieve her goal, she realized with sudden clarity, and in the same moment, she realized she was going to be sick again. Later, she would keep herself up at night thinking of many, many choice insults she should have hurled at this point in the conversation. Instead, though, she simply said, 'Fuck you, bye,' hung up, and then undid all the work she'd done in the bathroom by vomiting a torrent of iced coffee and yellow bile that splattered onto the wall beside the toilet seat.

Okay, cross 'call Steve' off the list.

She stumbled out of the bathroom and into the half-lit common area of the apartment, slumping onto the futon and turning on the TV in the same practiced movement. A *Seinfeld* rerun came on and soothed her agitated brain and body, and she allowed herself a few minutes of this intense recuperation before she moved on to her next duty.

She pulled out the stack of mail from under the coffee table and as quickly as possible tore the pile of bills out of their envelopes. Two credit card statements, two student-loan bills, the electric, gas, and wireless Internet bills that she was tasked with dividing among the roommates and collecting money from them to pay, her health insurance bill – she still had COBRA coverage from being in grad school, even though she kept making a mental note to find out whether Freelancers Union might be marginally cheaper – and her phone bill. She saved for last a red envelope from her bank that seemed likely to contain bad news, and she wasn't disappointed: a letter informed her that her repeated overdrafts were causing them to increase her overdraft fee.

She took out a piece of notebook paper and added everything up, then calculated how much she'd need to earn temping to pay it, and while the result was depressingly tight – and did not include such luxuries as food, toiletries, and abortions, all of which she would have to charge to her credit cards – it was manageable, as long as she didn't take any more days off this month or in the foreseeable future. She'd have to take next Thursday off, it was true, but hopefully not Friday. It wasn't great news, but it felt better to know.

Ever since her conversation with Amy on Sunday, there had been a thought in Bev's mind that didn't even qualify as a full thought – more of a sub-thought, a half-heard whisper thrumming under the surface of all her brain's other activity. It had been about the idea of her pregnancy as a baby, and as likely her only chance at having one. This hadn't made any sense to Amy, and Bev understood why; it wasn't the kind of thing you could expect someone from Amy's background to understand. But Bev's parents had been young and broke when they'd had her, and still young and still relatively broke when they'd had her siblings. And although it hadn't been easy not to have the same sneakers or breakfast cereals as other kids, she loved her sisters and her brother. Most of the time, she was glad she'd been born. Living in New York City was different from living in Minnesota, for sure, and she didn't have her parents' unwavering idea of Jesus as a busybodyish person who intervened in everyone's lives, which she knew made rough moments easier to survive. But there was still something about having grown up that way that was making her feelings less straightforward than the piece of paper in front of her – not to mention the conversation she'd just had with Father of the Year Steve – told her that they should be.

The thought was simply that if she could imagine a way of supporting herself and a baby, she would do it. But she couldn't, and so she wouldn't. It was – it had to be – that simple.

18

In the end, they didn't make Amy try to replicate the lo-fi viral success of 'Strawberry Cheesecake Yankee Candle AT LAST!!!' Instead Jonathan and Shoshanna had fun splashing out on equipment and rentals for the first Vyideo shoot. Like a lot of people who have always been rich, they had no problem spending money on onetime follies, but they balked at ongoing minor expenses, like better toilet paper for the Yidster bathroom. They'd hired a professional makeup artist as well as a cameraman, who'd already spent a couple of hours lighting the corner of the office where a roll of white paper had been gaffer-taped to the wall. This was where Amy was going to be shot.

Amy glanced over toward the white corner as she hunched at her desk, pretending as always to be super busy. She felt simultaneously clammy and hot, as if she were coming down with the flu. In the opposite corner the makeup artist was unloading her little rolling suitcase full of tubes and compacts and palettes. Lizzie and Jackie stared unabashedly at the proceedings from their desks. If Jonathan and Shoshanna had bothered to glance at Yidster all day (they hadn't), they would have seen that it had been updated just once, at 10:00 a.m., with a slide show about baby animals with spots on the tops of their furry heads that looked like yarmulkes. Amy had noticed but had not said anything about it.

Finally, Amy situated herself over in the corner in front of the camera. Jonathan situated himself in a swivel chair pumped up to its highest setting, to compensate for his short torso and maybe to make it seem more like a director's chair. The cameraman nodded. It was time to start.

'Okay, Amy!' Jonathan shouted, even though she was about seven feet away from him. 'We're rolling! Go anytime.'

'This is Amy Schein, coming to you live from Yidster headquarters with today's Yid Vid!'

'Cut! "Coming to you live"?'

'Sorry. What should I . . . '

'Just, don't be hokey. Be yourself. Okay, start again.'

Amy shuddered inwardly. 'Be yourself' was something she'd heard a lot in the early days of her job at the gossip blog; it had never meant 'Be yourself' then and it didn't now, either. Amy wished there were some way to explain to Jonathan that *real* directors, at least the ones who worked on those greatest-moments-in-pop-culture shows, lied to you and flattered you all the time to keep your confidence up: 'That was great! I think we can get an even better one, though. Want to try it one more time?' was their way of saying you had been abominably terrible and were about to do thirty more takes.

'I'm Amy Schein, and this is today's Yid Vid!'

'Cut! Ugh, can you just . . . say two words without moving your eyebrows? Two words. It's not hard. Look at me right now, saying this. Did my eyebrows just move?'

They had, actually, but Amy figured that pointing it out to him was probably counterproductive. She wondered whether she should get Botox, just once, just to get her through this day.

'I'm Amy Schein, and this is a Yid Vid.'

'Cut! Okay, that was better, but now it's a little flat. Can you just do "enthusiastic" without, like, "spastic"?' Jonathan paused. 'Heh, that rhymed. Sorry, hold on a sec.'

'Jonathan,' Amy said, finally losing her patience. 'Are you *tweeting* that?'

He didn't look up from his iPhone. 'Don't worry. I'm not saying it's about you.'

Amy's eyebrows did somersaults, but Jonathan was too immersed in his phone to notice. By the time he turned his attention back to Amy, she had made up her mind.

'Jonathan?'

'Yeah, okay, let's go again. The intro, and then just go right into the first segment.'

'No, Jonathan. Can we stop, actually? I have to talk to you about . . . I can't do this.'

He shrugged. 'You're right, you're pretty bad at it, but you can do it. We'll just edit it a lot. You can edit it, right?'

Amy's heart was racing; she was so angry, suddenly, that she felt as if she might spontaneously burst into flames. Jonathan was everyone she had ever hated: the gossip blog boss who'd hung her out to dry, the landlord who'd raised her rent, the parents who didn't even bother to humor her when she talked about her half-fledged dreams. She hated him so intensely, but not as intensely as she hated herself for putting herself in a position where she had no choice but to take orders from him.

She did have a choice, though. It was an idiotic choice, an overtly self-destructive choice, but it was her choice to make.

'Jonathan, this is it. I'm done. I quit.'

'Hmm?'

'I don't want to work here anymore. I'm quitting. I'm not giving any notice. Effective immediately, I don't work here anymore. You can find someone else to . . . ' Amy searched for the right words. She didn't want to confess that her job had largely consisted of doing nothing; it seemed undignified. 'To keep your website up and running,' she finished lamely. 'But this isn't me, and I can't pretend that it is anymore.'

'What do you mean, it isn't you? Amy, you *are* Yidster. You're the essence of Yidster.'

'What do you even *mean* by that?'

'You're, you know, our target audience. Young, upwardly mobile urban Jews.'

'Well, I'm officially mobilizing downward. As of right now.' She turned on her heel and strode purposefully past the foosball table toward her desk to grab her purse. Lizzie and Jackie, who'd been doing their best to pretend not to be listening attentively to every word, struggled not to swivel their heads toward her as she hurriedly pulled a few lingering office necessities – flip-flops, a pair of gloves, deodorant – out of her desk drawers.

'I should have known better than to hire you. Isn't this what you did at your last job, just flamed out? This is very unprofessional, Amy. You know that, right? And I'll tell anyone who asks that you're an unreliable employee.'

Avi, returning from a smoke break, caught the tail end of this sentence as he entered the office, just as Amy was about to walk out the door. 'She's leaving?'

'Good riddance to her!' Jonathan snarled.

Avi narrowed his eyes. '*Deserter*,' he hissed at Amy in a chilling whisper.

'Oh, get over yourselves, both of you,' Amy said, starting to feel a bit ridiculous. 'Uh, bye, Lizzie. Bye, Jackie. Good luck. See you on Facebook and whatnot.'

'Um, bye,' said Jackie. 'Good luck!'

Lizzie just stared, apparently too stunned to speak.

Waiting for the elevator was out of the question. Amy took the stairs two at a time, stopping to take deep breaths at the first-floor landing. Emerging onto the sidewalk, she decided to keep walking all the way home. She had to do something with this surplus of nervous energy; she had to stay in motion as long as possible.

It was cooler than she'd thought it would be when she left the house that morning; chilly air sliced through her light blouse – the unmistakable taste of fall coming more quickly than anyone had anticipated. Did she even own a good winter jacket? The one she'd bought a few years ago, at the height of her fiscal recklessness when she'd first gotten the blog job, was a piece of designer nonsense with detachable sleeves. Detachable sleeves! As if you'd ever think, *You know, what I really want is a jacket that will warm my torso but leave my extremities bare*. She had five hundred dollars in her bank account. Her rent and her credit card payments were due in a week.

If only she'd just been patient, feigned incompetence (really feigned it, not just *been* incompetent) until they fired her, so she could have gone on unemployment! She felt dangerously light-headed for a second and tried to force herself to notice her surroundings: the beautiful old houses, the deserted cobbled streets of Vinegar Hill, the stretch of scenic quaintness she was traversing between her work neighborhood and the industrial port of the Navy Yard.

There was a Buddhist temple on the corner, an anomalous multicolored cinder-block building that stood out among the brownstones. Its façade was covered by little Tibetan flags that fluttered in the wind. Impulsively, Amy sprinted up its front steps and tried the door, which was locked.

Just as she was poised with her finger over the bell, she heard noises coming from inside. She stopped. What had she even been thinking – that she would throw herself on the mercy of some wise old boddhisattva and learn to lead a life of mindful solitude? She ran back down the steps and kept running until she passed the tow pound and the Navy Yard, then jogged parallel to the BQE and finally up her own front stoop. A wave of exhaustion hit her as she unlocked the door to the building, and she dragged herself up the inner staircase with exaggerated, zombielike slowness.

When she arrived at her apartment door, she gasped: there was a letter taped to it. It was from Mr. Horton, or '99 Emerson LLC,' as he liked to call himself these days. It informed her that she had exceeded the proscribed amount of time in which to make her decision and was now being evicted. She had a month to gather her things, find a new apartment, and move.

Amy unlocked the door, fell into the bathroom, opened the medicine cabinet, and scrabbled around behind a box of tampons until she found her emergency Camels, stale but still smokable. She felt too weak to go outside again, so she knelt by the open back window of her apartment and chain-smoked until she was about to pass out, then lay down on the floor and stared up at the ceiling. How was it possible that in just a few hours she had gone from okay to destitute and homeless? How could a destitute homeless person be in possession of a Comme des Garçons wallet, a pair of Worishofer sandals, a fridge with Moroccan oil-packed sun-dried tomatoes in it – all these accoutrements of bourgeois stability, but none of the actual stability itself? Should she call her parents? She could not even bring herself to imagine the conversation. She would call Bev. No, Bev was dealing with so much of her own shit right now. Really, she should call Sam. What was a boyfriend for, if not to console you when you were having a crisis?

19

Sam's studio was in the Pencil Factory, a warehouse building in Greenpoint that reminded Amy of the best things about college. The stairwells always smelled like paint and hand-rolled cigarettes, and the whole thing was heated unevenly by big old radiators. Amy loved visiting Sam there, seeing all the other artists in the hallways and on the roof; it was so cheering to know that there were still people who made their living by creating physical things – even if some of them were commercial illustrators and graphic designers. Well, Sam wasn't, anyway! He was just a guy who made giant oil paintings of Cuisinarts.

They went up to the roof to talk. It was still cool, and getting dark alarmingly early. Amy pulled out her pack of stale Camels. Sam made a face.

'What? I told you, I'm freaking out! I'm allowed to smoke!'

'I'm not going to want to kiss you if you smoke that, baby,'

Sam said, pulling her close and pushing her hand away from the pack. Amy felt a stab of rage. Who cared about kissing? She needed to smoke more than she needed a kiss. But she put the Camels away. She also needed Sam on her side.

'Well, so ... I don't know where to begin, really, but you know how they were making me do those videos? I was doing one today, and I just stopped in the middle and announced my resignation, effective immediately.'

Sam exhaled slowly. 'Oh, wow. Wow. That is big news.'

Amy felt around longingly in her pocket for the shape of the cigarettes, the lighter. 'Yeah, I know. But I just couldn't risk ... I mean, the idea of putting myself out there like that, for Yidster? Even if no one saw it, I mean ... I'd still see it. And you know someone would find it. There'd be comments, and I'd read them, and I'd feel angry at myself for reading them, for letting that stuff in my head, and then on top of that I'd have that stuff in my head. You don't know what it's like ...'

Sam shrugged. 'I got a bad review of my last show on some website called Fartiste.'

'Well, okay, but what I'm saying is, you don't know what it's like to feel as miserable as I used to feel, because of the Internet.'

'You're right. I don't know, exactly, how that feels.'

Sam's family had been so poor that they hadn't had enough to eat sometimes when they first came to the United States, and his older sister had died of leukemia when he was a teenager. He never brought up either thing, of course.

'Look, I know it's not the end of the world. But also – and I guess this is the really bad thing – Mr. Horton's kicking me out. He says I didn't respond to his letter about the rent increase quickly enough.'

'Oh. Why didn't you?'

'Well, because I thought we were going to talk more. About moving in together, or not, or whatever. I thought maybe we'd end up finding a new place together. But now I guess I'm not really in a position to ... well, anyway, I was procrastinating about it. I don't think he's actually within his rights to kick me out. I mean, I can fight it ...'

'You live above him, though. He could make living there really uncomfortable for you.'

'Yeah, I've thought of that,' Amy snapped. She desperately ached for the click of the lighter, that first stinging lungful of smoke.

'You could just talk to him, though. Maybe he'd see reason. He probably just wants you to pay the new rent.'

'Well, I don't want to, as a matter of principle! And also I can't afford to.'

'Even with my help?'

'How much help are we talking about? I have one more paycheck coming from Yidster, but that's it, and I need to be able to, like, eat ... '

'Well, as long as you don't mean "eat at fancy restaurants," you should be fine, right? I mean, you must have some savings.'

They'd never really talked about money. Money had seemed like a part of the outside world, the world their relationship was a refuge from. Certainly the issue had reared its ugly head at times; they'd both eyed each other's respective stacks of bank statements and bills and wondered what was inside them. And there was Sam's charming Marxist thing of thinking that restaurants, new clothes, et cetera, were frivolities that only served to keep workers addicted and enslaved by Capital. Amy agreed with him about this, in theory, but she loved wearing a new outfit for the first time, ideally to a restaurant.

Now the moment of truth had come, and Amy decided – well, really, she had no choice – to trust Sam with the truth. 'I have the opposite of savings. I have to pay two hundred dollars a month to a credit card I can't even use anymore.'

'Is it debt you ran up because you were buying necessities with your credit card when you were unemployed, or because you didn't want to fall behind on your student loan payments?'

'No. It's from buying stuff that I couldn't afford, but that I didn't want to acknowledge to myself that I couldn't afford, because I just didn't want to think about money.'

'What kind of stuff? Clothes? You don't even dress that well!'

'Uh, thanks!' Fuck it, she was smoking.

'Amy, look, I'm sorry I said that. I'm not trying to judge you. I haven't always been responsible either. And I am willing to help you out. But I'm not exactly made out of money, either. Is there maybe someone else you could ask, like your parents or something? I'm just trying to save up for Spain right now and help my parents get their car repaired, and I can barely afford my own rent, much less yours.'

'So you're going to Spain?'

He refused to meet her gaze. She exhaled, trying to angle the smoke away from him, but the wind blew it toward him anyway and he unconsciously fanned at it, the gesture of swatting the air in her general direction making it seem as if he were shooing her away.

'Well, I didn't want to interrupt your bad news with my good news, but yeah, I got the fellowship! Isn't that great? I'm excited for you to visit.'

Amy stared at Sam, the cigarette cherry burning dangerously close to her clenching fingertips. They'd spent so much time together, breathing the same air, sleeping in the same bed, hearing each other use the bathroom and not really caring or even thinking about it. For the past few months it had seemed as if they were in each other's lives for real, maybe for good. But now it seemed that Amy might have made a mistake. Maybe she had assumed that what she and Sam had was veering in a permanent direction because they were at an age when people got married. She thought suddenly of how often during their relationship they'd found themselves at weddings, at dinners, surrounded by other couples, functioning as a unit and finding that it was easier to do so. Because couples were what society wanted, what it was built for. But maybe they hadn't been moving toward anything, maybe they had simply been coasting on inertia.

Amy looked at Sam's face and tried to find the familiar person she'd felt so tenderly toward. But she was looking at a stranger. A stranger who was about to go to Spain for two months.

'How would I visit you? I can't afford to visit you,' she said quietly, and started walking back toward the stairs.

'Amy, wait, I have my checkbook downstairs. Let me write

you a check. For the rent I owe you, because I've been staying at your place so often.'

Amy wanted to be dramatic and principled and keep walking, but of course she went downstairs with him and got the check (for seven hundred dollars) and even let him kiss her, which he valiantly did in spite of her cigarette breath. Then they parted without any more discussion, promising to call each other later.

20

Bev sat next to Amy in a magenta plastic chair, clearly trying not to puke. Her face was even paler than usual. She had acted nonchalant that morning, bustling around her apartment with her usual stomping efficiency when Amy came to pick her up, but now she was clutching Amy's forearm with a clammy hand.

'Beverly Tunney? Beverly?' a nurse finally called out from the doorway, and everyone in the waiting room tried to be subtle as their bored curiosity made them automatically turn toward Bev as she stood up. Amy gave her arm a last squeeze, then watched as she walked past the reception desk toward the hallway that led to another waiting room, a smaller one with a low couch and two chairs. This would be where Bev would spend the last ten minutes or so before her abortion, probably staring blankly into space rather than reading any of the celebrity or parenting magazines arrayed on the coffee table.

But instead of continuing into the hallway, Bev stopped walking. 'I'm really sorry. I'm not feeling well,' she said to nobody in particular before slumping to her knees, then sprawling faceup on the floor.

Amy ran across the room and crouched on the floor next to Bev's head. A girly susurration rippled through the waiting room as everyone gasped and murmured and whispered to each other, trying to be polite. The nurse knelt down next to Amy and took unconscious Bev's pulse. She was a serious-looking woman with big pavé-diamond rings cutting slices into her swollen fingers. 'Did she have anything to eat today, do you know?' she asked Amy.

'Probably not; she's been nauseous . . . '

'But you don't know for sure? Are you her partner?'

'No. I'm just her friend.'

'But you don't live with her.'

'No.'

'Okay.' The nurse sighed. Bev's eyelids fluttered. 'Beverly?'

Bev opened her eyes, squinting because she was staring straight up at the fluorescent lights. 'Oh shit. What the fuck? Did I faint? Oh god, I'm so embarrassed,' she said, and then started to cry.

'Beverly, can you stand up? I'm going to bring you back to one of the exam rooms and you can lie down there till you start feeling better, okay?'

'Can I come with her?'

The nurse paused for a second, then shrugged her assent.

'I can still get it done today, though, right?' Bev asked as the nurse helped her to her feet, and they started walking, slowly, down the hall. 'Oh, whoa. I feel weird. Can I sit down?'

The nurse opened the door to an empty exam room – there was a whiff of rubbing alcohol, a familiar crinkle of paper as Bev sat on the examining table – and instructed Bev to put her head between her knees until she stopped feeling dizzy. 'Don't let her get up and walk around yet,' she said sternly as she left the room, as though somehow the whole thing were Amy's fault.

With her head between her knees, Bev started sniffling again. 'I can't believe I even found a way to fuck *this* up.'

'Shh,' said Amy, paper crunching under her butt as she sat down next to Bev and started stroking her back. 'You haven't fucked anything up. You're very brave.'

21

Back when Bev and Amy worked together at the publishing house, there had been a bar on an otherwise highly gentrified stretch of Broadway about ten blocks north of their office, where the beers were so cheap and the patrons so poor and unattractive that it seemed like an elaborate re-creation of a bar in a different city (say, Philadelphia), or at least a different borough. This was where Amy and Bev and occasionally one other office friend, this slightly older gay senior publicist whose name was Adam, went after work to decompress and drink bottled Bud, which was two for one during happy hour, so you essentially had to drink four of them. One night, to everyone's shock, Adam brought his friend Todd, who also worked in publishing, to the bar with him. Even more shockingly, Todd was heterosexual, and his decent looks were set off to great advantage by the dim, scummy surroundings. By the second round, which Todd bought, Amy and Bev had both developed semiconscious romantic ideas about him, which made the evening much more fun: playing off each other and competing slightly for his attention made them feel brighter and funnier. The issue of a third round came up; it was only 8:30, but in early winter this felt like the middle of the night. None of them had eaten dinner. They decided to have the third round.

'I always imagine that if I were rich, I would have a big pool of cash to dive into, like Scrooge McDuck,' Amy was saying.

'Who's that?' said Bev. Her parents hadn't allowed TV in the house until after Bev had already gone away to college, at which point they'd somehow downgraded their religiosity to a setting where it was still intense but not actually culty.

Todd began gleefully to explain the cartoon duck family tree to Bev, who nodded as though rapt as he detailed the familial relationships that linked Scrooge with Donald, and Huey, Dewey, Louie, and (least credibly) Daffy, who Amy was pretty sure had been created by a different animation studio than his supposed cousins. She rolled her eyes, turned to Adam, and started a conversation about someone they mutually disliked at work. A few minutes later, when they finished their beers and Amy suggested all going to get slices or hot dogs or something, Bev and Todd demurred. 'I think we're going to stay here and hash out the details of this duck thing some more,' said Todd. Bev smiled and stifled a hiccup.

'Cool. Well, I'm just gonna pee – you wanna come pee with me, Bev?'

Bev did a split-second eye-widening expression to chide Amy for her obviousness, but then she mutely got up and followed her to the bathroom. There was only one toilet. Amy draped a mostly symbolic piece of toilet paper across the seat, pulled up her skirt, pushed down her tights, and sat to pee.

Bev avoided eye contact with her – probably because it would have seemed weird to lock eyes while she peed – and instead looked at her own reflection in the mirror.

'So you're gonna hook up with Todd, huh?'

Bev shrugged at herself in the mirror. 'Possibly. It's a possibility.'

Amy reached for the toilet paper roll, tore off a piece, and wiped herself. 'You don't want to, like, make him go through the formality of buying you a hot dog first or whatnot? Or maybe you should just go back to Brooklyn now, think about it sober, then email him tomorrow if he still seems appealing?'

Now Bev looked at Amy, who was straightening her skirt, flushing the toilet. 'I'm just wondering what's motivating this concern, Amy. Are you trying to protect me from Todd? He works at Putnam and wears Dockers; I don't think he's going to flay me and make my skin into a cape.'

'Fine, roll the dice!'

As Amy moved to the sink to wash her hands, Bev, businesslike, sat to pee. She didn't bother with the token seat guard; all the germs were on Amy's butt now, anyway. 'You're just irritated because you would have hooked up with him if he'd started paying attention to you first.'

Amy shrugged. 'No. I mean ... probably not ...'

'Even if I liked him, even if you knew it.'

They were silent, assessing each other. This was the stuff that was supposed to go unspoken between women.

'I wouldn't,' Amy finally said. 'I mean, not if I knew you liked him. Not if you told me and asked me not to. I wouldn't do that, I don't think. Not to you, anyway.' She moved away from the sink so that Bev could wash her hands.

22

Bev and Todd fell in love. Or at least Bev fell in love with Todd. Years later, after things had gone so disastrously badly, Bev would wonder whether Todd was capable of love at all, or even the barest baseline estimation of any of the things the word 'love' might be understood to entail, such as 'empathy.' But that spring, as she and Todd laughed over asparagus risotto at date-night restaurants on Smith Street and had more sex more times in the span of a few weeks than Bev had had in several preceding years put together, it had seemed unequivocally, to Bev, like love.

Theirs was a meeting of minds and bodies, the kind of passion you read about and saw in movies but never thought you would experience personally. Especially if you were Bev and had grown up with parents who, on anniversaries or other romantic occasions, had been known to pat each other on the shoulder companionably and mutter 'Love ya.'

Todd was devoted to the kind of gesture that, to a non-besotted person, might have seemed over-the-top or annoying. He brought Bev flowers and slightly damaged books from the Strand that he said reminded him of her. They went to museums together and sat together on park benches, assessing passersby and making up little stories about them in a way that Bev had done before only with women, namely Amy. They also did something together that Bev had to admit to herself that she'd fantasized about for years: they lay around on Sunday mornings with *The New York Times*, eating bagels and drinking coffee. This was one of the things that people who didn't live in New York – people like Bev's parents – probably thought that people who lived in New York did all the time, like seeing Broadway musicals. But until Bev met Todd, she'd never actually done it. Todd's apartment was great for lying around and eating bagels in: big east-facing windows let in the perfect amount of sun, and his leather couch invited lounging and napping and easily accommodated two people, especially two people who were so delighted with each other that they could lie entwined for hours, sharing the same section of newspaper.

Todd had somehow contrived to live by himself in an old doorman building in Brooklyn Heights; though he worked in publishing, previous generations of his family had not. A former version of Bev would have found Todd's neighborhood, like his Dockers, horribly dorky, but now she loved how close he was to the Promenade. And on the nights she spent at his place, she loved how close he was to the subway that took her to her office, wearing yesterday's skirt and a different shirt, looking so radiantly happy that people she barely knew in the production department commented on her glow. She muttered something about taking vitamins.

'Vitamin *D*,' said Amy with a disgusting wink. She had instantaneously gotten over her initial pique about Todd's preference for Bev over her and now was excited for her infatuated friend, but at this point she was so caught up in admiring the vista of new career prospects that had unexpectedly opened before her that she wasn't paying the closest attention to Bev's transformation. She took the gossip blog job just before Bev announced her own life-altering decision.

'You're moving *where*?' Amy had almost spat out her yellowtail scallion roll. They were having a celebratory lunch at Tomo during Amy's first week at her new job, and Amy had spent the morning being interviewed on MSNBC about some trouble Britney Spears was having. Now Amy was having trouble eating daintily around her TV spackle, trying and failing not to leave big smudges of industrial-grade lip gloss on the chopsticks.

'To Madison. Todd's going to law school at the University of Wisconsin in the fall. He didn't want to tell me till he knew he was accepted, but as soon as he found out, he asked if I would move with him and . . . '

'Madison . . . WISCONSIN?'

'It's small but it's a great college town. There are more NPR listeners per capita than anywhere else in America. There are farmer's markets and microbreweries just like there are here. And you can rent a house for what I pay to rent a room. I've been there before. You'd like it.' Bev tried to smile. 'I mean, you will like it. You'll totally visit, right?'

Bev squinted at Amy, hoping Amy wouldn't start crying. If she did, Bev would too, and also Amy seemed to be wearing false eyelashes, which would look terrible if she let the tears pooling in her eyes fall.

'You can't do this to me! I mean, sorry, obviously this is not about me. But your job and everything! You love New York City! You've always said that living here was the goal of your life!'

'I love Todd.' Bev said. 'I don't particularly love my job . . . '

'Yeah, I picked up on that,' Amy said. She'd started shredding the slim white envelope that had once contained her chopsticks into tiny pieces of confetti in her lap.

'I don't want to have a long-distance relationship, Amy, and I have never met anyone I want to be with nearly as much as I want to be with Todd. I can't lose him.'

'He's not planning to move back here after school?'

'He, uh – he really loves the Midwest. He wants to live near his parents. My parents live there too, obviously … eventually we might think about Chicago?'

'So, you're getting *married* to this guy?'

'Well, I assume we'll probably have that conversation at some point.'

Bev watched as Amy's face contorted fleetingly into hundreds of facial expressions at a rate of one per nanosecond.

'Just go ahead, Amy – get it out of your system now, and maybe we won't have to deal with it later.'

Sentences emerged from Amy in a relieved, vomitous gush. 'You're making a huge mistake, and I hate to see you sabotaging yourself like this. Todd is perfectly nice, but the world is full of Todds. There's only one of you, and you belong here. I'll be miserable without you. Um ... what else. Oh, yeah! Yes! What are you going to *do* in Madison? Are you going to go to law school too?'

Bev smiled; it was sort of nice to listen to someone else articulating your own worst fears.

'There's a university press ... If I can't find some kind of publishing job on the fringes of academia right away, I'll get a restaurant job for a while ... I don't really care what I do, Amy. I'm ready for a change. It'll be nice to live somewhere where everyone and their brother isn't vying for the same crappy twenty-five-K-a-year editorial assistantship that just opened up. And we're going to live in a *house*. Like, with multiple rooms in it!'

'Multiple rooms in Madison. Wisconsin.'

'I knew you would be like this.'

Amy had picked morosely at the edge of a filament of sashimi with her chopsticks, then put it in her mouth. 'Well, isn't this how you'd want me to be?' she said through a mouthful of fish.

The worst thing about Madison – and there were many bad things competing for the title – was that Bev was forced to take up jogging. Todd loved jogging. He loved entering marathons, loved nursing the same ninety-eight-calorie light beer at a party full of cheerful midwestern law students all night because he was 'in training,' loved subscribing to *Runner's World* and reading it on the toilet. Bev emphatically didn't love any of these things. Cheap, high-gravity microbrews were one of the best things about the Midwest, in her opinion, and if she was going to have to spend an hour talking about tax law with some wide-faced blonde who inflected her long *oh* sounds like Marge Gunderson, she was going to need to drink several of them. Also, jogging hurt. It was true that she'd gotten faster, but this victory was oddly unsatisfying. Getting incrementally better at something you had zero interest in doing made Bev feel as if she were back in high school. It was the same feeling she'd had right after taking the SAT2 in calculus; she had known at the moment she closed the test booklet that she would just scrap the calculus part of her brain and never use any of that knowledge ever again. She had imagined the now-empty drawer in her brain where she would one day shove another kind of knowledge. It would just clunk right into place, like a printer's toner cartridge. Back then, her goal had been pure, focused: chalk up achievements, win scholarships, get out of the Midwest.

And now she was back in. But at least she was no longer a pure annoyance to Todd on their morning two-mile trot around the perimeter of their cornfield-flanked town-house development. Sometimes she could keep pace with him for a few minutes before falling back and letting him sprint on ahead. Later she would find out that she'd rubbed away half the cartilage in her left hip socket during this period; something about her form had been off, or she'd been wearing the wrong kind of shoes. Or maybe some bodies were made to glide lightly along the earth's surface and Bev's just wasn't one of them.

She was on her way back from a particularly punishing run in the early autumn of their second year in Madison when she spotted Todd sitting on the stunted porch of their house with his head in his hands. His shoulders were heaving. When she realized he was weeping, she felt a surprising surge of glee.

Bev was still in love with Todd, but now the love was more complicated. It seemed to have mixed with a strain of seething resentment that resembled nothing so much as the frustrated rebelliousness she'd directed, in her teens, at her parents. Since they'd moved in together, the flowers and dates had slowed to a trickle and been replaced by a stream of Bev-improvement strategies, like the jogging. Todd would let his gaze linger on her round butt and the soft jut of her midsection and wonder aloud whether she ought to try cooking something slightly healthier every once in a while. She'd been filling her daytime hours, when she wasn't working at the wine bar, by frying and sautéing her way through classic cookbooks, and a lot of the old-fashioned recipes were loaded with meat and cream and butter. Todd had also bought her an unasked-for GRE prep book. She'd stood next to him at a party as he told his friends that she was looking into grad school, but she wasn't.

One time she'd been lying in bed beside him, staring into his eyes, thinking about how much she loved him, and he'd been staring back just as intently. When he opened his mouth to speak, Bev was expecting a compliment at the very least, or maybe the suggestion that they 'play kissy face,' his cute-shading-into-gross euphemism for sex.

'Maybe you should see a dermatologist, honey – I don't

think it's normal for a woman your age to have this much acne.'

Her skin wasn't even that bad, but she'd been picking at it, and after he said that, of course she picked at it more.

So it was nice for Bev to see Todd, perfect Todd, crying. She wiped her forehead with the sweatband on her wrist and trotted up the steps to the house, ready to comfort him. Maybe someone in his family was sick or he'd been unfairly accused of plagiarizing a paper or something. She would be a solid rock he could turn to in times of crisis, and he'd look at her the way he had on those mornings of lox-breathed make-out sessions back in Brooklyn and realize that he never wanted to be without her.

This vision was eradicated in an instant when he looked up and looked straight through her, as though she were a dog or a mailbox, some banal part of the landscape. 'I don't want to talk about it. It's nothing. Go take a shower.' His voice quavered like a teenager's. Dumbfounded, Bev obeyed him.

As she soaped herself, she imagined that she heard him, somewhere in their little house, wailing like an inconsolable child, but the noise could have been coming from the pipes. Probably it had been, because when she got out of the shower, he was completely dry-faced and fine, silently flipping through one of his textbooks at the kitchen table.

'Please tell me what you were crying about,' said Bev, naked in her towel.

'Oh god, honey, you know . . . it was something so silly that it's just not worth rehashing.'

'I don't care if it was silly. I want to know! I want to know everything about you! I want to be there for you.'

'And I don't want to talk about it, so the nicest thing you could do for me, honey bear, is respect that, okay?' He smiled with his mouth, but there was something steely and strapped-in that she'd never seen before about the upper half of his face. 'Now go put some clothes on, you'll catch a chill.'

Bev had a momentary flash of the early days of their relationship, when neither of them had worn real clothes indoors for basically weeks. She thought of walking toward him, touching the whole length of him with her warm, shower-damp body, but instead she went upstairs and put on her clothes.

Bev was in Pick 'n Save the next day, in the checkout line, when she grabbed the local paper and saw the story about the car accident that had killed Todd's classmate, the wide-faced blond future tax lawyer. A lot of things ran through her mind all at once, including a lot of completely reasonable explanations for Todd's behavior, but after she had loaded the trunk of her car (technically Todd's car, just as their house was technically Todd's house) with the makings for boeuf bourguignon and pulled out of her parking space and drove away from the shopping center and onto the little two-lane road on the way back to the town-house development, she plugged her cell phone's hands-free attachment into her ear and dialed Amy.

'Ahhh! Bev? Oh my god! What's going on? Hi!'

Bev heard Amy shuffling around. She imagined Amy standing at the window of her apartment, looking out at the BQE. She could see Amy's funny face in her mind's eye perfectly, and suddenly she missed her so much she almost couldn't speak.

'Hey, dude. Sorry I've been kinda incommunicado for the past few weeks.'

'No worries, I know you're busy at the restaurant and with Todd and stuff. I miss you, though.'

'I miss you too.' Bev would have called Amy every day if the pleasure of hearing her best friend's voice had outweighed the stress of feeling that she had to construct some kind of narrative that made the pointless midwestern life she'd chosen make sense.

'So what's up?'

Bev wound her way through the cornfields, taking the long route, the groceries in her trunk spoiling slowly in the Indian-summer heat, as she told her best friend about Todd's crying, his classmate's death, and her suspicions. Amy listened without interrupting, with uncharacteristic reserve.

'Did you take a Klonopin, dude?' Amy finally asked. A kindly midwestern GP had prescribed a generous supply of benzos to Bev, to take as needed, when she'd broken down crying during a routine exam.

'Two.'

'Do you have any evidence that he had something going on with this girl, besides the crying?'

'Well, I work most weeknights, and he goes to school in the daytimes; our schedules are totally opposite. He goes out with his school friends without me pretty often. It's hard to imagine anyone easier to cheat on than me, basically.'

'Do you guys still do it?'

'Um ... yeah. Well. Not tons. Usually, like, waking up in the middle of the night and kind of ... sleep-raping each other. The kind of sex where you wake up in the morning and are like, "Did that happen?"'

'Eugh.'

'Should I ask him about it?'

'Well, my impulse would be of course you have to confront him, but that's me. I mean, don't ask right off the bat if he was fucking her, obviously. Just ask if that's why he was crying. You knew her too, right? It wouldn't be so weird for you to be like "Hey Todd, I heard so-and-so died. Horrible – are we going to the funeral," et cetera.'

'And then what if . . . '

'Well, geez, Bev, if he was cheating on you with her, then you have to be jealous of a dead person, which is heinous, but I don't see any way to avoid it. And also you have to leave him, move back to New York, and live with me until you can manage to find a job here, but that's not all bad, is it?'

'It sounds pretty bad. I already moved to New York with nothing once, after college. I didn't anticipate having to do it twice. It wasn't fun. I ate peanut butter soup.'

'You ate what?'

'This recipe for the cheapest soup possible; it fills you up and it's really nutritious. I found it in a vegetarian cookbook. You combine a cup of peanut butter with whatever vegetables are on sale, plus a can of whole tomatoes. It's good over rice. Or, well, not *good* per se, but it's food.'

'Well, what else are you going to do?'

Bev thought about it. She could go home and never mention anything to Todd and quietly wait for things to return to what was currently passing for normal. That was one option. Another option was the one Amy had just suggested. A third option was driving her car into a tree, which under the circumstances seemed melodramatic, possibly unwarranted, and, if warranted, poetically just in a way that did not appeal to Bev. The accident that had killed the blond, smiley tax lawyer had taken place on the highway, had involved an overturned tractor-trailer.

'I guess I'll do what you said.'

'You guess, or you will?'

'I will.' Bev paused. 'Do you still have that same couch that's really uncomfortable to sleep on, or have you upgraded?'

'In part because of what you said the last time you visited, I am the owner of a pullout sofa bed now. It's all yours for as long as you need it.'

'Okay. It's a deal.'

What Bev found hardest to explain to herself, when she remembered this period of time, were the three days she had stayed with Todd after discovering his betrayal, before finally buying a plane ticket, packing up her minimal things, and moving in with Amy in New York. Partly it had seemed wrong to leave someone who was grieving, even if he was grieving for someone with whom he had been cheating on you (under your nose! for months! and all your mutual 'friends' had known about it!). When she'd finally come home on the day of the newspaper headline, after she'd driven through the fields for so long that she was low on gas and the backs of her thighs were deeply imprinted with the lines of the car seat's upholstery, Todd had been waiting for her on their stoop. He had embraced her somberly and led her to the kitchen, where he'd made dinner – Greek salad with grilled chicken and bottled low-fat dressing – and poured them both large glasses of white wine. She sat and ate mechanically and drank big, sour gulps of the wine as he reached his hand across the table to her and, with tears streaming down his face, told her everything. Really everything. At some point, much too late, she put down her fork and put up one of her hands to shush him.

'I don't need the details. You know? I would prefer not to know the details,' she said, and the sound of her own voice was like listening to someone else's voice on the radio, some reasonable NPR host's voice filtering softly in from another room.

'I'm sorry. I just needed to tell someone, and ... honey, you're the closest friend I have here.' He wiped his face with a paper napkin, paused, sniffled, and forked up a bite of salad. 'I understand if you want to leave, but I hope you know how much your support means to me. I feel so terrible right now. This is a very strange situation.'

It was a strange situation, to be sure. Bev had never experienced anything like it. How could she speak or think or make decisions while, in her brain, all her neurological furniture was being forcibly rearranged? Her memories of the past few months, her hopes for the future, and her assumptions about the present were all obsolete. Each conscious thought that occurred to her now prompted a strange kind of examination. Did the thought jibe with what she now knew, or was it outmoded? Most of them were the latter. But what would happen to those thoughts? Where would they go? She didn't want to give them up just yet. It was like owning a dress you knew no longer fit and never would again, but still not wanting to give it to Goodwill. But it was also like being repeatedly punched in the stomach.

Worse, somehow, on top of the druggy sense of constant

neural reordering was the weirdness of wanting to turn to Todd for comfort, forgetting – from one moment to the next – that he was the reason she felt terrible and so could not, by definition, make her feel better. She tried to say some of this to him, but instead she began to sob. He stopped talking and came to her side of the table and put his arms around her and also sobbed. Realizing that he was not necessarily crying for the same reason she was – was likely not – made Bev sob harder.

But on the third day, after Todd left the house for the first time for reasons he left vague but at an hour that Bev knew meant he was attending his classmate's memorial service, Bev put her clothes and books into a suitcase and a large green duffel bag and called a car service to take her to the airport. She called Amy as soon as she figured out when she would be landing and then called the owner of the wine bar and tendered her resignation. The owner assured her it wasn't necessary to be so apologetic, that it was a college town and people came and went easily in these kinds of positions.

'I just feel so bad,' Bev told her. 'I really thought I'd be here much longer.'

'No point in feeling bad about something that's a done deal,' the owner told her. 'You knock 'em dead in the big city!'

The flight was unusually turbulent, but for the first time in her life Bev experienced no terror that the plane might crash. Maybe she had attained the ideal state that Buddhists strive for: nonattachment, even to her own life. More likely she was going to need to see her old shrink when she got back to New York and to start taking antidepressants again as soon as possible. It couldn't be healthy to care so little about whether you lived or died.

Amy's apartment became, temporarily, Amy and Bev's apartment, a circumstance that by the third month had started to seem difficult to sustain much longer. Bev was trying to be a dream roommate, folding up the sofa bed every morning and hiding her bedding in the closet, cleaning up after herself and Amy without being asked and without making a big deal about doing so. But it was a small apartment, and Bev could tell that Amy was used to living in it by herself, that simply by being there, she was cramping Amy's style. She needed to move out, but without a job, that was impossible, and she hadn't found one yet, not even another service job. The restaurant managers who interviewed her seemed to intuit her fragility; they spoke to her with a gentleness that was more than professional. She was still crying a lot; anything could make her cry: a song sung by subway buskers, a dead pigeon in the gutter, an ad for life insurance with an older couple holding hands, talking frankly about what they wanted to leave as a legacy. No wonder she was blowing the interviews. It was impossible to seem upbeat and customer-service-oriented when you weren't really feeling sane.

But even though it was happening so slowly it was almost indiscernible, there were times when Bev could sense that she was making progress. She and Amy cooked meals and watched TV together, and Amy would make a joke, they'd laugh, and Bev would forget for a fraction of a second that she was in pain. In those moments she felt as good as she was capable of feeling. But sometimes Amy retreated into her room and Bev felt more alone and out of place in the world than ever. Everything that had happened to her in Madison seemed as if it had been her fault – her fault for going there in the first place, for trusting Todd so completely, and most of all for valuing being with Todd over her life in New York, over her friendship with Amy. She'd tried to explain this to Amy, and Amy just shrugged and told her that there was never any point in regretting anything, because you couldn't change the past, so it was a useless waste of mental energy to even think about it. It was basically the same thing her old wine-bar boss had said when she'd quit, and she hadn't quite bought it then, either. Bev got that regret was pointless, but she also didn't think forgetting everything bad that ever happened was the way forward. She didn't say this to Amy.

When Bev told Amy that Todd was coming to town for a weekend trip to see friends and that he wanted to see her and also drop off some of her stuff, Amy had been against it. She said the apartment had a 'no emotional manipulation' policy. But Bev had convinced her, of course, and now he was coming, under the condition (Bev's idea) that Amy be there to chaperone.

Bev and Amy sat at the kitchen table, a bottle of cold white wine between them, half an hour before Todd was due to arrive. The first time she refilled their glasses, Bev had put the bottle back in the refrigerator, but the second time she just left it on the table; she knew they would finish it before it had time to get warm. She felt oddly becalmed, but maybe it was just numbness. She'd imagined what it would be like to see Todd's face again. She had shower-monologued scathing condemnations of his behavior and his personality so many times that it didn't seem particularly relevant that the moment was on the verge of really happening; she'd almost lived it already. So when she heard the buzzer, the stab of terror that shot through her viscera took her by surprise.

'This was a terrible idea. Oh my god. I can't do this. Can you just go downstairs and get the stuff and tell him to leave?'

Amy wrinkled her forehead, her eyebrows – those hyper caterpillars – a-twitch. 'If that's what you want. Are you sure?'

Bev took a few deep breaths. The buzzer sounded again – a little obnoxiously, as though Todd were unused to having any of his needs go unmet even for a few seconds.

Amy rolled her eyes. 'Grow up, Todd.'

Amy's attitude, the way she'd summed up Todd's problem, gave Bev courage. She walked over to the intercom, hit the 'talk' button, and said 'Be right down' in an almost totally normal tone of voice, as though Todd were no more threatening than the FedEx guy.

On the stoop she barely looked at him, just said 'C'mon up' and stood to one side to allow him to pass. He paused, as if expecting her to offer to help with the giant cardboard box in his hands or to start climbing the stairs first, but she did neither. There was no way she'd kick off their interaction by turning her back to him, letting him climb a flight of stairs with her ass at his eyeline. He was wearing khakis, and he seemed, Bev judged, to have gained a small but consequential amount of weight.

In the apartment, she watched as Amy, still seated with her wine, returned Todd's mild, phony greetings with an icy stare. Finally she said 'Hi' in a way that made that single syllable sound sarcastic. Bev felt an odd mixture of awe and annoyance. Couldn't Amy just act indifferent and normal? No. She had to make it completely clear that she despised Todd, as though some imaginary audience were watching, judging her on consistency.

'Let's talk in private for a sec,' Bev heard herself saying. She was afraid to meet Amy's eyes as she led Todd back toward Amy's bedroom and shut the door.

He put the box down with a small grunt, and then they were unavoidably looking at each other. Todd attempted a smile, winced, but held her gaze. Just standing this close to him – close enough to smell his soapy, faintly milky, familiar body smell – brought Bev back to their earliest days together, those hallucinatory hours in bed and the brief and equally unreal-seeming times they'd had to be apart, when she'd floated through life lost in a fantasy of effortless and endless love. She forgot all her carefully planned insults immediately. She wanted to bury herself in his arms and die there.

Todd seemed to be on the same page. 'Bev, you don't know how much I've missed you. Feel free to say no, but . . . can we hug?'

Why deny him? Why deny herself? She stepped into his arms. She hadn't touched anyone or been touched in a while, unless you counted the horrible armpitty intimacy of the subway; and his body pressing against the answering areas of her own was too much. She started to cry. Todd smoothed her hair and whispered 'Shh' as her tears and snot soaked into the shoulder of his polo shirt.

When Amy slammed the door open, they broke apart as though they'd been caught doing something bad, which they had.

'No fucking way is this happening under my roof. Look, asshole, you are here to give Bev her things and leave, not to rip off the scab she's spent a lot of time and effort generating over the fucking gaping emotional wound you inflicted on her.'

'Ew,' Bev said under her breath.

'Well, I'm sorry I couldn't think of a less disgusting way of putting it, but you know I'm right! Don't get sucked back in. Todd has ruined enough of your life.'

'Please stay out of this, Amy. It really isn't any of your business,' Todd said quietly, and then both of them looked at Bev.

It was up to her, she realized, to align herself with one or the other of them. If she chose Amy, she was in for – in the immediate future – a lecture, more tears, cigarettes, more wine. Maybe ice cream. But beyond that point, the future was uncertain. If she chose Todd, her immediate future might contain apologetic, teary, possibly incredible sex, though it wasn't clear where they would do it. In the long term, though – that was the thing. She already knew what it would be like, in the long term, with Todd. She could pretend to herself that she didn't know for a night, but not for much longer. And what she'd be sacrificing, besides the months of scab generation that Amy had mentioned, would be Amy.

They would still be friends, but something would be lost. Obnoxious as she'd been about it, Amy had taken a risk to try to protect Bev – from Todd, and from Bev's own worst impulses. Amy had never done that before; if Bev rejected her help now, she probably wouldn't offer it again.

Bev left Todd's side and stood next to Amy.

'Of course it's Amy's business. And she's right, unfortunately.'

'You heard her! Get out of here! And I don't want to hear about any sappy text messages or anything like that, either – just leave her alone! I feel sorry for the next girl who comes into contact with your poison, you dickwad!'

'Okay, enough,' Bev said, though she was smiling.

Todd tried to give Bev a look, like *what a crazy bitch*, but she shook her head. She saw in his posture that he'd given up; cowed, he walked toward the door, wiping uselessly at the dark patch her tears had left on his shirt. 'If you change your mind, I'll be here another two days. I really think we should talk. We left things on such a bad note. Don't you want closure?'

'This *is* closure,' Bev said, reaching past him to open the door and let him out.

23

When Bev felt well enough to leave the gynecologist's office, they took a cab back to Amy's apartment. As soon as they walked in, Amy turned on the TV, then shuddered when it turned out that MTV was playing a marathon of *16 and Pregnant.* She flipped away quickly, but to no avail, because every other show was about pregnancy, too, or food.

Bev lay full-length on Amy's couch while Amy sat on a cushion on the floor near her feet. It was early, golden dusk, and they were both wrapped in blankets because the weather had turned colder but Amy's landlord hadn't turned the heat on yet. Dying sunbeams were coming in through the window and painting the floorboards with bars of light. They settled on an old rerun of *Keeping Up with the Kardashians.* The oldest sister was scared to have sex while pregnant, for fear of hurting her baby. She and her fiancé took a special sex class where a woman in a cape showed them how to use a foam wedge and a spooning position.

'Let's go home and [bleep] these pregnant girls!' the fiancé said at the end of the class.

Bev and Amy watched a couple of minutes of this in stupefied disbelief, and then Bev flipped the channel back to *16 and Pregnant*, where a girl with tears pouring down her face narrated the daily misery of her new fun-free life with her infant. 'It's too much, being a mom and a daughter and a wife all at the same time,' she told the camera, but then a minute later said that she loved her son and wouldn't change anything. Bev ignored Amy's attempt to catch her eye; she could tell Amy was trying to get some kind of read on her impassive expression, but Bev didn't feel like talking. It got darker and darker, and when the sun finally disappeared all the way, Amy went to the kitchen to start making some kind of dinner, and Bev was alone with her thoughts and the flickering teens.

She watched for a few more minutes, as much as she could stand, and then flipped the channel to the local news. A building had burned down in the Bronx and a botoxed TV reporter stood in front of it, trying as hard as she could to convey concern even though her eyebrows couldn't travel a millimeter downward.

Bev's familiar mental spirals were starting again, the habitual, incessant wish to be anywhere and anyone except where and who she was right now. In this mood, she could find a reason to envy anyone: the Kardashians, the pregnant teens, even the people wrapped in sooty blankets, smeared with ash, pouring wild-eyed out of the blackened building. They all had in common that they were not Bev, and she envied them for that reason alone. This was horrible, and she knew it, but then she felt guilty for having horrible feelings, and this just made being Bev more uncomfortable and put her back at the beginning of the spiral. She had to do something, anything, to wrench herself out of the pattern, and what she usually did was buy a pack of cigarettes and a bottle of decent red wine and lie in bed with them, watching *30 Rock* reruns. But the evil alien cell cluster inside her was exerting dictatorial control, making those sources of comfort (*30 Rock* excepted) seem worse than unpalatable. She was more trapped than ever, trapped in her brain and her out-of-control body.

Amy came back into the living room with two bowls of Annie's mac and cheese, and they picked at the bowls as they watched the weather report. It was supposed to be beautiful and sunny for the next week.

'I don't want to go back there,' said Bev finally.

'What? Why? Did you not like the office? I did think that one nurse was kind of brusque and rude.'

'I don't know. I'm just terrified of the whole thing.'

'Because you're afraid of it hurting, or . . . '

'I just really, really don't want to do it. I start to feel like I'm going to faint if I even think about going back there.'

'I don't get it. I mean I do, but . . . Bev, you have to! You don't want to continue being pregnant, right? You realize that the alternative to not being pregnant is tethering your life to another human's life forever, right?'

'I definitely can't handle that.'

'Well, I wish there was a magical spell we could cast, but there isn't. You have exactly two options.'

'Ha. So much for all this endless "choice" that's supposed to be available to me!'

'Well, you have one!'

They silently munched the mac and cheese for a minute.

'I wish I could just leave the baby on the doorstep of that couple we house-sat for in Margaretville,' Bev said.

Amy laughed, as Bev had intended her to. 'It's true. I should have said you have three choices. Adoption does exist. But think how weird your life would be for the next nine months. Explaining it to everyone you know. God, explaining it to your *parents*! Not to mention random strangers at your temp jobs or whatever. Random strangers who'd, like, congratulate you while giving up their seats on the subway.'

'Wait. So if this was happening to you, you'd have an abortion because you'd rather not have *awkward conversations*?'

'That would be one of the reasons!'

Bev tried to frown angrily at Amy but instead started giggling as she imagined Amy responding to a subway stranger's congratulations by saying that actually, she was giving up the baby for adoption. She would do it, too, that was the thing.

'What? What?'

Bev did her best Amy upspeak. 'Um, actually? I'm just kind of warehousing this baby for someone else? I'm not really in a place in my life where I want to have a baby right now? So, like, thanks anyway. Oh, and thanks for giving up your seat.'

They laughed somewhat hysterically for a minute, and then, when they calmed down, Amy's eyes were bright with laugh-tears.

'I'm not saying it's a *terrible* idea,' said Amy.

'Wait, what?'

'Adoption in general. And I think it would be nice to give it to people you kind of know, or are friends of friends. Not people you *actually* know, that would be weird. But that couple seemed cool. Or, well, not cool, but like good, interesting people.'

'Okay, no, let's stop talking about this. I'll suck it up and take a Klonopin and go back to the clinic.'

Amy hesitated, about to say something, but then decided not to.

'What?' Bev said. 'I'm not going to be insulted.'

'Uh, okay, this is insane. But what if someone wanted to, like, pay your medical expenses and also pay you for your time and, you know, mental anguish?'

'Like, what if someone wanted to buy my baby.'

'Well . . . yeah.'

'Ha!'

'Okay, whatever, just think about it.'

'I am thinking about it, and I think you are completely insane!' But Bev was smiling, and as she smiled, she realized how long it had been since her face had made this shape.

Amy was also grinning. 'Dude, you know what? I think we should have a drink.'

'What? No. Yuck.'

'No, come on! It'll make you feel better. French people drink when they're pregnant all the time.'

'It just doesn't sound appealing.'

'One little glass of wine doesn't sound appealing? It'll be good for us to get out of the house, too. Let's go to a bar! Be around people! Let's just go to the Mexican restaurant at the end of the block and get one margarita. *One.*'

'Ughhhh.'

'Just come sit with me while I have one, then!'

Two margaritas later, Bev and Amy were not at the Mexican restaurant anymore but in a cozy corner of the art school bar five blocks south, which was having a special on shots of whiskey and cans of PBR. Bev's nausea had melted away with that first drink; she felt that it would be a public service if doctors would just tell miserable women that there *was* a surefire cure for morning sickness, but she guessed there were laws against it.

The bar's ceiling was decorated with crepe paper and tinsel, and as Bev looked up at it, she fleetingly thought of how tacky and sad it would look in daylight. But it wasn't daylight, and the mirrors and neon reflected off the tinsel and lent everything a glowy dimness. With her Irish tolerance, Bev was barely buzzed. But she felt more comfortable in her skin than she had in days, which was a miracle. She was pretty sure that even the French would disapprove of drinking a shot of well whiskey while pregnant, so she gave hers to Amy, who definitely didn't need it; she was almost slurring her words. For some reason they had googled Sally and Jason on Amy's phone and were now squinting to read a *New York* magazine profile on the tiny screen. 'Urban Rustic' was the headline.

Sally Katzen and Jason Park had rehabilitated every inch of their Victorian house themselves after buying it in 2003 for what they seemed to think was a 'small' amount of money. Their initial plan had been to live in it during the summer months, but after a while they realized they loved the area so much that they wanted to live there all the time. So they sold their loft on Great Jones Street ('Ugh! *Why?*' Amy said) and moved to the mountains, coming into the city frequently for nights out and to explore their favorite neighborhoods. They also spent a lot of time at the upstate antiques fairs and outdoor flea markets in search of the unique decor finds they'd filled their space with, such as the copper drawer pulls in the kitchen, the old barn door that was now a desk ...

'Do you think they do it?'

Amy pinched the photo, then moved her fingers apart to enlarge it, and they scrutinized Sally and Jason, who were posing ironically with a pitchfork in their sunny garden. 'No. Look at his Rag & Bone work boots. There is no way that man is heterosexual.'

Bev sighed. 'So Sally has the perfect life, essentially.'

Amy spluttered, spitting out PBR. 'Perfect how? Married to a gay dude, living miles away from anything, writing epic emails about the specifics of her house's septic system?'

'Well, but they must be good friends, at least, right? Living in this gorgeous house with your best friend ... I don't know, what could be better than that?'

'Oh, Christ, Bev, did you read this part? This is creepy. "Park and Katzen's simple design sense would be marred by boxes of plastic toys, it's true, but while they're particular, they hope not to be anal-retentive if they become parents."'

'But she totally will.'

'She absolutely will. But more important: they want to have kids!'

'Amy, you're drunk.'

'So? That doesn't automatically make it a bad idea.'

'Trying to *sell a baby* to people we've met once? I think that is categorically a bad idea.'

‘What if they paid all your expenses and, you know, some extra? What if you could talk them into paying off your school debt?’

‘What’s in it for you?’

‘Jesus, Bev, nothing! I’m just trying to help, and it seems like selling a baby would be preferable to your … *having* a baby. I mean, Jesus Christ.’

Bev sighed and took a dainty sip of her PBR. ‘First of all, my life … Well, it’s not like things could get much worse, you know? Maybe somehow this would be what I need to stop sinking lower and lower. Because I don’t know what else would ever motivate me to finally get my life together.’

‘Oh, don’t say shit like that, Bev. You’re having a rough patch, that’s all.’

‘I’ve been having a rough patch for as long as we’ve known each other.’

‘I think you might have been having one before that, too.’

‘Right, well, that’s not a rough patch. You, on the other hand, are genuinely having a rough patch right now, I think.’

‘I don’t even want to talk about it. Tonight is about you,’ Amy said, and then spent the next half hour complaining to Bev about how she was probably breaking up with Sam, who was abandoning her for Spain, and she was getting evicted and had quit her job and had no money.

Bev nodded and was understanding and asked the right questions as she waited for Amy to finish talking. This was how their friendship had always been.

24

Incredibly, there were no cafés or libraries in Margaretville that would allow Sally to get work done on her novel. Not in neighboring Roxbury or Fleischmanns either. There was one in Woodstock, but once you were thinking of going that far away, why not just go ahead and drive into the city and go to the library at Judson Memorial Church and see if the old magic was there, and if it wasn't, or if it was closed for renovations (again!), Sally might find herself, the way she had today, in a café in the East Village that several incarnations ago had been a bar where Sally herself waited tables and go-go danced twenty years earlier. At this point it would be about four in the afternoon, *which was crazy*, certainly a crazy time for Sally to be just opening her laptop for the day. It meant she wouldn't be able to have dinner ready until maybe ten at the earliest. Of course Jason wouldn't say anything, but obviously he'd be irritated; being served dinner at ten was objectively irritating. It was one of their things that she did the cooking, another vestige of his patriarchal-culture upbringing that Sally had at one time found exotic, thrilling. They were leaving for London on Friday, and she hadn't packed at all yet. He would do something to show his irritation, but it would be subtle and interpretable as a nice gesture, like maybe she'd arrive home to find some Jasonish utilitarian meal already cooked, or all their bags packed and waiting by the door, so that she'd have to wear her worst underwear and skip her hair products for the rest of the week rather than pack them again.

The other option for Sally had been to sit in her study in their house in Margaretville and write there, but obviously that was never going to work. She would have just ended up sitting down at her antique oak desk at eight in the morning with a steaming cup of jasmine tea at her elbow, flexing her fingers over the keyboard, and then spending the entire day – without even breaking for lunch – on Facebook, looking at what her college classmates were doing now. She envied the ones with major museum retrospectives almost as much as she envied the ones with little kids or big, almost teenage kids. As much as she didn't want to admit it, considering her recent decision to stop pursuing a pregnancy, she envied the ones who were knocked up. Did they have to be so show-offy about it? 'It's hard to work when a baby is kicking you behind your belly button!' one of the pregnant women had written the other day. That update had gotten so many likes, and Sally had felt like punching herself in the face. It made her wish she still had easy access to opiates. She hadn't dosed herself with anything stronger than red wine in years, but reading that status update made her want to inject herself with pure oblivion. Instead, she had eaten a piece of frozen organic cheesecake and looked at Facebook for three more solid hours, as though the bad experience could be obliterated by additional ones, if she could just rack up enough.

So today she'd rolled out of bed, eschewed her felt slip-ons for No. 6 clogs, and headed out the door without even drinking a cup of coffee. She paused in the driveway to say goodbye to Jason. He was heading out for a run, after which he would spend the day happily engrossed, as always, in editing the design magazine that funded their life. He was wearing leggings, his nutsack making a goofy little knot in them that, as she hugged him goodbye, she tweaked gently, mindlessly, the way you'd tuck a stray strand of someone's hair behind his ear. Then she'd gotten into the car and headed for the city.

There was a dingy Italian pastry shop where she ritualistically made her first stop before she settled down with her laptop somewhere less old-fashioned. She felt a strange obligation to the place, as if she were the only person keeping it in business, though of course elderly Italian people did that. She sat, as usual, at the bakery's counter and drank a watery espresso and ate a little plate of odd-shaped cookies slowly, counting the bites toward the end, before ordering a box of cannoli to take home, even though Jason never touched them.

If she was extraordinarily lucky, she might run into someone she knew; this happened less and less often, though, and lately it hadn't happened at all.

With the string-tied box of cannoli swinging in a plastic

bag at her side, occasionally banging against her thigh, Sally walked briskly south on Second Avenue. She maneuvered around slower-moving walkers as though she were a car in traffic, crossing the street sometimes in order to avoid waiting at a stoplight. She had nowhere pressing to be, of course, but this somehow made her more determined to keep her pace up.

As she approached the corner of Houston Street and Second Avenue, dimly wondering where she'd go from there, an older couple caught Sally's eye. A college kid was shrugging at them apologetically as he continued on his way across the street; they'd clearly just asked him for directions. 'What are you looking for?' she asked them, unprompted. 'St. Mark's Place,' said the man; he was wearing stylish glasses and had a neatly trimmed white beard. Sally pointed north. 'It's the same thing as Seventh Street,' she offered helpfully. As the couple walked away, she heard the woman saying, 'I thought it was the same thing as Eighth Street.'

'I mean Eighth Street! Eighth Street!' Sally shouted after them, unwilling to believe she'd made such a dumb mistake. Even actual tourists knew her old neighborhood better than she did now. She couldn't believe it had really been almost twenty years since she moved into that second-story loft on Second Avenue. There had been a dress form in one corner, not because Sally ever sewed, but because she loved the way the form looked when she peered up into her own window from across the street. It was like a slightly eerie presence in the loft, beckoning her home.

Now, sometimes a chance errand – or, like today's, a largely invented one – would lead her close to the building, and if she was in the mood, she'd walk past it. On the sidewalk across the street from her old apartment, attempting to be casual, she'd look up at the window, half expecting to see that headless woman's shape somehow still there. The current occupants, whoever they were, had installed thick drapes that were always drawn. She wished someone would tear the building down.

The building would inevitably be torn down – so many of the surrounding old tenements and lofts already had been. Someday soon she would walk by and find the weathered brick structure replaced with one of the new black-and-silver towers named Azure, Core, Cerulean, Glaze, Spire. But while the stretches near Houston to the south and Fourteenth Street to the north had already been colonized in this way, her old building still stood, looking almost as it had when she moved in. She hadn't really appreciated its beauty then. For all the pleasure she took in talking about her first years in New York, she barely remembered any specific moments in time. She remembered sensations, blurrily. The fuzzy, overheated warmth associated with the loft: a daytime feeling. And the neon, adrenalized nighttime feeling she associated with the streets and the bars. Sometimes she would get a hit of that feeling in the oddest places. The quality of light in an airport bar could do it, or the halo around a streetlight illuminating a deserted stretch of sidewalk in her sleepy town upstate.

She had assumed that staid adulthood came for everyone eventually, without exception or much effort – like a bus, if you just waited around for it long enough. It had taken meeting Jason to show her that she was wrong.

Their first night together they hadn't had sex, just talked endlessly on her pink velveteen couch, amphetamines combining with the natural high of their easy brand-new intimacy to keep them awake till the sunrise turned the cut-glass ashtray they'd been filling into a prism that projected blinding splinters of light onto the wall behind them. A moment came when Jason asked Sally point-blank how she planned to sustain herself in the future. Did she think she would grow old here in this loft, handing her landlord envelopes thick with rubber-banded fives? He forced her to articulate her vision of gala receptions at museums in European capitals, and even on drugs she realized how ridiculous these fantasies sounded. Everything she'd thought of before as a 'plan' was revealed to be more of a vague whim, but the weird thing was, she didn't really mind. It was immediately clear that Jason had a plan. Jason had enough plans for both of them.

He had been six when his family moved to Queens from Seoul, and his earliest memories were of filling paper tubes with coins behind the cash register at the first of his family's produce markets. Now they owned forty. He'd gone to Harvard and was finishing up a master's in architecture at Yale, which he talked about as if it were a hobby, a fun diversion from the real work of running his design business. Unlike all of her friends, he was willing to admit that money was necessary, even important. Planning, perseverance, and money: with these, Jason turned what had seemed to Sally like an unpromising one-night stand into a relationship that had, at this point, spanned almost half of Sally's life.

She remembered the moment of his leaving the loft that morning, after it had become clear that they'd been through too much together, now knew each other too well (and also were too sober, shading into hungover) to have the meaningless sex that had been their flirtation's initial goal. He had smiled and touched her face after putting on his coat, then held up his palm and showed her the piece of glitter he'd removed from her cheek. 'Sorry. That's been bugging me since about two a.m.,' he said. 'You have such soft skin.' After Jason left, she lay down to nap until her shift started that afternoon, but even though she was exhausted, she couldn't fall asleep. She hadn't been attracted to him initially, or so she'd thought. Bringing him back to the loft had been almost random; she'd liked their conversation, and he'd seemed so safe, so small and nonthreatening. But his chaste caress had communicated a huge amount of restraint, somehow. What depths of violent passion was Jason restraining? She imagined them and imagined them and then couldn't nap, and went to work afterward in a daze of exhaustion, compounded by the kind of infatuation that feels a little bit like the flu.

Remembering that she'd once found the idea of sex with Jason mysterious and irresistible made Sally almost giggle now. She still wanted him, of course, but he was so familiar to her; the same person he'd been that night, but also completely different, kind of like the block she was walking down. Every inch of Second Avenue was rife with associations from Sally's old life in the city; she remembered many aimless afternoons like this one, spent visiting various friends at the cafés and boutiques and bars and video stores where they stood behind counters all day. She remembered how she felt virtuous for distracting them for a few minutes, as though this were some kind of necessary work. Now everyone who worked in these shops and restaurants – indeed, nearly everyone who was walking down the street around Sally – was fifteen years younger than she was.

It was amazing how quickly you went from feeling uncomfortably stared at and catcalled every time you left your house to being functionally invisible. It seemed to have happened on the day Sally turned thirty-five. Or maybe by leaving the city she had broken some spell. Even though there was nothing about her clothing or her demeanor that marked Sally as a visitor, the suspicious natives could sense her foreignness, could maybe smell it. Perhaps it smelled like a humid suburban laundry room, that warm, damp, homey smell you almost never got in the city.

There had been an intermediate time in Sally's life, before she and Jason had decamped to Margaretville, when she thought she had finally mastered life and was poised on the verge of fame and success, was indeed already a little bit famous and successful. It started after their wedding had been written up in the *Times*, with the headline 'Designer and Painter Make Bohemian Living an Art.'

She had decorated Jason's loft on Great Jones Street in a Day of the Dead theme and worn a Mexican wedding dress that she knew was slightly too transparent to wear without a slip, but she'd foregone the slip anyway, and in the *Times* photograph you could just make out one of her nipples denting the fabric. Jason's friends included lots of semi-famous painters and playwrights and magazine editors, and in the months after the wedding Sally had devoted herself to entertaining. Jason loved having people over to the loft because it functioned so exquisitely as an advertisement for his design skills; invariably their richer dinner guests would end up hiring him to redo their own spaces in his trademark spare yet distinctive style. Jason's signature quirks became quirks for many other people. He would tell them what to say about the oddball pieces, whether to claim them as family heirlooms or flea market finds. Sally spent her days shopping for perfect outfits and fresh flowers and occasionally even painting. Her mixed-media canvases – she had begun making them again – hung on the walls of the loft, and she remembered the excitement she'd struggled to conceal beneath a veneer of coolness when a photographer from *Paper* came to photograph her next to one of them. The brilliantly sunny loft with its huge west-facing windows had lent itself so well to photo shoots; she wished there had been more of them. They'd devoted a whole page to her profile, focusing a little bit less on the art than they did on the phenomenon of Sally and Jason's parties and her interestingly seedy past (she had been candid about the stripping).

The move to the country had seemed like a victory lap: Jason had parlayed his business into the editor-in-chiefdom of an international design magazine, Sally could do her work anywhere, and of course their friends would visit all the time. Their friends would stay for weekends, like in a country-house novel. They'd toyed with the idea of keeping his loft as a pied-à-terre – how Sally wished she'd hung on to the lease at her rent-controlled Second Avenue loft! – but it had grown to be worth so much more than what Jason had bought it for that it seemed ridiculous not to sell. Plus, there were the theoretical eventual children to consider; Sally had her dated *Harriet the Spy* notions about the enriching aspects of city-kid life debunked by Jason, who had spent his formative years in Flushing, yearning to play outdoors while standing behind a cash register. They'd fought about it at the time, but eventually Sally had come to see the wisdom of the move. Now she loved the gentle rhythms of country life. She loved tending the garden, loved working when she felt like it. She had painted, then got bored with painting and got into ceramics, which led to a period during which she had run a small store showcasing work by local artisans for a few years – until it became too depressingly obvious that no one local wanted to buy any of the artisans' work – and then finally settled into the idea of being a writer. She plugged away at her book every day, and she was confident, on a good day, that something worth showing would eventually come of her efforts. Everyone in her little town asked her how her writing was going; to them, at least, she was a writer. She didn't miss the sense she had in the city that everyone crowded around her was brimming with shrill, seething ambition. She had long since canceled the subscription to *Paper*.

And now here she was, at the reincarnated café, finally sitting down to write. If she could avoid Facebook and focus, she might be able to make some kind of breakthrough this afternoon. A new energy, or maybe just the two espresso drinks, hummed in her veins. She felt on the verge of some kind of change. She would just quickly check her email and then begin.

Her email contained a message subject-lined 'thank you!!!' and it was from Amy, the taller of the two girls who'd house-sat. Really late, but better late than never. With a twinge of embarrassment Sally remembered her wish to be friends with the girls, as though she could befriend a younger version of herself. But as she read Amy's email, which was several paragraphs long, chatty and conversational about books she'd noticed in the house and full of charming, irrelevant personal details, Sally's embarrassment faded: it seemed as if Amy, at least, wanted to be her friend, too.

25

It had been easier than Amy thought it would be to ask Sally if she and Bev could come up and visit while she and Jason were there – she said they were coming upstate for a leaf-peeping weekend and staying nearby – and Sally had offered (as Amy suspected she might) that they stay with them instead: 'Plenty of room!' Sally sounded really excited. Amy almost felt sorry for her.

They sat down at the long glass dining room table to have lunch with Sally and Jason but without a plan in place about how they'd bring up Bev's pregnancy and the idea that Sally and Jason might want to adopt the baby. Amy didn't have a plan. It wasn't in her nature to have plans, and she imagined that she knew why Bev didn't have a plan: the idea of having this conversation, which would make the baby a concrete thing, a real future, was so terrifying that Bev refused to think about how the conversation itself might work out. But maybe Amy was wrong, and Bev *did* have a plan – a plan that she hadn't shared. That was also a scary prospect. Bev and Amy were supposed to tell each other everything.

Amy looked at Bev across the table, but Bev wouldn't make eye contact. Getting up and running out of the room at any moment seemed very possible, just on the verge of happening. Amy could feel the springiness of her leg muscles as they tensed. Next to her, Jason cut his chicken breast into thin slices, anointed each slice with a smear of arterial-red chutney, then used a deft fork-knife combo maneuver to marry it with a bit of salad green from the other side of his plate before slipping it into his mouth. He either chewed noiselessly or swallowed each little perfect bite whole, snake-style. It wasn't disgusting, but it wasn't appealing either. It made you feel that he might have a method like that for everything.

Sally was talking even as she came up the basement stairs; she'd been bustling around in the 'wine cellar,' searching for the perfect bottle. 'Honey, do you remember whether we liked the Grüner Veltliner that Augie sent from Munich? We have a whole case of it. Want to try a glass? Would anyone else like wine?'

'Yes, please,' said Amy. She darted a questioning eyebrow Bevwards, daring her to use not drinking as an excuse to mention her pregnancy.

'Too early in the day for me,' Bev said, wrinkling her forehead at Amy for a split second.

Jason just nodded and nudged his glass toward Sally, who situated herself at the head of the table and poured for herself first, then for her husband and Amy.

'Delicious chicken,' Amy said after a moment.

'Thanks! It's local,' said Sally, then laughed at herself. 'God, I'm sorry. I hate to be that person. But it is one of the cool things about living in the boonies – the local stuff. I mean, I got the chicken from my friend Diane. I probably *met* it.'

'Have you guys thought of raising chickens?' said Amy, and felt Bev's foot nudge her ankle.

'I would really like to, yeah! I mean, but we travel so much, it would be hard.'

'Eh, we could travel less. I for one would like to start traveling less,' said Jason.

'Well, we don't want you to start traveling less. We loved house-sitting,' said Amy.

'We're so grateful, really. It's so nice to get out of the city,' Bev said. Amy could sense her trying to compensate for her rudeness.

'Ha, well. Maybe you guys could man the coop when we're in London! I don't know, though. It seems like a lot of work, and they do smell terrible. Though it would be fun to go and gather the eggs every morning. I'd really feel like a farm wife.'

The conversation veered to other agricultural topics and from there to sites of interest nearby; Amy and Bev had already seen most of them, and Amy enthusiastically seconded Sally's opinions. Bev pushed bites of chicken around on her plate, smearing the red chutney. *Are you okay? Is this okay?* Amy tried to telegraph to her friend mentally, but Bev seemed not to receive the psychic message. Instead, she pushed her chair back and left the room without saying a word. Amy tensed, half expecting to hear the front door slam.

Instead, she heard – they all heard – the unmistakable

sounds of vomiting coming from the opposite side of the house. Bev had made it to the downstairs bathroom in time, it seemed, but not quite in enough time to close the door.

Jason didn't bother to conceal his disgust. 'Ugh, that's not appetizing,' he said. His plate was spotless.

'Is she okay?' Sally said, the three light lines across her forehead deepening momentarily in concern. 'Wild night last night or something?'

'Oh god, I'm so sorry. I'm gonna go take care of her. Please don't get up.'

'I'll come with you,' said Sally, and Amy didn't bother to try to dissuade her. They left Jason at the table – he picked up a magazine – and went into the bathroom, where a pale Bev was sitting on the floor.

'Sorry. I couldn't close the door in time,' she said. 'I pulled on it and it only, like, half slid.'

'Oh god, that fucking sliding door! It's been on our to-do list for ages: normal bathroom door for the downstairs bathroom. I didn't poison you, did I?'

Bev looked up at Amy, who widened her eyes and inclined her head slightly, not quite a nod of approval, more like the nudge you'd give a balky animal.

Then Bev looked at Sally. 'I'm pregnant,' she said.

For the first time in their friendship Amy felt that she had no idea what Bev was thinking.

Nobody spoke for a minute, and then Bev straightened herself up to hork into the toilet again. Sally tactfully turned away, but Amy was experiencing that thing where you can't wrench your eyes from wherever they happen to be focused without an extreme effort of your tiny facial muscles.

Jason's footsteps were already audible on the second floor; clearly, the whole situation offended his sensibilities. With a forcible head shake Amy snapped out of her momentary paralysis and bent to rub Bev's back. Bev slumped over the bowl. Sally caught Amy's eye and mouthed something inaudible.

'On purpose?' Sally said it just slightly louder, loud enough for Bev to hear.

Bev laughed. 'Yeah, I thought it would be a good time to have a baby. Since I had this downtime between dropping out of grad school and trying to restart my failed career. You know? It just seemed like a perfect opportunity.'

'She's kidding,' Amy felt the need to clarify.

Sally was silent for a second; Amy thought maybe she was mourning whatever perfect hostess plans she had for the afternoon. Then she straightened up.

'I have some saltines in the cupboard. Bev, the best thing is to just nibble one of them slowly, and then you won't feel as queasy. It's totally abhorrent at first, but it works.'

Bev allowed herself to be led to the kitchen table, where she sat with her head in her hands as Sally pawed through the cupboards behind her. Amy sat down opposite Bev.

'You sound like you know what you're talking about,' Bev hazarded after a minute.

Sally looked at the girls, as if she were deciding how open to be with them, but of course she was going to tell them everything. 'I've had a couple of miscarriages. We've stopped trying. Your standard story. We thought of embarking on the whole high-tech thing, but I was just grossed out by it – injecting yourself with hormones, walking around with this big, sore lump of bloated ovary inside you. It offended my hippie sensibilities.'

She put a plate of crackers in front of Bev, who picked one up and watched it crumble.

'These seem old,' Bev said.

'They're three years old, yeah.' Sally was smiling, but Amy saw her jaw clench around the words. 'Like, almost exactly. Anyway. So, you're getting an abortion?'

Bev nibbled the disintegrating cracker tentatively, then with more gusto. 'Well, unless you want to adopt my baby.'

'Um?'

Amy, unable to stand the weirdness of the situation, burst into nervous giggles.

Sally looked at them both coldly. 'Did you come up here to offer me the baby? Is the baby-shaped hole in my life that obvious?'

No one said anything. Sally grabbed a cracker from the plate and chewed an edge of it thoughtfully, staring out the window over the sink that overlooked the backyard.

'You barely know us. Why did you think ... Is it too late to ...'

'Nope. I have a few more weeks. I just thought it was worth a shot.'

Amy felt sick. She scrutinized Bev, taking in her pallor and dark eye circles. She'd lost a little bit of weight in the past few weeks; the loss of flesh was starting to subtract a little of her face's childish roundness. But she had a new beauty, a kind of physical authority she'd lacked before.

Sally abruptly got up from the table and walked into the dining room, where the table was still set with the remains of their lunch. Amy caught Bev's eye and suddenly sensed her fear. They followed Sally into the dining room, where she was pacing. She didn't look upset anymore, though. Instead, she seemed excited.

'Do you guys believe in God? Or, like, fate, or the universe or astrology, or anything?'

Bev shrugged. This was weird, but no weirder than anything else that had just happened. 'I don't. I mean, I was raised to, but now I don't believe in anything. Amy believes in astrology, to some extent. And I guess Judaism?'

'Mostly astrology,' said Amy. 'I mean, but not really. You know. As one does. Why, what about you?'

'Oh, I'm totally not into any of that stuff, but I do think you guys came into my life for a reason. I feel like I'm supposed to be involved in your lives. Is that super weird?'

'Does that mean you want the baby?' Bev said, all business.

'I don't know ... maybe? Or maybe there's some other way of doing it, like, not adoption, but maybe I could just be really involved, like an aunt or a godparent?'

'Why would you want that? I mean, no offense, but you barely know us – I mean, me.'

'I don't know. I like you guys! You remind me of ... a younger me. Is that weird to say? But you do. And I would love to, like, support you, however I can, if Bev decides she wants to have the baby.'

Amy's eyes narrowed. 'Support, like, emotionally?'

'Sure, but maybe I could also help in other ways, if that makes sense? I could babysit, take the baby on weekends. It would be like I had a baby, but part-time. And actually, it would be the same for you. How ideal does that sound? God, you wonder why people don't do it all the time.'

Amy and Bev looked at each other. 'Well, but it would be a strange situation for the kid,' Bev finally said. 'And also, I'm still not sure that I want to have a baby, even part-time.'

'Really? Why?'

'Uh, because choosing to have a baby seems completely insane even in the best of circumstances? Which, mine are not, especially financially.'

Sally shrugged. 'Well, I'm sure everybody feels like that, yet the human race persists. And money's not a problem for me. It's like, the one problem I don't have, you know? I don't know. I think we should keep thinking about it. It could be fun!'

'Okay, but what about Jason? Do you need to consult him?'

'Consult me about what?' Jason said. He was standing in the stairwell. 'I'm about to head out. See you at dinner? Is everything okay, honey?'

Sally walked over to her husband and, with an effort that would have been awkward if it hadn't been smoothed by years of practice, leaned her head down very slightly to peck him on the cheek. 'Totally. Go ahead out, baby. We'll talk about it later.'

26

Late that night, Amy lay sleepless in Sally's guest room for several hours. Every time her thoughts started drifting and morphing into dreams, she was jarred awake by a pastoral noise that shattered the otherwise total stillness of the night. A crow would caw or an insect or frog would shriek or croak. It was almost unbearable. She missed the steady white-noise hum of traffic on the BQE.

Finally she got out of bed and tiptoed to her door. Opening it a crack, she saw a ribbon of light leaking out from under Bev's door across the hall. Tentatively, she knocked.

'Come in,' Bev said. She was in flannel pajamas that Amy hadn't known she owned, baggy ones patterned with lipstick kisses. Her blond hair was loose and crimped from the braids she'd had it in earlier, and she looked innocent, almost angelic. She patted the bed next to her, and Amy got in. They lay next to each other, staring up at the ceiling.

'I miss you,' Amy said.

'I miss you too,' said Bev. 'What happened?'

'I'm just weirded out by the idea of you having a baby. I mean, are you really considering it? I know talking to Sally about adoption was my idea, but that doesn't mean I think it's a *good* idea. And whatever she's talking about seems like an especially not good idea. Who ever heard of a time-share baby?'

'I haven't made up my mind about anything yet. I guess I feel insulted that you're not trusting my judgment. Like, no offense, but it is my decision. It doesn't really affect you at all, either way.'

Amy didn't know what to say. She felt that it actually did affect her a lot, but obviously it affected Bev a lot more – so much more that it seemed somewhat monstrous for Amy to even talk about the impact it would have on Amy's life.

After a minute Amy held her hand up toward the ceiling. Her nails were painted brown. 'Hey, did you notice I got a manicure?'

'I did notice. I like that color, actually. I usually never like your nails.'

'I got them done at this salon in Williamsburg; it's set up like a bar, with stools, so you can chat with your girlfriend who's next to you while a team of silent Asian women sit across the bar from you and tend your cuticles.'

'Creepy. This is why I don't get manicures.'

'Well, yeah, totally creepy. Anyway, so I was alone, and I had no choice but to eavesdrop on the conversation of the group next to me. One of them was a handbag designer, and I think they all had kids. They talked about their other friend who was pregnant and how it was *the best news*. The best news they'd ever heard. And about giving her a shower, and how one of them was a "domestic diva," and how the handbag designer named one of her handbags after somebody's daughter. Oh, and the cute, stupid things their husbands did, sort of bragging about their husbands' ineptitude with cooking or taking care of the kids.'

Amy glanced over at Bev to make sure she hadn't fallen asleep, but her eyes were still open. She was staring up at the ceiling fan; the only sound in the room was the gentle swoop of its blades cutting the air.

'I guess I'm talking about this weird vapidity that women seem to aspire to,' Amy said. 'This kind of *Us* magazine editorial voice that infects people's actual conversations and lives. Just fetishizing . . . *children* and *domesticity* and making it seem like they are the goals of women's lives, the only legitimate goals women's lives can have.'

'I am the furthest thing in the world from being in any way like those women,' Bev said, yawning.

'I know, I know. But no matter what, if you decide to have this baby, you're going to, like, *have a baby*. That's going to mean something. Just because . . . like, it's a baby. No matter what, it's your baby. Your child. Doesn't that fuck with your head? I'm just worried now about all the things that could go wrong. I just want things to go back to how they were before you got pregnant.' Amy was getting too tired to think straight.

'I want that too, but there's no point in wanting something

impossible. I also feel like this might be my chance to change the direction of my life,' said Bev. 'If you had one of those, you would take it, right?'

'I don't know,' Amy said. After a while, when it seemed that Bev had drifted off, she went back to her own room to sleep.

27

It was weird how long it took to get anywhere in Margaretville, considering how little of it there was. As Amy walked down the hill away from Sally and Jason's house, she felt as if she were breaching some veil between postcard scenery and reality with every step. The town was totally surrounded by mountains but somehow not in their shadow. The sky was full of bright, pale autumn sunlight. There wasn't another human being in sight, and Amy imagined that all the houses were empty, that the whole picturesque thing was a show put on for her benefit.

For the minutes it took Amy to hike to the main street, she tried to occupy her mind with something besides Bev's situation. She purposely stepped over the lines of weeds sprouting out of the cracks in the sidewalk. She tried to make herself think about her apartment search, her job prospects. *Please, God, let me get a new job soon,* she thought.

Amy's impression of God was more or less that God was a

reasonable guy/gal, a very wise yoga instructor type, who knew that you had done and thought some heinous stuff but didn't take it personally. Or maybe there was no God, no personified intelligence, but it was still important to have some internal moral code that you would be rewarded for sticking to. Doing unto others. Not fucking other people over. It was weird that in all their years of best friendship, Amy and Bev had never discussed morality, or whatever you wanted to call the rules they, respectively, lived by. When Bev had talked about feeling that she would faint if she went back to the gynecologist's office, Amy had been shocked to realize that there was a vestige of Bev's extremely religious upbringing left in her. Or – well, that wasn't quite true. Before, Amy had thought that Bev's evangelical childhood resulted in what sometimes seemed like amorality, as if instead of rules, Bev had a lacuna where rules had been and where there was now something slightly too vague – something that made Bev vulnerable to impulses because there was nothing inside her telling her 'no' except something she didn't trust, something she fought with in order to live.

But now Amy thought that maybe Bev – despite not believing in a devil who would punish her or a hell she was doomed to go to after she died – did believe there were things you simply could not do, and having an abortion was one of them. And if that was the case, it wouldn't be possible to talk her out of having the baby.

Amy wandered up and down the main street, peering into the windows of businesses that seemed mostly closed. Idiosyncratic hours of operation were posted in their windows: 11:30 to 4:15; noon to 6:00 on Thursdays. She finally wandered over to the block behind the main street, where the quaintness ended and was replaced with bland suburban utilitarianism. She walked into the supermarket. Its wide aisles, made to accommodate two carts side by side, filled her with hunger and nostalgia, and she was struck by an impulse to call Sam, just to hear his voice, an impulse she quickly gave in to.

He picked up on the second ring, but his voice was tinny, and wherever he was sounded windy. 'I'm on my way to soccer, baby, so I only have a couple of minutes. Where are you? I miss you.'

'I'm in a grocery store in upstate New York, near the cheese island. They have samples. I just ate some local chèvre; it was okay. Super salty. I'm glad you got out of the studio, baby. How is your soccer career going?'

'We won last night, but today I think we're going to lose. Are you and Bev having fun on your vacation, baby?'

Amy hesitated. She actually had no idea why she was hesitating to tell Sam about Bev's pregnancy. In the past, she'd told him gross and revealing details about her best friend's romantic life all the time, the way people in relationships always gossip about their single friends to compensate for the lack of sexy scandal in their own lives, in between watching episodes of *The Wire*. But this felt different, more private and serious than Bev's usual indiscretions and debilitating crushes. And besides, she wasn't sure what was going on with her and Sam's relationship.

'Yeah, we actually ran into those people we house-sat for before, and now we're, like, visiting them.'

Sam's end of the line grew windier. 'Sorry, baby, I have to

catch this bus or else I'm going to be late to soccer. I don't want to be that annoying guy talking on his cell phone on the bus. Will you send me one of your beautiful emails later?'

'Okay. But I would rather talk, I mean ... I have all this stuff I want to tell you, and you're never around. And you could send me an email too?'

'I'm sorry, baby, I've just been trapped in the studio. There's so much amazing light this time of year. Okay, I'm on the bus, baby. Wish me luck in the game!'

Coming out of her telephonic fugue state, Amy realized that she'd been standing there by the cheese island, fondling the same piece of string cheese for a long time, squeezing the firm knot from one end of its plastic package to the other. An aproned supermarket staffer was eyeing her from the other side of a row of bagged yellow onions. She shoved the phone to the bottom of her pocket and smiled at the guy, who stopped stacking the onion bags and gave her a halfhearted wave.

It was really getting old, this business of Sam being the only person besides Bev whom she most cared about and wanted to confide in and Sam's perhaps not feeling the same way. She needed to break up with him, but she needed some other arena of her life to improve before she relinquished the support, however minimal, she was getting from him. For example, she needed a new job. Or a new apartment. Or a new boyfriend. She bought a can of organic fruit juice soda with her credit card and began trudging back up the hill.

When Amy got to the house, Bev was lying on the couch in the living room, nursing a ginger ale and flipping idly through an issue of Jason's magazine. Sally was plopped down in the wing chair opposite Bev, busily scribbling some kind of list.

Amy stood in the vestibule, one hand reflexively teasing the screen of the phone in the depths of her coat pocket, as though she might be about to call someone who'd be able to come and rescue her. They'd done what they came here to do. Couldn't they now, non-awkwardly, say their goodbyes and get back to Brooklyn? She suddenly felt frantic about her job search, her apartment search, her broke-ness. The first chance she got, she'd talk to Bev about leaving. Meanwhile, she forced a smile, took off her shoes and coat, then retreated to the guest bathroom upstairs, where she self-consciously ran water during her entire toilette.

When she came back downstairs, Bev had pried herself up off the couch and was in the process of tying her ratty high-top Converses. 'I'm feeling a little cabin-fevered, dude. And the nausea seems to have subsided for the moment, knock wood. Want to go on a bike ride? They have like ten bikes; Sally is going to show me her favorite trail.'

Amy knew that she should force herself to go on the bike ride, that she would feel much better if she got exercise. She looked at Sally, who was reaching down to lace up sneakers that had no overt brand insignia on them but still managed to look incredibly expensive. Amy knew she should go, and just as clearly, she knew she wasn't going to.

She told Bev and Sally that she would hold down the fort and that she was glad Bev was feeling better. As an afterthought, she asked what Jason was up to.

'Oh, he's down in the basement,' Sally said. 'He's working on one of his little projects.'

Half an hour later, without quite knowing how she'd ended up there, Amy found herself knocking on the door of Jason's basement workroom.

He was straddling a bench, wearing protective goggles and holding some kind of tool. His ratty T-shirt was a little bit tighter than it needed to be, but otherwise this was the butchest Amy had ever seen him look. When he glanced up at Amy, she understood him to actually be heterosexual in a way she hadn't before.

'What are you working on?'

He pushed his protective goggles up and wiped his brow with an exaggerated Diet Coke commercial-ish gesture, and Amy giggled, as he'd intended her to. 'Come over here and take a peek,' he said.

She stood behind him and looked at the object on the bench. It was a tiny replica of the couch Bev had been lying on earlier, the one in the living room upstairs. Jason was using a Dremel tool to create a tiny version of the intricate pattern on the real couch's wooden frame.

'Whoa. That's amazing! And sort of bizarre,' said Amy.

Jason stroked the mini couch, looking at it as though it had appeared suddenly in his hand via magic. 'Yeah. It's so nerdy, I never tell anyone about it. I don't have a dollhouse for them or anything. I just learned how to make scale replicas of stuff by building architectural models in design school and sort of fell in love with it. Now I do it sometimes when I'm feeling stressed-out.'

'It's good to have a project,' Amy said. She was reaching.

'Do you have a project?'

It was the first time they'd made eye contact. It was a basic question, and he'd asked it only to make conversation, but it caught Amy off guard.

'Um ... no, not right now.'

'What do you do, again?'

'Oh, stuff with the Internet. Editing stuff, mostly, like blog posts. And sometimes I write stuff. I immerse myself in each little project completely while it's in progress, but then the moment it's finished, I don't want to have anything to do with it. I mean, I want to cash the check and that's it.'

'Huh! You have one-night stands with your work.'

Amy wrinkled her nose to show that she thought he was being slightly inappropriate, but the allusion to sex gave her a tiny, queasy thrill, and a secret underlayer of her mind started doing math about how much longer Bev and Sally could reasonably be expected to ride bikes.

'Not quite. It's just like, once something's done, it's no longer a part of me. I would sooner keep, like, a box full of my old fingernail clippings than read an old blog post. Don't you ever feel like that about old issues of your magazine?'

Jason was looking at her now with total engagement. 'I don't. At all. When I do a layout for the magazine, I want to look at it again and again. I'll wake up in the middle of the night and flip through back issues to lull myself to sleep. It's like: I exist, I exist, I exist.'

Amy grinned. 'I do that too, compulsively, but all I ever feel is disgust. Like, I exist, I exist ... ugh.'

Jason turned his gaze back to the tiny couch in his hands. 'Sally's more like you, I think. She's always revising; it's why she's taking so long to finish her book. She doesn't ever want to get to the part of the process where something stops being, like, still potentially perfect.'

He had mentioned Sally at the exact point in the conversation at which it would have become weird if he hadn't acknowledged the existence of Sally; at the same time, he'd known, on some level, that their being alone in the basement together required him to mention her.

'Uh, well, maybe I'll become more like you as I age. You know, I'll grow up,' said Amy lamely.

Jason smiled. 'Yeah, you've got time. How old are you, anyway, early thirties?'

'Thirty,' said Amy. 'So, yeah. Early thirties. Wow, when you put it that way, it sounds old.'

'You seem very youthful, actually.'

'What do you mean? Like, that I'm immature?'

'Kind of. Not in a bad way. There's something about you that seems ... unformed. Like, impressionable.'

'Uh, thanks?' Amy frowned. 'I don't know, that seems like an insult to me.'

'No. It's not,' Jason said. He looked up at Amy, really scrutinizing her, and for a strange moment she thought he might stand up and kiss her. She wasn't even attracted to him, not really, but the basement and the specter of his wife gave the situation an adrenalized zing. But then he turned his attention back to the miniature couch and she decided she had imagined the entire thing.

28

Sally was in the middle of telling Bev that she had been a stripper when she'd lived in the East Village. Looking at Sally now – flushed from the ride up the steep hills behind Margaretville, wearing spandex bike tights, a portrait of athletic suburban wholesomeness – it was almost impossible for Bev to imagine this. But it had been a different time, when breast implants and fake tans were not yet de rigueur accessories for the professionally attractive. They were sitting in a clearing and eating the picnic Sally had packed: little crusts-off cucumber sandwiches, dill from the garden, home-made bread.

'Um,' said Bev. 'Why were you ... I mean, were you on drugs or something?'

'No! I mean, a little, but not more than anyone else. It wasn't a problem.'

Sally seemed to be enjoying Bev's discomfort; the novelty of being able to shock someone was, Bev could tell, a big part of why she'd unfurled this confession. It seemed certain that Bev wasn't the first person she'd revealed her stripper history to. It was her friendship test, designed to reel you in by making you feel privileged to know insider info; you were supposed to suddenly think of Sally as a transgressor, possessed of sexual bravado and vulnerability you hadn't previously suspected her of having. But knowing you weren't remotely the first person who'd heard the confession made it seem like imitation intimacy. Like stripping, Bev supposed.

'I had been a painter before that, that's actually what I studied at Brown, fine art, but then I became a performance artist, and I was making a lot of work in those days involving nudity, and I figured, fuck, might as well make some money! And all my friends were doing it.'

'Wow,' Bev said, smiling at Sally to let her know she was impressed and not weirded out.

'Have you ever, you know ... done anything like that?' Sally said.

'Oh god no. No way. I get self-conscious even thinking about being onstage.'

'You totally could, you know. You have a great body.'

'I don't think now would really be the time to start,' Bev said, pointing at her stomach.

'Huh. I even kind of forgot about it for a second,' Sally said. 'Sorry. Do you ever? I remember times when I was pregnant, I would go whole days without thinking about it once.'

'Nah,' Bev said. 'I'm always thinking about it.'

'You dropped out of grad school, right?'

'Yeah. I have half an M.F.A. I guess that makes me not quite a master of fine arts.'

'It's cool. I'm more of a servant of fine arts myself.'

'Did you get an M.F.A.?'

'No. I don't have any credentials. I decided I wanted to write only after we moved up here, and to be honest, it's not like I'm that serious about it. I try to do it every day, though. I keep thinking that if I keep doing it, maybe one day some perfect story will just come to me.'

'So you're writing fiction?' Bev asked.

'Yeah.'

'Yeah, me too. Though I don't really think it's a meaningful distinction.'

'Right? Like if I tried to write about stripping, now . . . I mean, fuck, I don't remember anything that happened. I would just be inventing it.'

'Maybe you should do that.'

'Write about stripping?'

'Yeah, people love that. Or, like, the bad old East Village. Write about that, and make shit up.'

Bev finished her sandwich and rolled over on the grass. It was getting chilly, and the sweat from the bike ride was cooling on her skin, and as she looked off into the woods, she caught a flash of movement. Not fifteen feet away from them, a family of deer stepped into the clearing: a big buck, a smaller doe, and a faun – white-tailed and beautiful with their wide-set, stupid eyes staring directly at Bev and Sally. Bev caught Sally's eye and they grinned at each other. She felt sorry for Amy, back at the house, missing this moment.

29

There was a baby drowsing in the stroller pressed up against the booth next to them at the restaurant where Sally and Jason had taken Bev and Amy for dinner, and they were all trying and failing not to look at him. Amy thought she could tell, based on Sally's and Jason's body language, that they'd discussed Sally's proposal about the baby, though no one had mentioned it. Bev had convinced Amy to postpone the end of the weekend, spend Sunday night in Margaretville before heading back to the city midmorning Monday, so this dinner – at a ski lodge–style restaurant named Moose Ridge – was their last meal together, for now at least. The baby had abandoned himself to sleep and lay perfectly still except for the rise and fall of his contented belly. His arms and legs were splayed at perfect right angles. Amy envied him.

Jason was in a great mood. He enthused over the wine list and menu and then, when they arrived, over the food and the wine. 'I think they gather these mushrooms near here. They grow near the hot spring – it insulates them, like a natural greenhouse.' He waved a forkful in Amy's direction. 'Want to try them?'

Amy didn't really want the mushrooms, but she also didn't want to make a big deal of anything. She caught herself glancing in Sally's direction for approval as she accepted the bite from Jason's fork. Sally was smiling into the distance, vaguely in the direction of the baby. Amy made eye contact with Jason as the fork entered her mouth. 'Mmm, tasty,' she said.

After dinner, back at the house, Amy stood in the backyard in the waning sunlight, her stomach uncomfortably full of morels and wine, and called Sam again. She had felt some pressure to help Sally drink the bottle of wine they'd ordered. Jason had held back because he was driving; Bev had abstained completely, despite Sally's exculpatory declarations about 'the French.' Now the ground was soft and a little unsteady under Amy's feet. The ringtone sounded again and again, and she was just about to give up when Sam finally answered the phone, sounding groggy.

'Hi, baby,' she said, all overcompensating crispness.

'Baby.' He sighed. 'I'm working. Can we talk some other time?'

'I know, babe, but we haven't talked in so long!'

'We talked earlier today.'

'I mean really talked. *Talked* talked. Let's talk!'

Sam sighed again, and she could hear him shifting around, maybe getting out of bed. It felt like New York was so incredibly far away. Sam always slept in an old T-shirt, and she imagined him wearing her favorite one, the one with the lion-head mascot of his high school, holes around its collar she could stick her finger through to feel his warm, muscled skin underneath. She was wandering around the way you do on the phone, reaching out and plucking leaves from low branches of the saplings at the yard's border, then crumpling them in her palm. As she wandered, she realized how drunk she was, and also why she had really called Sam, and even as she spoke her next sentence, she began to wish she hadn't called him, but now it was too late. She'd started.

'So, I've been thinking a lot about, you know, us.'

There was silence, more readjustment. 'Baby. Listen, I leave for Spain soon. I just can't think about the future right now. Also, I think this is the kind of thing that would be better to talk about in person.'

'You won't talk about it in person, though! You never want to talk about the future!'

He stayed silent.

'I mean, do we *have* a future?'

They had reached the familiar weird impasse past which any conversation would have to include either a marriage proposal or a breakup, and neither seemed exactly possible at that moment.

There was silence on the line until Sam broke it. 'Baby, you know I love you, right?'

Amy stubbornly stayed silent. She knew she was being childish, but as long as she was being childish, she wanted to go all the way with it: throw a tantrum, say unforgivable, stupid, illogical things.

Luckily, some telecom god spared her this indignity, and

the line went dead; the cell signal had faded again. Ugh, but what if Sam thought she'd hung up on him? Desperately, she redialed, but to no avail.

After a few more minutes she stopped wandering around the yard clutching her phone, willing it to ring, and slunk up onto the porch and into the house. She was shivering. The meager warmth of the day was disappearing as the sky began to darken, and inside the house it was barely warmer than it was outside.

In the middle of the night Amy woke suddenly and then couldn't shake the idea that there was some kind of creepy presence waiting silently outside her bedroom door. This house was so old; maybe it was haunted! More probably, it was Bev, hesitating over whether to disrupt Amy's slumber with a session of midnight confidences. But no: it was too silent to be Bev. That left two options: ghost or Jason.

The floorboards creaked slightly, and Amy immediately became one hundred percent more conscious, her earlier drunkenness completely out of her system. She hadn't been imagining the noises. There really was someone out there. She remembered in a flash that she hadn't showered, and she put her face under the covers for a moment to make sure she smelled okay, then rolled out of bed and tiptoed to the door and opened it slowly and soundlessly.

Jason smiled and raised his fingertip to his lips. Amy crossed her arms and pretended to be confused about why he'd come, but she let him walk past her into the room. He was wearing drawstring pajama pants and a tank top, and the sparse hair on his forearms was straight and black.

He sat down on the edge of the bed, and she closed the

door – they both winced at the tiny latching noise it made as it shut fully – then sat down next to him. When she opened her mouth to speak, he shushed her by putting his finger over her lips, the same way he'd touched his own mouth a moment earlier.

If she spoke, or made any noise at all, Amy knew that she risked waking Bev and Sally, and then how would she explain Jason's presence in her room? Clearly Jason knew this too. He smiled again, a slightly nasty smile. He still had his fingertip at her lips, and without breaking their eye contact he began to increase the pressure, force it past her teeth, which parted in shock and curiosity, and then his finger was in her mouth.

Tentatively – was this what he wanted? – she touched the intruding finger with the tip of her tongue and felt herself respond to this weird gesture with a surge of physical hunger that was even more intense because it was a surprise. With his other hand he reached under her T-shirt, between her legs, shoved her underwear to one side, and pushed two fingers inside her vagina in the same peremptory way he'd put his finger in her mouth. Amy would probably have made some small surprised noise at this, but she couldn't because there was a finger in her mouth (maybe that was why he'd put it there).

Usually Amy had to focus on some fantasy in order to come, but this reality was fantastic enough to do it for her, apparently, because she clenched around Jason's rhythmically jabbing finger more effortlessly than she'd thought possible. Feeling that she owed him, she reached for his crotch, but he pushed her hand away, and she was grateful;

it was always hard to know how to touch someone, easier to sense what they wanted from you and just try to do that. Smiling a bit impersonally, Jason set to work getting them both completely naked, moving around as little as possible to minimize bed creaking. His body was smooth, cool-skinned, and somehow expensive-looking; his dick especially had the ergonomic look of a high-end sex toy. Amy had one final moment of tension, of thinking, during the condom-related pause, about how her actions could affect Sally and, in turn, potentially, Bev. But then the pause was over, and there was nothing to think or do for the foreseeable future besides what Jason wanted, which was violent and strange and somewhat degrading and entirely thought-annihilating, a blessed relief.

30

In the moment of waking up, Amy's first thought was to be grateful that she didn't believe in Bev's parents' punisher God. Her yoga teacher God would not exactly be thrilled by what she'd done either, though, and she certainly wasn't thrilled with herself. For one thing, it meant that she definitely had to break up with Sam as soon as possible. She wasn't a cheater; lying and sneaking around lay far outside the range of her acting ability. She allowed herself a brief teary moment of lying in bed and feeling terrible about losing Sam. Beautiful, brilliant Sam, with his perfect butt and force field of mystery that she would now never be able to penetrate fully! She'd spent so much time feeling jealous about him – of his accomplishments, of the paintings whose company he prized over hers, over the feelings he'd had for his ex-wife – that she'd never imagined that *she* would be the one to betray *him*. She had never even thought about betraying him. That was how the betrayal had been able to happen:

she hadn't had time to weigh her options, make a decision about whether or not to commit the act. The act had presented itself to her and made itself irresistible.

Well: no, not true. Not technically true. She could have kept her arms crossed at the threshold of her room. She could have shaken her head once, a decisive nonverbal 'nope.' She could have drawn the line any number of places: this far, no further. There had been infinite opportunities for line drawing and she hadn't availed herself of any of them.

She stopped crying, wiped her eyes with the antique quilt, listened for sounds of stirring in the waking house, and rolled over and stretched, intrigued by how abnormally energetic she felt about getting out of bed. She still felt full of strange pockets of conflicting feeling: sadness about Sam, mild disgust and a queasy throb of lust about Jason. But underneath everything ran a low hum of exaltation. Things were happening to her. They were bad things, but at least they were happening.

31

The kitchen was at its best in the early morning, with white light bouncing off the glass-fronted cabinets. Sally and Bev were sitting at the table in their pajamas, drinking from oversize coffee mugs and waiting for the catalog-ordered frozen croissants to come out of the oven. When the croissants were done, Sally arranged them on a clean dish towel in a basket and put them in front of Bev with a jokey little flourish. 'I thought we deserved something a little bit special for breakfast, since you guys are headed out today.'

Bev was already munching gratefully on one of the croissants. 'This really hits the spot.'

'I remember being able to handle pastries even when other food seemed universally unappealing, so I thought . . .'

'You mean, when you were pregnant?'

'Yeah.'

Bev brushed crumbs off the front of her bathrobe. 'Is it

weird for you if we keep talking about it, or is it not a big deal to you?'

'It's not weird. I mean, now when I think about it, it seems like a big deal, but it wasn't at the time.' Sally paused to take a bite of her croissant, which she'd torn into halves and daintily placed at right angles on her plate. 'Actually, besides the more recent times, there was one time right after I met Jason that I found out I was pregnant. Not with Jason's kid, actually. There was really never a question of whether I'd keep it. Not only had I just met this wonderful guy, but I had done all kinds of bad things to that little fetus without realizing it. I still think about that when I hear my friends talk about their no-caffeine, no-soft cheese, no-sushi pregnancies – like, I would have given birth to a *crack* baby!'

Bev widened her eyes a little bit, unsure of whether to laugh.

'Well, not literally crack, but you know what I mean. Definitely not the most deluxe accommodation, my uterus,' Sally said. She munched her breakfast and looked up at Bev brightly, smiling with a glimmer of something sharp and not okay in her eyes.

Without premeditation, Bev put her hand on Sally's, on the table. 'Think of all the stuff that would never have been able to happen if things had gone differently back then, though, you know?'

'God, you're so mature, you know that?'

Bev waited a decent interval before removing her hand. The back of Sally's hand was dry and a little bit scaly. With her other hand, she brought a bite of croissant to her mouth. *Enjoy the croissant, hypothetical baby*, she thought. *This is the kind of thing Sally would be able to help me give you. You could go to Paris and eat croissants there, probably. You could be born a sort of rich person, and then you wouldn't be worried all the time, which would make you fun to be around. You could grow up to be nothing like me.*

32

They drove over a covered bridge and out onto the highway and away from Margaretville, getting a slightly later start than they'd wanted to, but Bev felt more relaxed about missing a day of temping, it seemed to Amy, than she would have before the weekend's events had taken place. Sally had insisted on loading them down with a picnic lunch, hugging each of them several times and exacting momlike promises that they'd call when they got back to the city, to let her know they'd arrived safely. Jason had been MIA for their leave-taking; Sally explained that he'd left early for a meeting in the city.

It was beginning to seem as if they might spend the entire drive back to the Zipcar lot in silence when, finally, Bev spoke.

'Okay, out with it. Whatever it is that you don't want to tell me but are also kind of dying to tell me, just do it now, even if it's horrible, please.'

Amy half suppressed a shocked laugh. How pleasant it was to be so known. 'Ugh, it's bad. You're going to be mad. I feel like I should preface this by saying that I had no intention of doing it and I have no intention of doing it again, but . . .'

'Jesus, Amy, you're going to make me get into an accident! Just spit it out!'

'Jason came into my room last night and we did it.'

'You did *what*?'

'Um? It?'

Bev guffawed. 'Jason isn't gay?'

'I know. I was shocked too!'

As the information settled into the car's interior, the initial shock of it dissipated, but the change in the atmosphere lingered, like a bad smell. 'I have a million questions about this, but I'm just, like . . . I mean, do you get the sense that this is the kind of thing Jason does all the time?'

'Like he'd tell me, you know – "Don't worry, I'm serially unfaithful to my wife so it's not like this is a big deal to me"?'

Bev shrugged. 'Well, not in so many words, or not in those words exactly.'

'We didn't talk about it – we didn't talk at all. He walked into my room and sat down on the bed and it was, like, a foregone conclusion that we would – um, the whole thing just felt very inevitable.'

'That sounds hot.'

'It was. I mean, it was crazy. I have no idea why I went along with it – it was dreamlike, in a way. His confidence was so appealing.'

'You did it on purpose, so it would be harder for me to have a relationship with Sally and accept help from her, et cetera,' said Bev dully, not in an accusatory way at all.

'But I didn't do anything!'

'You did.'

'I didn't make an *effort* to do anything. And there's no reason anything has to get fucked up.' She glanced over at Bev, who was gripping the steering wheel with the grim determination of a boat captain in a thunderstorm.

'Well, it won't.'

'Good!'

The gears turning, the processes of rationalization happening in Bev's mind – Amy imagined that she could hear Bev's thoughts in her own mind. But the next time Bev did speak, several exits later, what she said was nothing like what Amy had imagined she was thinking.

'I'm really touched that you'd go that far to protect me, Amy. I know you want what's best for me, and you feel like you have to do whatever you can to try and keep me from making a bad decision. I wish you didn't think you knew best about what decision I should make, but I am grateful that you care.'

'Are you being sarcastic?'

'No! I wish you had a different way of showing it, but you do care about me. And that means a lot to me.'

Amy felt like the shittiest imaginable shit. She was used to Bev always giving her the benefit of the doubt, but this was much more benefit than she was used to. She did care about Bev, of course she did, but she hadn't had sex with Jason in order to complicate things with Sally and dissuade Bev from having the baby. Or had she? Who knows, maybe subconsciously she had. And there was no point in telling Bev she hadn't, no point in actively *trying* to make Bev think less of her.

'You're a way, way better friend than I deserve,' Amy said.

'I don't know about that,' said Bev.

But Amy saw her face and knew she was thinking that Amy was right.

33

There was a magazine in the waiting room called *Conceive*, and Bev stared at its cover in disbelief for a few seconds. The woman on the cover wasn't obviously pregnant, but she was beaming. Were readers meant to assume that she had *just then* conceived? Bev had brought a book, a collection of 1980s short stories that had been assigned reading for one of her workshop classes, but even the idea of opening her bag and unearthing it seemed too taxing. She just wanted to stay perfectly still for the moment. But she also needed to avoid making eye contact with anyone in the waiting room, so she was going to have to read something. The magazine she picked, *Disney Family Fun*, was innocuous enough. There was a two-page spread on how to throw a 'Reading Is Fun!' theme party, complete with invitations that looked like library cards along with instructions for using fabric paint to print book shapes on canvas tote bags. Bev sensed herself filing the information away for future reference; the tote bags were cute, though she had a hard time believing that kids would think so. She was halfway through the following article, about healthy new ideas for sandwich fillings, when the receptionist called her name, held out a specimen cup to her, and gestured wordlessly with her head in the direction of the restroom.

Afterward a nurse took her to a little alcove near the restroom, where she took her blood pressure and gave her a form to sign. The nurse didn't ask any question more personal than 'How tall are you?' but Bev was still careful to answer her as brusquely as possible; she was in the kind of mood where a simple 'How are you?' might elicit an unstoppable torrent of intimate information. There was no point in humiliating herself any more than was absolutely necessary. The nurse's touch, when she removed the blood pressure cuff, was kind and soothing, and Bev realized that aside from Sally's unwanted hugs, she hadn't touched or been touched by anyone in days.

The nurse brought her back to an exam room, instructed her about what portion of her clothing to remove, then left her alone. There was a *New York* magazine near the little alcove where she left her clothes, as well as another issue of *Conceive* with a different beaming woman on its cover; this one had a slightly convex stomach, which she was accentuating with tight blue yoga pants. Bev busied herself removing her pants and underwear, folding them in a neat pile, and situated herself on the exam table with the paper wrap she'd been given loosely draped around her pelvis. How much longer would the doctor keep her waiting? Should she get up and grab the *New York* magazine? What if the doctor came in while she was walking across the room to get it?

The doctor made her wait for what seemed like much too long, and during this interval Bev thought of getting up and putting her underwear and pants back on and leaving at least four or five hundred times.

The doctor who came in was young, blithe, stylish, and visibly just slightly pregnant. 'Hi, I'm Sandy,' she said, reaching out to shake Bev's hand, then immediately turning to the sink to wash her hands and pull on latex gloves. 'Everything going well?'

She didn't even look at the chart, Bev thought. Years of paying for all her medical care out-of-pocket had made Bev highly attuned to inconveniences and flaws; she felt like writing a bad Yelp review. 'Uh, so. I'm pregnant, and I just need to know if I can change my mind about it without its being totally traumatic and horrible. I tried googling it, but that was just too … uh, there's a lot of really bad Internet out there about abortion, and I got too horrified to continue.'

'Do you know how many weeks you are? Lie back and put your feet in the stirrups.' Sandy stared fixedly at the corner of the room as she palpated Bev's abdomen, touching her brusquely, verging on roughly.

'Eight and a half.'

Sandy treated her to a forced smile. 'Well, you've still got options. But if you do decide to terminate, you'll have to schedule another appointment, as you know. It's a routine procedure, but it's still surgery. You have to abstain from eating beforehand and we have to confirm that there's someone waiting to take you home, all that stuff.'

Bev felt relieved and disappointed. She had kind of known that she couldn't just walk into the doctor's office and walk out un-pregnant. It was another of those vague myths about New York that still lingered in the collective imagination, that it was a city where you could get anything you wanted at any time, as long as you were willing to pay for it. But you could no more impulse-buy an abortion than you could get good take-out Chinese food at any hour.

'If you decide not to terminate, though, we should set up a schedule of appointments and consult about your nutrition, and we should really do that soon. So – I mean, I hate to state the obvious, but it would be good to decide as soon as possible, either way.'

'But how much longer do I have before I won't be able to . . .'

'I'd have to do an ultrasound to give you an ironclad number, and you're out-of-pocket, right? So let's not do unnecessary stuff. Is ASAP going to be good enough, or do you need a deadline?'

Bev forced a short laugh to defuse the awkwardness, then felt even more awkward about how laughing like that had made her muscles contract around Sandy's gloved finger, which was now in her vagina, pressing upward to feel the shapes of Bev's organs from the inside. As if responding to the pressure, the finger withdrew. Sandy made eye contact with Bev for the first time as she stripped off her gloves.

'Do you want to talk about it more?' Her voice sounded sincere, as if she was ready to deviate for the first time from an established script.

'Not really,' Bev said.

'Okay, then you can get dressed. Make another appointment with the receptionist on your way out, or you can call and make one in the next couple of weeks. But Beverly? The next *couple* of weeks, okay? Don't let the decision be made for you.'

Bev shed her gown and stepped back into her clothes, feeling the gross gooey warmth left by Sandy's lubricated finger between her legs as she slipped her underwear back on. Her breasts hurt as she put on her bra; she looked in the mirror in profile to see if she could discern any change in her silhouette, but of course there was none. She ran her hands down her body, feeling strangely distant from it, as if it were a robot she could control. She felt detached from her body's fate.

She finished dressing and took her body back out onto the street. As she started walking downtown, she noticed the warmth of the sun on her skin, alternating with the cool shade generated by the tall trees of Gramercy Park. She was back in her skin again, and she felt reassured and happy for no reason she could name. Happy and ravenous.

There was a raw juice and vegan salad place nearby that was, improbably, really good, but it constituted a big splurge for Bev: the salads and juices were all in the eleven- to fifteen-dollar range. But for the first time in a while Bev felt like spending money, not because she had any more of it than usual – in fact, if she didn't pick up a temp assignment this week, she was going to bounce her rent check – but because the future seemed promising in some inchoate way. She felt genuinely uncertain about her pregnancy, but also newly confident that whatever she decided would turn out to be right.

As she stood in line at the juice bar, she checked her phone: no emails, no texts, no missed calls from Amy. They hadn't hung out since they got back from Margaretville over a week ago. Sally had texted her a few times, not about anything in particular, just older-person-style sentiments like 'Hope your Monday's not too much of a Monday' and stuff like that. Bev had appreciated it. She wondered if maybe she could just ask Sally for a check. Not for a lot, for like five hundred dollars, just to give herself some breathing room. She felt as if she probably could.

After she placed her order and settled into a seat to wait for it, she became aware that a beautiful woman with a huge amount of curly black hair was watching her from the next table over, and with a shock she realized why the woman was familiar: it was her favorite professor from her one year of grad school, Elise. 'Beverly Tunney! Oh my god! I'm so delighted to see you here! How are you?' Without waiting for an answer, Elise swooped Bev into a bosomy hug.

'I'm good! It's really good to see you!'

'Isn't this place amazing? I love what they do with nuts.'

'Totally.' They beamed at each other. Elise had written several well-received books and was married to a banker, but despite being successful, beautiful, and rich, she'd been Bev's nicest teacher by far. Or maybe that was why she'd been nice: teaching was a lark for her, whereas for everyone else, you could tell, it was a burdensome and ill-compensated necessity. The sense that her teachers were marking time and that they thought checks were the most important thing she and her fellow students were writing had been a big part of why Bev had left school. But Elise had been so encouraging that Bev felt slightly guilty about not living up to her expectations.

Elise furrowed her brow cutely. 'You claimed you'd stay in touch! But not a peep. What gives? What have you been up to? I hope you're getting lots of writing done.'

'No, I totally haven't. I've been more, like, accumulating material,' Bev said with a slight eye roll to show that she was kidding.

'Don't roll your eyes! That's a legitimate thing for you to be doing. Listen, I'm going to sit here and eat fifteen dollars' worth of kale and hazelnuts, and you're going to tell me absolutely everything that's been going on with you.'

Ordinarily Bev would have told what was appropriate to tell and left it at that. But she was in a strange, expansive mood, and Elise was just far enough outside of Bev's life that she *could* tell her everything. Elise's eyes got gratifyingly wider and wider, and when Bev finished, Elise seemed genuinely awestruck. 'Oh, wow. That's a weird one, huh? I don't know whether to congratulate you or console you.'

'I don't know either. Um, I know it's a bizarre thing to ask, and obviously you shouldn't feel pressure, like my whole decision is going to hinge just on what you say, but . . . what do you think I should do?'

'Well, primarily I think you should get a job.'

'Ha! That's definitely true.'

'No, like, a good job. No more temping. And nothing to do with books, or publishing, or teaching or tutoring, or anything like that. You just won't make enough money doing any of those things to be able to have a baby on your own, even with some help from this wannabe godmother.'

'I'm with you so far,' Bev said. 'Except that I've never done anything besides those things, unless working in a wine bar counts.'

'It does,' Elise said. 'In fact I think it's the most important thing on your résumé. Okay. Here's my idea: my friend Anna owns this high-end maternity boutique in Carroll Gardens, and she's trying to hire a manager right now so that she can spend more time with her own kids.'

'Which one? Where is it?'

'It's on Smith Street.'

'Oh my god, your friend owns Push It?'

'I know it's a punch line, but here's the thing. They do like half a million dollars in sales every month. It's insane. She gives her employees health insurance, paid vacation ... and maternity leave, needless to say! It's hard work, of course, and you have to be nice to a lot of ... people. But I think she'd hire you.'

'Why? I have no retail experience ... '

'You have customer-service experience out the wazoo. And you have the right look. Especially pregnant. I know that's weird to say, but I just imagine you in that store, maybe with your hair in two braids, wearing J Brand maternity overalls and maybe a sleeveless button-down – you have just the right mix of edgy and wholesome. You'll inspire those mommies to spend.'

'Um, thank you?'

'I know it's a bizarre thing to say. But I'm right, though.'

'Okay, well ... I'm in, I guess. Are there any conditions?'

'Yes.' Elise pulled down the corners of her shapely mouth and became serious. 'You have to promise me you won't give up. If you have the baby. You won't let that be your excuse. It's a great excuse, and you already have so many. But you have to make it something else instead.'

'The opposite of an excuse, maybe?'

Elise smiled, and Bev tried to remember whether she had kids. 'Okay, call your friend. I might as well at least interview.'

After they'd finished their salads and Elise had given Bev a big, sincere goodbye hug, promising she'd be in touch about the job by the next day at the very latest, Bev immediately pulled out her phone and called Amy. On the third try she finally picked up.

'Now you call me! Well, it's done now, so don't bother coming over here.' Amy sounded bad, peeved but trying to hide it under a veneer of manic cheer.

'What's done? Did I miss something? I'm sorry, I was at the doctor.'

'The doctor! Are you okay?'

Good, she's not a complete monster, Bev thought. 'Totally fine. Just, you know . . . '

'Oh, did you finally go through with the abortion? Jesus, Bev, you should have told me. I could have put Mr. Horton off a couple more days if I'd known it was today.'

'No, I . . . it wasn't today. Mr. Horton?'

'He evicted me, remember? I had to move out today. I hired movers. I didn't want to be pathetic and ask people for help, but anyway I'm putting all my stuff into storage. I'm cat-sitting for a friend of a friend from Yidster while I look for a room in Bushwick or whatever. I'm at the storage place now. Actually, can you hang on one sec?'

'Sure, I just wanted to . . .'

But Amy had turned away from the phone and was talking to someone else. 'What do you mean, it didn't go through? Here, try this one,' Bev could hear her saying. 'Sorry,' Amy said to Bev. 'Jesus, it's taking forever to get out of here. Thank you for calling me, anyway.'

'Oh, I was actually calling because I wanted to tell you . . . Okay. Well, so I just ran into my old teacher Elise, and she's going to help me get what sounds like this great job, and I think if it works out, which she seems sure it will, I'm going to have the baby.'

'Have the baby – like, give the baby up for adoption or to Sally or whatever?'

'No. I was more thinking I would, like, have the baby.'

'*Keep* the baby.'

'Yup.' Bev had been so happy a moment ago. Something about the compliments and the reassuring, stable presence of Elise had made it seem that anything was possible. The silence on the line, the face she imagined Amy making – she didn't have to imagine, she knew exactly what face Amy was making – were undoing her good mood. But not, weirdly, her certainty.

'Look, can we talk about this later?' Amy said. 'I'm in the middle of all this shit. I'm really sorry. I just can't even handle talking to you about this right now. I'll call you tonight, okay?'

'You will? Okay, talk to you then.'

Bev bussed her salad tray slowly, meditatively, and walked out the door of the restaurant into the sunlight. Some words were forming in her mind, but she didn't quite trust herself to think them, not yet. They had to do with Amy, with the baby, and with all the variables sliding into place at the moment. She felt a sense of nervous, slightly far-fetched anticipation, as if she'd entered a sweepstakes or made a bet. And she felt coldness around her heart, numbness, a feeling of loss that was more anticipation of loss, really, but it amounted to the same thing.

34

Eleven o'clock found Bev on the subway, on her way – like the three other people in the subway car carrying rolled-up PVC mats – to yoga. Her stomach was noticeably rounded now. Although she could still pass for simply chubby, lately some perceptive strangers had begun to discern her pregnancy, and she had started to gratefully accept seats when they were offered and mildly resent it when they weren't.

This time, she got a seat, and the intra-Brooklyn commute passed in a flash; fifteen minutes after leaving her apartment, Bev was situating her mat near the back of the classroom. She'd chosen the studio primarily for its interior design and its proximity to Push It; the teachers, she figured, would be fine, good enough, and she would get to spend time in this big sandalwood-scented room in a DUMBO loft building, looking out across the water at Manhattan as she stood in mountain pose. Today would be her first class, though, and she wasn't sure what to expect. She hoped there would not be sharing or deep eye contact or anything else that might rattle her; lately the dumbest things could move her either to white-hot rage or tears. She had been trying not to think at all of Amy, for instance, because Amy seemed not to be thinking at all of her, and as sad as this made her, she also felt almost as if she understood. She was traveling into a different world now: a Lycra-clad, jargon-filled, slightly ridiculous but decidedly adult world, and it was not a world where Amy belonged.

Bev hoped to spend lots of time sitting in meditative silence, feeling obscurely virtuous and soothed but not really having to *do* anything, as the rest of the class chanted in Sanskrit. She didn't believe in any of the stuff yoga teachers talked about, all their various babblings about reframing negative thoughts and sending good vibrations out into the universe and returning always to the breath. But whenever she'd dabbled in yoga in the past, during phases when she had the necessary spare cash or spare time, she always left the classes feeling better, both in her hip, which still creaked sometimes from whatever she'd done to it with all that poor-form jogging in Madison, and, though she hated to admit it, in her mind.

The teacher introduced herself as Sky and started class with everyone sitting upright, cross-legged, and om-ing 'like you're having a conversation with that little one inside you, sending him or her that vibratory energy.' Bev dutifully om'd, but in her mind she refused to participate in the creepy ritual of pretending that what was inside her somehow had thoughts and feelings and whatever kind of sensory abilities might be able to perceive 'vibrations.' It seemed as dumb and wishful as imagining your cat or dog talking to you in a funny little voice, asking you to buy its favorite brand of treats. Opening her eyes, Bev stole a glance around the room and inspected her knocked-up, tight-lidded fellow students, resting their palms on their Crenshaw melon or watermelon or barely rounded bellies and softly smiling as they om'd, as though they all shared a delicious secret.

There was no real option but to join them. For the duration of the class Bev would have to drink their brand of organic agave-sweetened Kool-Aid. She would dedicate her practice to world happiness and send healing love out into the expanding universe and down into her own expanding uterus. She came to the front of her mat, bent her knees, and bowed forward as Sky led them through a sun salutation. 'Draw energy up through the soles of your feet!' she intoned. 'In-heeel. Ex-heeeeel.'

Bev focused and went inside herself, emerging only at the end of class as everyone lay in corpse pose. She was among the minority of students who were still early enough in their pregnancies to lie on their backs; her vena cava was still unencumbered by her unborn baby's weight. Everyone else lay on their sides, with bolsters between their knees. Bev looked up at the ceiling, unable to relax enough to allow her eyes to close. The ceiling was nice: white-painted pressed tin. Then it was obscured by Sky, who loomed over Bev and straddled her as she adjusted her shoulder blades. Bev tried to keep her gaze on the ceiling, but Sky insistently caught her eye. The whites of Sky's eyes were very white compared with her turquoise pupils. Was she wearing *colored contacts*? 'Allow your eyes to gently close if you wish!' Sky whispered.

Bev blinked and realized that her eyes were full of unshed tears. Rather than shed them, she closed her lids and tried to go limp as Sky adjusted her occiput with patchouli-scented fingers. A few minutes later they were allowed to sit up, om one last om, bow forward, thank themselves for coming to class, and then get up and start making their way back to their jackets and shoes.

When Bev looked up from lacing her sneakers, a watermelon-bellied woman who'd come in late and positioned her mat toward the front of the classroom locked eyes with her as she pulled her blond curls into a tighter ponytail. 'Oh my god. Bev Tunney! What are you doing here? Oh my *god*! Congratulations! I didn't even know you were married!'

'I'm, um. Hi! From Oberlin, right?'

'Allie Heffernan! Formerly Allie Singer? We had that Dante seminar together junior year. The one where that kid had a seizure?'

'Ah! Right.' Bev had been jealous of the kid who'd had a seizure; he'd gotten an automatic A.

'I didn't even know you lived in the city! What are you up to, besides . . . ' And here Allie Heffernan gestured to her own gigantic Lycra-covered stomach.

'I, you know, this and that. Grad school?'

'Amazing! Wow! Well, listen, I have to pick this one's older sister up from preschool, but do you want to come get a smoothie with me, or something, on the way? I mean, we don't have to get a smoothie.' Allie put her hand over her mouth and whispered dramatically, 'I could go for a burger, to be honest.'

They'd probably exchanged ten sentences in college. 'I

have to go to work, actually,' said Bev, grateful for the easy out.

'But you have to eat! What time do you have to be there? Come on, walk with me. We need to catch up!'

'One thirty. I guess I could get lunch on the way.'

Against her will and her better judgment, Bev found herself following Allie, who walked more quickly than her bulbous middle seemed likely to permit. As they sprinted down the stairs to the F-train platform, Allie caught her up on their classmates' doings; they'd known such completely different types of people that the news wasn't already familiar to Bev from Facebook. Allie had been friends with private school and boarding school kids who'd gravitated back to the New York area, where they'd originated, the type of people who'd gotten all the performance art and lesbianism out of their systems before graduation and had gone on to law school or management consulting and in due time had, like Allie, forged unions with men as practical and well-heeled and boring as they were. Bev's friends from college had mostly been midwestern, like her, and most of them were in the middle of the country getting doctorates in some useless branch of the humanities, or in someplace like Laos, studying hard drugs, or in San Francisco, living in shared houses and still drinking as much as they had at twenty-two.

And where did Bev fit into this continuum of outcomes? Talking to Allie made her feel uncomfortably aware of the possible Bev futures she'd scrapped or that had been pulled out from under her feet: the Bev who lived happily in Madison, married to a lawyer, was someone Allie would have an easier time wrapping her mind around than the Bev who, four months pregnant by a random stranger, lived with roommates and worked in a maternity boutique called Push It. Or, for that matter, the Bev who had an M.F.A. and published short stories in obscure but impressive-sounding periodicals. But boutique Bev was the real Bev, and her life was the life she was going to have to describe to an increasingly uncomprehending Allie.

'So what does your husband do?' Allie asked as they emerged from the subway. The wintry day had turned chilly, and they huddled in their coats and walked quickly toward MooBurger Organic.

'Oh, I'm not married.'

'Sorry, your ... partner? What sort of work—'

'No. I mean, I'm single.'

Allie paused in her determined march toward the burger place's counter to place her order.

'Oh my god. You don't have anyone to help you? Does your mom live nearby?'

'No, I ... you know, I'm from Minnesota. I'm not really that close with my family.'

'Do you live by yourself?'

'No, with roommates. But I'm saving up to move into a place of my own soon. I work at Push It – you know, on Smith.'

They ordered their free-range, grass-fed Whopper equivalents and sat down to wait for them to be ready.

'Sorry to be so nosy. I'm just ... kind of in awe! I mean, you're doing something pretty unheard-of.'

Bev laughed out loud; she couldn't help it. 'I think, statistically speaking, it's incredibly more common than, you know—'

'What I'm doing? Yeah, I guess you're right. I mean, I read the newspaper!'

Bev was willing to bet that Allie didn't read anything but the Sunday magazine and Styles, but she tried to quash her negative thoughts.

'You must think I'm really boring and suburban,' Allie said, as if reading her mind.

'No. I'm just really jealous of you,' Bev said without thinking.

Allie grinned. 'Ha! Uh. You won't be, soon. I mean, I think I know what you mean, but there are things about pregnancy, motherhood, you know, the whole thing, that are the same for everyone. But it's important to have help. I don't mean, like, paid help – necessarily. You need good friends, the kind you can call if you haven't slept and just need to take a shower. Do any of your close friends have kids?'

'My closest friends? No. They're still more in the ... behaving like infants themselves stage.'

'I think that's why I decided I wanted to have kids,' Allie said. She gazed past Bev out the window of MooBurger, and her expression transformed from bovine content to super serious and sage. 'There didn't seem to be any other way to snap out of that. I didn't want to just segue from that into, you know, death.'

'It's as good a reason as any.'

'This is very personal, but ... what was your reason?'

'I hated my life, and I wanted it to change,' Bev said.

'Samesies, basically.' Allie shrugged, and suddenly Bev didn't dislike her anymore. She was starting to see that what

Allie had said about motherhood being the same for everyone – though it was still a lie rich people told themselves to feel morally okay – was also partially true. What was happening to her body and Allie Heffernan's body was a great equalizer in some ways. Already Bev could see that and viscerally feel it. She felt part of the great undifferentiated mass of humanity in a new way. It wasn't altogether pleasant, but it was interesting. The novelty of getting all these tacit nods of what felt like approval or at least understanding was a little bit overwhelming. She supposed it was because she was visibly doing what women her age were expected to be doing, and regardless of how she'd gotten there or how she would pay for it, she had a new status in the eyes of the world: Mother.

Their order number was called, and Allie sprang up to fetch the burgers. Bev's came in a bag, and she grabbed it, poised to make her exit. She hadn't even unzipped her jacket. Allie unwrapped her burger and immediately started tearing into it so ferociously that it took her a second to register that Bev was leaving. 'Oh, do you have to go? No, come on, stay!'

'I do. Sorry – the store gets really busy around now. Hey, come in and visit me sometime. I'll totally give you the friend discount.'

35

Amy was lying on the ominously sagging futon in her creepy sublet with her eyes closed and her mind racing, trying to pretend to herself that she was asleep, when her phone came alive with a text from an unfamiliar number. 'In Manhattan. Meet, chat?' With a hint of wariness in case it *wasn't* Jason, she wrote back: 'In Brooklyn. Some other time?' Within seconds, the reply came: 'Shipping out tomorrow, London calls. I could come to your place.'

Amy's heart somehow plummeted and sped up simultaneously as she scanned her field of vision. There was no way she could invite Jason or anyone back to this place. For one thing, she would inevitably encounter one of her eight roommates. For another thing, there was no window in this attic crawl space, for which she was paying five hundred dollars a month (futon included).

The price had been the main attraction of the weirdly chopped-up loft – and the fact that they hadn't checked her credit, were okay with her renting month to month, and permitted her to bring Waffles because they already had four cats and so didn't mind one more. Everything else was not an attraction.

She texted Jason that she would meet him at a bar a few blocks away.

She was going to have to find somewhere even worse if she didn't get a job soon. She had spent the last of her final Yidster paycheck on December rent, but now the new year loomed more forbiddingly than it ever had in her life. Seeing Jason would take her mind off her problems. He might even take her to his hotel, if she could make it seem like a kinky treat and not a pathetic necessity.

She still couldn't quite believe that this was where she'd ended up, but after she'd quit her job and lost her apartment, the dominoes had fallen with increasing speed. Sam had gone to Spain, telling her, before he left, that it was important for his work that she not contact him too often. She surprised herself by not even wanting to. She felt guilty for cheating on him before they'd officially broken up, and they weren't even officially broken up now, or maybe they were; she hadn't wanted to ask. He didn't know she was living in a crawl space. She missed him, but it was as if there were cotton batting around her thoughts of him: she couldn't get too close to them, it hurt too much; thinking about him would allow all these other thoughts to escape too, and it was better and easier to remain numb.

It was bizarre to think that just a few months ago she had thought that she and Sam would move in together, get married, and have children. If he called her on the phone right now, it would take her a moment to recognize the sound of his voice.

Amy walked to the bar, where she ordered a double Jameson on the rocks. She sat at a little table in the corner and surveyed the scene. There were a few underage-looking students and a little group of the bartender's friends at the bar, chatting and keeping her occupied on this slow night. The bartender was low-light beautiful, with a swooping wedge of pink hair. She'd called Amy honey when she gave her the drink. People like this bartender made her feel at a disadvantage for not wearing makeup, but Amy had never figured out how to walk around in eyeliner and lipstick without feeling clownishly costumed. The pink-haired bartender probably did not worry about feeling costumed, or maybe she relished the feeling. Amy felt suddenly as though a costume would be perfect for the circumstances she found herself in. She ought to be wearing a pencil skirt, seamed stockings, blue-red lipstick. Maybe then, instead of being lame and nonsensical and hopeless, her circumstances could begin to seem glamorous, decadent.

She looked down at her drink and was surprised to find that it was mostly gone. She looked up and saw Jason walking toward her, wearing almost the same outfit he'd worn for the photograph Amy had made fun of, with Bev, in this same bar. She wished she was hanging out with Bev tonight, but instead she was getting drunk and getting ready to have sex with a married man. She didn't even really understand why she'd been avoiding Bev. Maybe for the same reason, months ago, that Bev had resisted telling Amy she was pregnant: because telling her would make it real. At drinks with acquaintances and on job interviews, insofar as those things were still happening, Amy had been able to portray her circumstances as madcap and fun – situations someone confident enough not to give a fuck found herself in all the time. The problem was that Amy *did* give a fuck. She gave many. She hadn't completely failed to notice that her life had escaped her control. Bev would home in on this and, without meaning to, force Amy to come to terms with reality. So even though she missed her friend desperately and craved nothing more than to dial the phone and hear the sound of her voice, Amy kept not dialing. Seeing Bev would be like opening her credit card statements and really knowing, instead of just being vaguely sure, that she owed too much to ever repay.

She didn't want to see Jason anymore at all. She could just get up and leave at any time, she told herself. She knew she wouldn't leave, though, because it would mean going back to the attic.

And then he was there, anyway. Jason smiled at her, the same catlike, serene smile he'd smiled when he'd pushed his finger past her lips. 'Another?' he said, gesturing to her drink.

'Yes, please. Jameson,' she said. 'Um, I was bracing myself.'

'I hope this won't require being braced,' he said, and went to get the drinks. In his absence, she glanced at the label of the trim-fitting leather coat he'd left on the back of the chair. It was Prada.

As he took the first sip of his beer, Jason made a face. 'Oof, this stuff is skunky. She needs to change the keg.'

Amy looked at him in disbelief. 'Are you going to ask for a new one?'

Jason sniffed his drink. 'Well, yeah, I can't drink this. Is yours okay?'

'Of course it is! How can you fuck up a whiskey on the rocks?'

Jason shrugged. 'I dunno. Too much whiskey, not enough rocks, vice versa.'

'It meets my exacting standards,' Amy said.

'Good! Well, maybe I'll have one too,' he said.

Amy watched as Jason ambled over to the bar and explained the situation to the bartender. There wasn't the faintest flicker of annoyance on the bartender's face. In a moment he returned, bearing a glass that matched Amy's.

'Free! I like this place,' he said.

'She likes *you*,' Amy said. 'If I'd tried what you just pulled, she would have just stared at me silently until I apologized and slunk away.'

'Not a big deal to ask for what you want,' Jason said lightly. 'Also has to do with how you ask for it.'

'Sometimes you don't even have to ask,' Amy said, hearing the forced jollity in her voice.

'Mmm. Yes, right. Well, I hope you don't feel bad about what happened in Margaretville. I don't. I really like you, Amy.'

'Of course I feel bad! I sort of . . . I mean, I pretty much have a boyfriend.'

Jason pantomimed looking avidly around the room, then smiled his slightly evil smile again. 'Do you? I don't see any boyfriend.'

'Well, we're sort of on a break right now. I mean, he's not in the country. I don't know, I think we're not really together.

But I'm not exactly single. And I definitely wasn't single when we . . . '

Jason's eye crinkles conveyed understanding that verged on condescension. 'Okay, fair. You might have noticed that I'm not single, either. But I would suggest that none of that has much to do with our current situation. In my experience, it's not a good idea to expect one relationship to bear the burdens of all your various . . . needs.'

'I never thought my needs were so burdensome! And anyway, I don't. Expect that. I have what I need. That should be enough.'

'I don't suppose there's really such a thing as "enough," at least not in this context,' Jason said, and put his hand on Amy's jean-clad knee under the table. She almost laughed – everything he was saying, the whole situation, and the knee grab, it was all so textbook – but then he moved his hand up her thigh, and then he was pressing his thumb along the fly of her jeans with pinpoint accuracy.

They drove in Jason's car to the Wythe Hotel. In the lobby, Amy wished again for high heels and a skirt, an appropriate disguise for the stranger she was becoming. There was a panicky moment as they passed the restaurant when she thought she'd made eye contact with one of Sam's friends, but she reassured herself with the fact that there was nothing obviously inappropriate about what she was doing. As far as that guy knew, she was just walking around in a public place with some man who wasn't Sam. She felt excited, verging on panicky, but the whiskey muted the shrilling of her nerves just enough that she made it into the elevator and up to the room, and soon Amy found that she was nowhere, that she had sort of ceased to exist except as a related constellation of sensations. Occasionally her consciousness resurfaced to make a mental note of how good she felt, and this meant losing the mindless good feeling for a moment, but it always came back.

It lasted a long time, and then, when it was over, she felt depleted, endorphin-drained, as if she'd come down from Ecstasy. Jason had to leave; he was expected back upstate. He told her to stay in the hotel room as long as she liked, and she wished he really meant that she could stay there indefinitely.

As soon as the door clicked shut behind him, Amy rolled over and fished her phone out of her purse and, rushing so she wouldn't be able to stop herself, texted Bev, asking her to meet in the morning at the Brooklyn Flea. Then she set an alarm, shut the blackout blinds, buried herself under the sex-smelling covers, and tried to burrow into sleep, which finally came in its most thin, nightmare-filled, and restless form. As she drifted between states of consciousness, a thought kept repeating: the uncomfortable realization that despite all the adventure of the past few hours, her circumstances had not changed at all.

36

The outdoor flea market had moved indoors for the winter and had lost a lot of its charm in the process. The vendors and shoppers were now crowded together in the massive basement of a former bank, and the enclosed space made the goods look tawdrier. Why were people lining up to get a closer look at some overpriced old T-shirts? The basement's lighting didn't flatter anyone, either. Amy caught a glimpse of herself in an antique mirror that was for sale for three hundred fifty dollars. She winced. Compared with the very young crowds milling through the market, she looked about a thousand years old. Well, she had barely slept. The young Fleagoers probably hadn't slept much either, but they could still bounce back, whereas Amy was thirty, too old to drink as much as she'd drunk, eat as little as she'd eaten, and have sex for as many hours in a row as she'd had sex. She hastened toward the food area, where Bev was waiting.

Bev looked great, glowy and shiny-haired, wearing a new shirt that matched her pale blue eyes. She smiled radiantly at Amy, and Amy felt like rushing toward her and throwing herself into her arms and crying on her shoulder. And she could have, but she checked herself in deference to all the people around them. What if someone she knew saw her weeping in the middle of the Flea? She bit her inner cheek and took a seat in a folding chair opposite Bev.

'I missed you, dude!' Bev said, reaching out to touch her knee.

Amy almost started crying again but instead bit her cheek harder.

'I mean, I know we've both been busy, though. How have you been? How's the job search?'

'Terrible. There's really nothing right now – no one's hiring right before the holidays. I've just been emailing people I know, trying to get them to have coffee with me, and massaging my profile on LinkedIn, which is more depressing than words can say. Sorry. This is so boring, let's not even talk about it.'

'Stores are hiring right before the holidays,' Bev said. 'I mean, temporary positions mostly. But if you just need something to help you pay the bills while you look for your next real job . . .'

'Well, that's exactly what I need. But I can't work in a store, Bev. I mean, what if someone found out? It would be so humiliating.'

'Someone who? I don't mean this as an insult, but like . . . no one cares if you work in a store, Amy. Plenty of writers have service jobs.'

'At the beginning of their careers, sure. Not in their early thirties. Or, well, not after they've already . . . '

Bev didn't say anything. She didn't look at Amy, either – instead she scanned the perimeter of the room, as if she were looking for someone.

'Look, I know it doesn't seem like I did anything important. But there was a time when people totally recognized me on the subway! I got thousands of emails. Thousands! They were so mean, too. Everyone was so mean to me. That has to have meant something. It has to have happened for some reason; there has to have been some payoff for that, and it can't be that I work in a *store*!'

Bev turned her gaze toward Amy again.

Maybe it was being pregnant that made Bev seem so distant and foreign, but Amy felt that in the past, she'd been able to count on her for immediate reassurance that she was doing the right thing, that she was right, just in general. And also, it was usually Bev who'd needed help in the past. But now it was all Amy being uncertain, being in trouble. And she thought she could see in Bev's squinting, impersonal gaze that she just wasn't up to being leaned on.

'Hey, I meant to mention this earlier, but Sally's meeting us here. Is that cool?'

'What?'

'I wanted to hang out with you, but I also wanted to see her, and this is my one day off. Sorry, but my hours are nuts. Because, uh, it's the holiday season. And I work at a store.' Bev smiled, but her tone of voice was slightly tart.

Too late, Amy realized how insulting she'd been. 'I didn't

mean to imply that working at a store was somehow … anyway I didn't mean … Well, it's different for you!'

'Okay. Whatever, Amy. We definitely need to talk more about what's going on with you. But look, for right now, be nice to Sally, okay? And I'll try to steer the conversation away from Jason, so you won't feel too weird.'

'No. I can't do this. I'm sorry. I really don't want to hang out with her. It's too weird. I know you guys are friends now, but I'm not … I can't handle seeing her right now. I just wanted to hang out with you!'

'Is it because you feel awkward about what you did with Jason, or because she's going to help me with the baby, or what?'

'I guess both of those things, and also because she's this random person who's invaded your life – our lives, and I feel … usurped by her.'

'You're being crazy. You could never be usurped.'

'Really? Why? I feel like I've been being pretty much the worst friend, and she's giving you everything I can't, like money.'

'I don't want money. Well, not from you. I want you to think about me. Call me, text me. Be curious about what's going on with me, not just use me to unload all your bad feelings, like I'm your therapist. I need you to care about me, not resent me.'

'What, like I'm jealous of you?'

'You're jealous of everyone.'

'*You* used to be jealous of *me*!'

'Not really, Amy.'

'You're full of shit. You were jealous.'

'Maybe sometimes. But I'm definitely not right now. But that's okay, right? We don't need to feel mutually superior to each other. That's not the point of friendship, Amy. I mean, maybe it is for you, but it's not for me.'

'All I'm saying is I want to talk to *you* and not you and *Sally*!'

Again Amy felt as if she was about to start crying, like a toddler having a tantrum. Rather than make a fool of herself in front of Bev and all the Fleagoers, she jumped up and started making her way toward the exit of the underground mall. As she pushed her way through the crowds, she hoped that Bev would chase after her, ready to help and fix and make sense of everything. But of course Bev wasn't following her, and it took forever to escape the crush. Tides of people surged through the halls, and it seemed to Amy that everyone was pregnant. She walked out of the bank vault feeling invisible, like a ghost, alone in a sea of couples and children and happy, rich friends.

37

The email from Jackie arrived at a particularly bleak moment. Amy had been sitting around the creepy loft all morning in front of her laptop, headphones on to foreclose the possibility of conversation with the hippies, telling herself she was gathering her strength and was just about to go to the café around the corner, where she'd disable her computer's access to the Internet and spend time revising her CV to reflect her newly adjusted set of goals. She wanted to position herself as someone who wasn't a writer so much as a 'content creator' or, better, a 'content strategy consultant' – someone who might be able to work for brands or ad agencies, not blogs like Yidster. It was getting close to noon now, she was hungry for lunch, and her limbs twitched restlessly because they craved motion, but somehow she couldn't stop mindlessly scrolling through Tumblr, liking photographs of food and animals. Her actual cat lay at her feet, occasionally pawing her and trying to engage her in play, but she fobbed him off with some desultory petting and then continued to ignore him in favor of the cats on the screen.

So when Jackie's note popped into her in-box, she found herself grateful and relieved. Even better, Jackie wanted to have lunch as soon as possible; she knew it was 'a long shot' but maybe *today* – because she was 'having trouble figuring out some of the loose ends you left behind.' Possibly she also had a vulturish interest in seeing how Amy was doing, so she could gossip about it with Lizzie. But who cared: it would mean getting out of the house. Amy accepted readily, with the stipulation that the restaurant be nowhere too near the Yidster offices. They agreed to meet at a down-home southern restaurant in Carroll Gardens. Amy noted with a twinge that it was near a Starbucks and a Trader Joe's, both places where she should go and fill out job applications. Bev was right: she just needed something to get her through the month, and no one cared if she worked retail; it was pointless to keep living on her almost maxed-out credit cards out of some kind of misplaced pride.

Jackie, sitting at the restaurant's bar waiting for Amy, looked shockingly great. Her curls were less frizzy, her retro-red lipstick was applied more evenly than usual, and she was wearing a polka-dot dress that accentuated her small waist and concealed her large, flat behind. When the waitress dropped off two menus and a cocktail list, she grabbed at the cocktail list. 'We have to toast your quitting, right?'

Amy nodded, realizing that she shouldn't drink if she was serious about applying for cashier jobs after lunch. Well, she promised herself, she would do it soon, almost certainly tomorrow.

They ordered Manhattans, and two sips in, Amy began to imagine that the whole afternoon or maybe her whole life would be like this: hard, bright winter light slipping into the dim, cozy restaurant; hilarious chitchat with Jackie, who turned out to be so much happier and so much more fun than she seemed when she and Amy had been coworkers. Jackie launched immediately into an anecdote about Avi losing his temper and attempting some Krav Maga-type maneuver on the malfunctioning copier before the editorial meeting that morning. Amy was almost sorry she'd missed it. Her laughter seemed to please Jackie so much, and it was refreshing to be around someone who, for whatever misguided reason, admired her and wanted her approval. Halfway through her drink Amy caught herself thinking about how lucky she was to be unemployed, with a vast sea of possibilities opening up in front of her. She didn't know what any of the possibilities were, but that seemed exciting, not terrifying, in this moment.

Their sandwiches arrived, and they set about consuming them ferociously, Jackie smearing the bread with red lipstick as she ate. Amy tried to be more restrained, but they were very good sandwiches. As she tried to avert her gaze from the little slices of pickle and flecks of coleslaw falling out of Jackie's roll, though, her gaze stuck and fixed for a moment on Jackie's engagement ring, which shimmered with a rigid intensity in the golden restaurant light.

Amy felt a visceral, impulsive pang of desire, the kind that could make someone grab food off a stranger's plate. She wanted the ring so badly. She thought, crazily, of stealing it. She wanted to take it off Jackie's finger and put it in her mouth. Would it be completely weird, if she were ever rich, to just go ahead and buy herself an engagement ring? She loved how it gave Jackie, this totally unspecial person, a sheen of value. Because it actually meant that Jackie *was* valued. It was a symbol, and it was the thing it symbolized. Someone thought Jackie was worthy of wearing a little rock worth thousands of dollars. Amy found that she wanted to cry. This kept happening lately, more and more often. She took a large sip of water and heard the satisfying crackle of ice in her water glass, the cubes like giant diamonds catching the light and refracting it. She wanted a diamond as big as an ice cube, and she wanted the kind of endless, outsize love such a diamond would symbolize. Seriously, had her drink been drugged?

'These are really strong, huh?' she said to Jackie, trying not to slur her words.

'Yeah, but it's good. I needed to steel my nerves for this conversation,' Jackie said. 'Okay, Amy . . . I didn't bring you here to ask you about Yidster loose ends. I could give a fuck about Yidster.'

'I thought that was bullshit. So what's up?'

Jackie cleared her throat, seeming nervous for the first time. 'I interviewed for a position at . . . okay, basically, your old job. I just got the offer this morning. They seem really cool, and it's much more money than I've been making at Yidster, which I could definitely use . . . I mean, Amy, the handmade napkin rings alone! You don't want to know . . . Anyway, I was worried, though, because of your experience there, and I just . . . wanted to know if you had any advice. Or, like, words of warning?'

Amy shrugged. 'I don't know. It's a job. It wasn't the right job for me, but I'm sure you'll be fine. Besides, I hear things are really different there now.'

Jackie forked around a bite of slaw. 'Yeah … well, anyway, they actually asked me if … uh, well, they asked me what you were up to, and I told them you had left Yidster. It seems like they would be interested in your working there again, in some capacity, if that was something you wanted.'

Amy snorted. 'Are you kidding? You couldn't pay me to … '

'Well, the thing is, they *would* pay you. A lot. I mean, they just got that big investment from GigaWatt. I probably shouldn't say how much they're offering me, but. Uh. Let's just put it this way … When I told my brother, who went through eight years of med school, he said, "Wow, Jackie, if I'd only known that I should have just been joking around on Twitter all those years instead of dissecting fetal pigs, I would have done things very differently!"'

Amy laughed. At least it was partly a laugh. It began as sort of a gag, but she managed to make it sound credibly laugh-like about halfway in.

'I thought you should know, anyway. I mean, I know you probably have lots of offers, and this is just something to consider. I'd love to work together again and … you already know the lay of the land there. I don't know, I just wanted to know if there was some horrible secret reason not to work there, I guess!' She smiled as though this had been a joke, but Amy knew she was really imagining some kind of blog-business Bluebeard's closet.

'No, they're fine. I had a bad experience there. It'll be totally different for you.'

'You should call them, Amy. I mean it, they would take you back in a heartbeat. I mean, they might make you grovel a little. After all, you did get fired. But you're a big girl, anyway, you can handle it. Oh, and the commenters will love it! They always loved you.'

'Ha. Uh, if by "love," you mean "thought of inventive ways to murder daily," then sure, they adored me.'

'Well, that's inevitable, right? I mean, you're a woman, it's the Internet ... and you're getting combat pay, basically, to deal with it.'

'Have you experienced that kind of thing before, Jackie?'

'Oh, totally! You know how various zealots and neo-Nazis and Zionist wackadoos home in on Yidster once in a while. I'm not unfamiliar with trolls.'

'Yeah, but it's different when it's about you.'

'Well, it's ... not really ever about *you*,' Jackie said, and sat back, took a meditative sip, and looked very pleased with her wisdom. 'So you'll think about it?'

'Sure. I mean ... I have a lot of other stuff going on, but it's definitely worth thinking about.'

Jackie smiled. 'Good. I hope we can work together again. It'll be good to have another woman there, if it works out. We can have each other's backs.'

Amy swallowed a surge of BBQ-bourbon bile and pushed herself away from the table. As she stood and tried to walk calmly toward the restroom, smiling, she passed their waitress, on her way to drop their check. The door to the bathroom closed behind her, and Amy noted in the last second before she dropped to her knees that there was a fan loud enough to obscure any noises, and she knelt on the sticky floor and watched her lunch unspool in reverse into the bowl. She tried to do it quickly.

When she came back to the table, Jackie had already paid the check. 'Oh, you didn't have to,' Amy said weakly, but Jackie just gave a little *Oh, it was nothing* hand flick and her ring caught the light again. Amy fought back another surge of nausea.

They hugged and parted, and Amy turned and walked down a leafy side street, setting out to walk home, not wanting to chance the subway in case she threw up again. She would try to duck into an alley or behind a parked car. People would just think she was pregnant, in this neighborhood.

She walked and walked and didn't start feeling better, though she did stop feeling drunk, which actually made her feel worse. When she got to a little minipark, she paused and sat on one of the benches, hoping her stomach might settle down if she rested.

All her problems could be solved in a second if she simply apologized to everyone she'd offended and asked for one or the other of her old jobs back. Not only – if Jackie was to be believed – could she potentially go to work in the blog big leagues, but if she didn't feel up to that, she could even potentially sucker Jonathan and Shoshanna into rehiring her at Yidster; with Jackie gone, they'd be desperate. Either way, it would be like going back in time. And either way, she realized, it would be impossible. On paper, those ideas seemed exponentially better than whatever she had lined up (nothing, Trader Joe's). But when she imagined the moment of walking back in the door at either place, she felt like actually killing herself. Deep down, Amy knew that all her compulsivity and procrastination had been about avoiding one simple, fairly obvious truth: her life in New York, in the form it had taken since she graduated from college, was over. The lies she'd been telling herself about job applications and reinventing herself as a consultant were just that: lies. A change was looming, as necessary and unpleasant as vomiting in the restaurant just now had been, and like the vomiting, it would happen whether or not she wanted it to. The only thing she could control was whether it happened sooner or later, in private or in public.

In search of soothing familiarity, she pulled out her phone, as though it might ever be the bearer of good news. She had five missed calls, all from a number she didn't recognize. The area code was familiar, though, and with a sinking feeling Amy realized why: it was the same as Jason's. The caller had to be Sally.

38

They had arranged to meet for lunch the next day at the Roebling Tea Room in Williamsburg. Amy had tried to put Sally off, but Sally insisted that they needed to meet in person, and as much as Amy dreaded the telling-off that she knew was coming to her, she was pathetically enticed by the idea of another free meal, which, in spite of everything, she imagined Sally would pay for. Aside from the Jackie lunch she'd vomited up, Amy had been living on bits and pieces of her roommates' vegan nightmare leftovers, snagged from moldering Tupperware in the fridge when they weren't looking. She couldn't keep it up much longer, healthwise or practically: already, Sage had wondered aloud more than once what happened to the remainder of his previous night's stir-fry.

She arrived at the café early and ordered a glass of Sancerre and a starter of deviled eggs, eating them all before Sally even got there, and then ordered more.

She'd expected Sally in a mantilla and sunglasses or something, but she looked exactly the same as she always did: groomed, pretty, with a slight shrug to her shoulders or cringe to her mien that made her seem physically smaller than she was. She wasn't quaking with rage or glaring at Amy, but she did look tired and, as usual, a bit sad.

As soon as they made eye contact, Amy knew for sure that the jig was up.

'I'm sorry,' she said, before Sally could say anything.

Sally sighed. 'It's okay. It's not a big deal. It's not the first time. I'm not angry with you, really, but I did want you to know, well, two things. One, that I'm divorcing Jason, and two, that it has nothing to do with what he did – or is doing, or whatever – with you. Oh, actually, three things, but I guess I can get to the third one after we order. Do you want another glass of wine? Maybe we should just order a bottle?'

'Um, sure. Yes, please,' said Amy.

They managed to find other things to talk about while the waitress was near their table, filling their glasses and bringing them bread and little plates, and Amy felt almost as if the situation were normal. But then the waitress left and Sally continued with her speech, which seemed to have been practiced in advance, possibly in the mirror.

'Okay, so, obviously things between me and Jason have not been perfect, but I just don't believe in infidelity as a deal breaker. Some of the happiest couples I know are in open relationships. But when you really think about it, they're all gay men. And what does that teach us? That part of the reason nonmonogamy doesn't work for heterosexual couples, or at least not for heterosexual women, is that there's this social stigma associated with being "betrayed" that is really only a problem for women. Because it's humiliating. But it's not humiliating for men when their male partners cheat, at least not in the same way. And why is that?'

It was a rhetorical question; Amy shrugged.

'It's because of the patriarchal social construct that men are fiscal providers, inherently desirable, and that women are interchangeable and valueless! Like, if your husband cheats on you, it means he's demeaning you by exposing you as inadequate in some way. But it doesn't have to mean that. I mean, if we decide it doesn't mean that, it doesn't mean it.'

Amy, sensing that some kind of thumbs-up was called for, nodded vigorously.

'But, this situation is different because I've been thinking about a lot of other things that are not exactly perfect about our relationship – besides which, I really feel that being in the city and around its creative energy is better for me, and to give myself a chance to experience that, I really feel like the best thing is to get away from Margaretville and Jason and just ... soak this up, you know? I mean, this neighborhood specifically. Isn't it just vibrant and pulsing with new energy? Even all the construction, it's, like, about novelty and growth.'

'I guess so.' Amy hadn't spent a lot of time in Williamsburg, even when she had a job; she didn't feel that she could really afford to. What Sally saw as a hotbed of youth and culture, Amy saw as a hotbed of European tourists and restaurants with thirty-five-dollar entrées. But there was clearly no point in mentioning this. Their food came, and

Amy tried to maintain her respectful, slightly ashamed look while devouring her cheeseburger.

'So I'm moving out, which Jason is fine with. Uh, I guess that's … oh, right, the third thing!'

'Mmm?' Amy dipped a small fistful of fries in ketchup.

'Oh, just … well, I have no right to ask this of you as a favor to me, but I am hoping you'll do it anyway, for yourself. Can you please, if you can, just not see Jason anymore? I don't think what you two have is a genuine love connection or whatever. And I just think as far as you and I and Bev are concerned, it would be so much better, so much less weird emotionally, for me, and probably for you too, if you could just … not continue any kind of relationship with him.'

Amy was dumbstruck, which Sally must have mistaken for resistance, driving a hard bargain, because she sighed and took something out of her purse.

When Amy realized it was a checkbook, she gasped. 'What is with you? You can't always pay people to do what you want them to do! I mean, sometimes you can, but why is that your default means of solving problems?'

'Because it works?' Sally said, all hippieish clumsiness gone. Perhaps it had served its purpose.

'Maybe on Bev, but not on me,' Amy said. As she pushed her chair away and tried to pull on her jacket as quickly as possible, she looked down at her plate: half the burger was still there, and a lot of the fries. Not to mention the full glass of wine. She briefly considered grabbing the burger, but stopped herself and headed straight for the door.

39

Bev was still pleasantly shocked to find that she hated working in the boutique way, way less than she'd thought she would. There was an inherent satisfaction in rearranging the display cases, refolding the clothes customers disarranged, checking inventory against what was in the computer, and doing the rote procedures of opening and closing each day. It had been only a month or so, of course, and she could foresee this getting stale. But for now it was blissful. She felt a little bit less exhausted than she had in her first trimester. Sally had bought her a book about pregnancy and childbirth – 'Not the fearmongering one, this is a hippie one, but not too hippie, like you. You'll like it' – and she'd read it, and it made her feel much less terrified, so that was cool. She had been going to her appointments with Dr. Sandy and had seen the baby on a sonogram for the first time. The baby was going to be a baby, and it was going to be her baby. It was almost too bizarre to think about, but it was true, and it seemed, for the moment, as if it would be okay. Her parents might never speak to her again when they found out, but in a way, that would also be okay. The only thing that really bothered her was what was going on with Amy, who was supposed to come by the store today. It would be her first visit.

Bev hadn't spoken to Amy since their fight at the Flea the previous Saturday, which felt awful. But Amy had been awful. Amy didn't want Bev to be a mother, Bev had seen this so clearly in her face that day. Amy would never say so, but she was so terrible at hiding anything, terrible at telling anything but the complete truth. Once, Bev had seen this as a good quality: Amy was trustworthy, if only because she couldn't get away with being otherwise. But right now Bev wanted to surround herself only with people who supported her wholeheartedly.

Bev was sitting behind the cash register, ringing up a customer's shoe purchases, when the store's door chime rang out and Bev saw that Amy had just walked through the door. Bev looked up at her and smiled. 'Hi there,' she said in what she hoped was a casual voice. 'I'll be with you in a sec.'

Amy made an exaggerated tiptoeing show of not wanting to interrupt Bev at her work. 'Nice place,' she mouthed, then walked off toward the racks. Bev printed out the customer's receipt and presented it for her to sign; the woman's handwriting was big and loopy and childlike. She had just spent four hundred and seventy-five dollars the way someone might buy gum. It would take much longer than a couple of months to get used to that, but Bev imagined that she would eventually.

The door chimed again and the rich woman was gone. Bev had to wait another fifteen minutes at least before she could start emptying wastebaskets, straightening up the dressing rooms, doing the kind of purposeful puttering around that would let customers know it was time to quit browsing. There were a surprising number of people in the tiny store, considering that it was 8:30 on a weekday evening. For some of them, maybe, it was a reward after a long workday, and others had probably snuck out of their nearby brownstones for a stolen half hour of Me Time after putting the kids to bed, leaving their husbands half drowsing in front of a DVD of *Mad Men*. The store was lovely, full of carefully chosen clothes that looked good on most pregnant women, and it smelled wonderfully of beeswax candles and expensive fabric, silk and linen and warm, soft cotton. Bev was mostly hoarding her paychecks for the baby, of course, but she had allowed herself to buy one of the T-shirts, the one she'd been wearing when she fought with Amy at the Flea. It cost ninety dollars, even with her employee discount, but the difference between it and every other T-shirt Bev had ever owned was that it was silky soft and looked phenomenal on her, setting off the blue of her eyes and cupping her swollen breasts, squeezing them together just slightly so that subtle, unslutty cleavage was visible in the shirt's V-neck. Yesterday she'd worn it again, and three people had bought one.

Amy was fingering the same shirt now. 'This seems like something even a non-preggo could pull off. Can I try it on?'

'Sure. Any dressing room you like,' Bev said, gesturing.

Gradually, all the customers filtered out, and Bev pulled

down the gate outside after the last one left. Amy was still in the fitting room.

'Okay. Everyone's gone, we can talk,' Bev said. There was silence behind the heavy curtain, and she pushed it aside. Amy was sitting doubled over on the bench, wearing the shirt – it fit her perfectly, wasn't noticeably a maternity shirt in any way. She was silently weeping into her hands.

Wordlessly, Bev rushed to her friend's side, folding her arms around her, holding her as she cried. She patted her back and whispered, 'Shh, shh, it'll be okay.'

'I really want this shirt,' Amy finally said.

'I can give you twenty percent off.'

'I can't buy it. I don't have any money.'

'Are you trying to drive a hard bargain? Twenty percent is the best I can do.'

'Dude, I'm literally completely broke. The last of my cash went to this month's rent, and I haven't even made it past one interview at any real jobs. And you're completely right about service jobs, but I haven't found the right one yet. How did this happen, Bev?'

'Well ... sorry, I know you aren't actually looking for an answer. But ... you quit your job even though you had no savings at all, and not even enough money to pay your rent.'

'Um, yes.'

'Can't Sam help you?'

Amy looked down. 'Shit, I'm getting tearstains on this fucking shirt. I have to take it off before I end up having to buy it.' She pulled it over her head and kept crying in just her bra, which had once been a nice one but looked to Bev as if it had been accidentally put through the dryer.

'Amy, did you tell Sam?'

'I don't want to talk to Sam.'

'Are you guys broken up?'

'Yes. No. I don't know. Probably. He left for Spain and told me he needed to focus on his work, but lately he's been calling me and I've been ignoring his calls.'

'Did you tell him you slept with Jason?'

'No. I mean, that's why I haven't wanted to talk to him. I'm worried that I inadvertently will.'

'You shouldn't.'

'I know.'

They sat on the thin ledge. It was hard not to look at themselves in the mirror opposite: red-eyed Amy in her dingy bra, looking like she hadn't slept, and rosy Bev, groomed and pretty enough to inspire other women to buy clothes. There were fingerprint-shaped bruises on Amy's upper arm, and her worn-out winter coat splayed next to them, the once-stylish one without sleeves, smelled like cigarette smoke. The light in Amy that had drawn people in – that had drawn Bev in – was flickering, dim.

'I came here to ask you for money, Bev. Look, I will pay you back really soon. I just need a loan. I need to be able to stay in the sublet another month and to buy food and stuff. I'll apply for seasonal gigs at stores, like you said. I'll get something soon. But in the meantime, if you could just give me maybe, like, three hundred dollars, I just . . . I wouldn't ask if I didn't really, really need it, Bev. You know that.'

'I really wish I could, dude, but I just can't. I need to save every penny that I'm making for the baby. I can't help you out.'

The first expression that crossed Amy's face was terrible, as Bev had known it would be. *She feels sorry for me,* Bev thought, *but not as sorry as I feel for her.*

'So you can't help me because of the baby? This is exactly what I knew would happen: you're choosing the baby over me, and it's not even born yet.'

'Are you hearing yourself? Of course I'm choosing the baby. It's my *baby*.'

'You're choosing Sally over me, too. You made a bargain with this person you barely know. You're in this situation because of Sally's money!'

'I'll pay back the money.' Bev said. 'When I'm ready to, I'll make money and then pay her back. She knows I will.'

'Bev, you are fucking nuts.'

'Well, thanks for being honest with me about your feelings, dude.'

Amy shook her head. 'I didn't mean it like that. I'm sorry, I'm not ... I'm really sorry. But I wouldn't be asking if I didn't really need your help. It's my last chance. I will pay you back! It won't affect the baby at all!'

'Look, I have to finish closing up.'

Amy still sat there, staring at Bev in the mirror, then at herself.

'So ... really, the answer is no?'

Bev just shook her head. 'You need to leave, Amy.'

So Amy left. After she walked out the door, she heard the lock turn behind her: Bev must have thought there was some chance she would come back to beg some more.

Amy had always thought she was too vain and selfish to seriously contemplate suicide, also too afraid of pain. She realized now that when she'd thought that, she hadn't understood how painful existence could get. It could get so painful, it turned out, that any other kind of pain began to seem preferable. She felt ridiculous thinking these goth-teenager thoughts, but they were real. Bev was right: she did need to leave – not just the store, but the city. Her life. Before anything else was taken from her or before she gave up anything else. Whichever was happening, she had to find a way to make it stop.

40

To her credit, Amy's mom hadn't said anything too underminery when Amy had called from the BoltBus (not the nice bus) and informed her that she and a heavily sedated Waffles were en route and would soon arrive at the small split-level house where Amy had grown up. Amy's mother hadn't even asked how long they would be staying or what had happened. She just said, 'You're bringing the cat, mmm,' not even making it into a question.

The bus ride had been fine until the third hour, when the recirculated air and its heavily disinfected smell had begun to make Amy feel sick. The bus was packed with college students coming home for Christmas. The flexible polyester cat carrier was sticking to her legs. She wished she had been able to afford the train. Well, she wished she had been able to afford not to leave New York.

But just as she started to feel that she wouldn't be able to survive another minute on the bus ride, it was over, and she was walking from the Takoma Park Metro station toward her parents' house, cat carrier slung over one shoulder and LeSportsac duffel over the other and a backpack with her laptop in it on her back. These bags and their contents were all her remaining possessions in the world. She opened the front door with a key her parents kept in an obviously fake rock and walked into the empty house; it would be a few hours before her parents got home from work. She felt as if she were coming home from high school. She unzipped the carrier and watched as her dazed cat sniffed and explored. Amy sniffed too, smelling the house's familiar smells of cedar shingle and eucalyptus potpourri from the downstairs bathroom. She felt incredibly tired, as though her body had been on high alert and now was systematically shutting its alarm systems down. After she fished an old bag of cat litter out of the basement mudroom and set up a makeshift litter box for Waffles, she dragged herself upstairs and lay down on the carpeted floor of her childhood bedroom, now an office, and fell fast asleep.

When she woke, it was winter early-dark outside, and she could smell onions being sautéed downstairs. The horn fanfare announcing the beginning of *All Things Considered* floated up to her. Amy sat up and looked down at her limbs, almost surprised to find them adult size.

At dinner she was ravenous. Her parents treated her like an invalid and spared her the awkward questions she assumed they'd ask immediately. They talked about themselves: the problems her dad was having at work, the difficulty her mom was having in getting her grandmother to stop antagonizing the other women who wrote for the community newsletter of her assisted living facility. At ninety-three, Nana still insisted that she wasn't retired; she had missed her opportunity to have a journalism career in her youth, because she'd had to raise Amy's mom and her siblings, and now she was making up for lost time. Hearing her mom gently make fun of her own mom was hilarious, and Amy was shocked to hear herself laughing. Her life was a shambles, and she was supposed to be miserable, and her parents were supposed to be disappointed and guilt-tripping her, but somehow they didn't seem to realize this.

'We're happy you're here, sweetheart,' her dad said when he came into his office – converted now via foldout couch back into her bedroom – and kissed her good night on top of her head. She watched five episodes of *Arrested Development* on her laptop, Waffles purring alongside her. She began to feel bad again only when she'd closed the laptop and tried to sleep. She reached into her backpack for her phone and flicked her fingertip once, twice. Another flick could dial Bev, but she put the phone down. She might call tomorrow, or the day after, but first she had to figure out what to say.

41

For a moment, every morning as she was waking up, Sally still thought she was in Margaretville. With her eyes closed, it still felt as if she might climb out of bed, go down the creaking stairs to her sunny kitchen, and slide the bathroom door open to pee in the resounding old toilet – her own sounds the only human sounds, it had once seemed, in the world. Now, though, as soon as she opened her eyes, she sensed the thrumming life around her, and even at the very moment of waking, she was made aware, beyond a shadow of a doubt, that she lived in New York City.

Sally's new apartment was at the top of a glassy tower that overlooked the East River from Williamsburg's northern edge. The apartment was huge and slightly tacky and absolutely perfect. Jason had loaned her the down payment; he'd been very reasonable about the whole thing, so far, in part because he still didn't seem to quite believe that she was divorcing him. But soon he would: she had hired a wonderful lawyer, who'd assured her that more than half of what was Jason's and hers would soon be all hers. Jason hated confrontation and would do anything to avoid it. It could go badly, but for the moment everything was in abeyance, and she felt rich and free.

She imagined all her hundreds of neighbors waking up too, cells in a hive thrumming with activity. All those neighbors were making coffee, ripping open the plastic on their bags of dry cleaning, plugging in their flat irons to style their hair. She imagined that she could smell their coffee, their warm, freshly straightened hair, their breakfast smoothies, the expensive, understated perfume they sprayed on their wrists. 'A lot of women live by themselves in this building,' the broker had said. 'I think because the neighborhood's so safe and the commute's so easy, it attracts professionals. That, and the gym.' It was just what Sally wanted, what she'd been owed.

Compared with the Margaretville house and all its details – all Jason's details – her new place had no character. There were no soft nooks, no centuries-old polished doorknobs, no wainscoting or paneling or original wallpaper faded just the perfect amount. Sally had bought all-white furniture at West Elm. She had just pointed at the living room display, said 'that whole set, and the table,' and told the salesperson where to have it delivered. She didn't often feel inclined to sit on those pristine couches, or linger at the kitchen counter over coffee. She didn't procrastinate for hours by wandering from room to room readjusting picture frames that had slid slightly out of alignment. She didn't even make coffee at home anymore, actually. She just laced her sneakers and went for a run along the waterfront, all the way to DUMBO, aiming to arrive just in time to meet up with Bev as her pre-natal yoga class was getting out.

This morning, Sally ran toward Bev with the wind at her back, loping gently past commuters in their sleek jeans and heels, past the wobbly herds of little Hasidic kids shepherded to their bus stops by chattering mothers. Sally smiled and nodded at them, and sometimes they were befuddled enough by her attention to smile back, though mostly they ignored her. She felt benevolent toward everyone, especially mothers.

Thanks to Bev's ingenuity – well, her neediness, but also her generosity – Sally had found a way to be a mother without being one, a privilege few people got. Well, some lesbians. It was as if she were going to be a dad. A divorced dad.

They had met up recently to hash out the details of their arrangement. Sally sat on Bev's couch in the windowless common area of her apartment, and while they talked, a roommate had walked through to the bathroom and then stayed there for a weirdly long time. Bev had offered her tea, which they drank out of stained mugs. Sally could, if she wanted – if she was interested – help take care of the child, babysitting while Bev worked and even some weekends, and could also help with stuff Bev couldn't afford. What if she wanted to help Bev more? Sally had asked. Bev frowned and said she would think about it. She wasn't sure she wanted help that came with strings of any kind. She suggested that it would be good for Sally to think about what she was really prepared to offer and what she really wanted in return.

And Sally had been thinking about it. She'd had time to

think since then, though not the kind of endless, unlimited time she once had, because now she had a job. She worked behind the cash register of a bookstore where she'd once browsed aimlessly, feeling jealous of the authors whose books' spines she had fondled. Now she didn't have time to feel jealous. During the workday, at least, she didn't have time to think about anything abstract or non-immediate. There were always people talking to her, people who needed or wanted something, coworkers or customers or her boss. Of course she was still jealous sometimes, during readings or afterward as she stood next to the signing table and flipped books open to the first title page so that the author could sign them as quickly as possible. But this new jealousy was more concrete and could be transmuted into action, and it was also finite, grounded in reality, the reality of the numbers she saw in the computer when she did orders and inventory; she knew how many of the pretty new hardcovers sold and how many got shipped back to their publishers.

It was really only on these long jogs that she had time to think about the terms of her life, and she had discovered a capacity for generosity and okayness in herself. She didn't need to be the subject of a reverent profile in a magazine. She didn't need to be in *Paper* or *New York*, and she definitely didn't need to be in *Plum*, the magazine for older mothers. She would be Bev's baby's fun Aunt Sally, the one who took the baby to museums and plays; Aunt Sally whom you had to send thank-you notes to because she paid for summer camp or ballet or indoor soccer. 'But why?' Bev had asked her on the day they sat in her dim, depressing living room, the strange, dry heat from the radiator tinged with a gross breath of damp from her roommate's lengthy shower. 'I mean, we still barely know each other. We might as well be strangers.'

'But we're not,' Sally had said. 'We're not strangers. Now we're friends.'

42

The room was giant, gilt and dark wood, the furniture upholstered in a tiny leopard print trimmed in red. A small brunette about Amy's age arrived with tea in cups whose edges you wanted to bite and crack, they were so thin. The interviewer smiled at Amy over the rim of her cup. She was wearing a red St. John Knits suit that matched the furniture trim, and a big, thick golden necklace, like a piece of armor protecting her clavicles. Her hair didn't move. She set down her teacup with one decisive sweep of her arm, without regard for its delicateness, but of course it didn't break.

'So, Amy! Your dad says you're interested in working in advertising. Can you tell me a little bit more about what you'd like to be doing?'

Amy tried to keep her eyes focused on the interviewer's unwavering blue ones, but she couldn't help but dart her gaze around the room as the sunlight caught different golden objects and set off gleaming flares. She wasn't sure whether she was supposed to actually drink the tea.

'Well, I don't know how much my dad told you about my background, but even though most of my work experience is editorial, I've mostly worked online, in social media, so I thought that might be useful.'

'But what is it that you want to accomplish, Amy? I'm not really concerned with what you could do for us. I'm sure you could do whatever we'd ask. But in order to know if you're a good fit, I need to know more about your personal goals.' The interviewer smiled and took a deep sip.

'I was hoping to find a way to put my expertise in action in a way that could help unite consumers with the brands that are the best fit for their needs,' Amy said, as sincerely as it was possible to say something like this.

The interviewer put her teacup down and laughed. 'Oh, sweetheart, cut the crap, pardon my French. You're here because you're thirty and you just realized you actually care about making money.'

Amy could feel her face shifting through several expressions in rapid succession, trying to find one that wasn't outright offensive. 'Um. I guess I thought that went without saying.'

The interviewer cackled. 'Honey, I was just like you. I lived my twenties in New York City, thought I'd be a little Joanie Didion, packing my suitcase for reporting jobs with a leotard and a bottle of bourbon and two pairs of nylons or whatever. Typing away at my novel on my lunch hour and working as a secretary at an ad agency. Lucky for me, I moved up at the ad agency, because it wasn't a very good novel. Now I own the agency. Do you know what's glamorous about living in New York City and having no money?'

'Um. I guess there's—'

'After you're thirty, exactly nothing. A girl like you needs either a rich husband or a great job, and I don't see a ring on your finger.'

'I don't think I would even be good at having a rich husband,' Amy hazarded.

'Better to be in charge of a bunch of other women's rich husbands, in my experience. Now, the social media thing... I don't think that's how we position you. You'll just get stuck working your way up the rungs of creative alongside a bunch of twenty-two-year-olds. You'll find it degrading and get discouraged. Do you think you have management potential? It says on your résumé you ran an editorial team at your last job.'

Amy thought of Lizzie and Jackie, whom she'd managed for about ten minutes a day by Gchatting them, begging them to do their godforsaken jobs. 'Absolutely, I think so.'

'Great. I'll set up some interviews. Get a better suit, please, and some real shoes. Nothing edgy.'

Amy looked down at the shoes she'd found in her childhood bedroom closet. She'd worn them to the homecoming dance junior year. 'Okay. Wow. Um, thank you so much.'

'Aw, it's nothing. I owe your dad a favor, and I like helping gals like you. I should warn you, though, you can't half-ass this. If you're going to do it, do it one hundred percent. No typing in the Starbucks across the street when you should be at lunch with clients. No secret blog about how ridiculous your clients are. No writing of any kind, except memos and emails and presentations, from here on out. That's the bargain.' The interviewer drained the last of her teacup, and the brunette appeared from thin air to take it away. Amy held on to her full cup helplessly, not wanting to seem ungrateful and not knowing how to signal that she didn't want it. The secretary saved her, though, grabbing it from her hand and leaving the room as quickly as she'd come.

'Can I think about it?' Amy heard herself saying.

'No,' said the interviewer, smiling. 'If you have to think about it, then I know you're not cut out for it.' She stood and held out her hand to Amy, who also stood and tried to impress the woman with the firmness of her handshake, though there was no point in doing so now.

Amy's mom picked her up from the interview, and they drove away from the Georgetown town house via traffic-clogged Wisconsin Avenue. Amy watched the commuters in other cars, sipping coffee, inured to the gridlock, probably listening to NPR. Amy and her mom drove in silence, in traffic that flowed smoothly in the unpopular direction.

For the first time in a while, Amy had a flash of what it had been like to drive, for those few learner's-permitted months as a fifteen-year-old before she'd failed the test for the third time and given up completely on the idea of being a driver. 'Some people just aren't meant to drive,' she'd told various people in various situations over the years when called upon to explain herself. 'And a lot of them are on the road anyway,' the person usually said, and if the person didn't, Amy would sometimes say it herself. 'I'm doing everyone a favor, really.'

What exactly was it about driving that was beyond her? At

fifteen she'd thought it was mechanical, that she actually lacked the reflexes and the layers of attention necessary to be aware of shifting speeds and angles of her own vehicle and the vehicles around it; this had seemed like a very small, very specific form of mental retardation. But now she realized that everyone felt that way about driving at first, until they got used to it. Her fear of driving (because that was what it was, not incapacity: *fear*) stemmed from a feeling of being somehow responsible not just for her own car and its actions but for the car and actions of everyone on the road. This was manageable on a two-lane neighborhood side street or a country road, difficult on a three-lane highway, and nigh impossible on the six-lane permanently clogged Beltway where the driving instructor had taken her during her second driving lesson of all time. Signaling, checking her blind spot, getting over into the next lane, then the next, then the next lane to exit – how could she do that, all while simultaneously willing the cars behind her to let her in and to avoid suddenly speeding up and crashing into her? It was too much. She had stayed on the Beltway until traffic thinned, then exited with a heart-stoppingly dramatic swerve at the final possible second. Her instructor had been pretty inured to nearly dying at the hands of phobic fifteen-year-olds, and he hid the tremor in his hands almost completely as they slowly drove back to Amy's house through the backstreets of suburban neighborhoods, coming to a complete stop at every single stop sign.

Fifteen years had passed, but to be fair, Amy had spent ten of them in New York City, pretty much the last city in America where relying entirely on public transportation didn't automatically mean that you were poor. But now she was exiled, at least temporarily, and it was probably time to learn to drive for real. Just the thought of going to the MVA filled her with white-hot dread. She thought of how differently the interview might have gone if she'd arrived for it under her own steam instead of being dropped off like a child by a mother who'd gone and gotten them both Starbucks lattes before coming back to pick her up. Possibly not all that differently, but who knew?

Learning to drive would mean admitting that she was living in Maryland for a while, and maybe that was part of why she didn't know how to do it. Not knowing how to drive was a way of binding herself to New York. But it was a sad kind of bind, less like a pact and more like a trap.

Amy's mother had to go to work, so she dropped Amy off at the Kiss and Ride with a reassuring smile and a hand pat. Amy had a choice now: another informational interview, this one at an M Street law firm for paralegal work she wasn't even slightly qualified for – a friend of her mother's this time. Or, by taking the red line two stops in the other direction, she could go back to her bedroom, where she could eat whatever was in the fridge and watch bad TV and check her email for any signs of hope. Both options were depressing, and for a bleak moment Amy just stood staring into the maw of the Metro, borne along toward the turnstiles by the commuter tide.

She felt the bleak tally of all her losses pile up in the center of her chest and seep out toward her extremities, a physical pain that was inescapable for a moment and so horrible that it left her breathless. Again she thought of what it would mean to harm herself. An infinite eternity or probably more like thirty seconds later, the pain ended by itself, leaving only a lingering ache in some undefinable part of her (her soul?) as she slipped her flimsy paper card into the machine, taking care to replace it in an outer pocket of her bag so that she'd be able to find it easily at the end of her journey; you swiped while entering *and* while exiting here, another dumb thing about D.C. that she would never get used to.

Amy got off the Metro at Takoma Park, but instead of going straight home to her laptop and a cold Tupperware bowl full of last night's leftovers, she decided to take the long way, past her old middle school and Takoma Park's meager little main street intersection. Maybe she would pick up a flyer from the yoga studio. The weather had turned spring-like, just slightly: sunny and cool. Someone somewhere was already cutting grass. A block later this smell was eclipsed by a muggy smell of industrial food, and Amy deduced its source: a piece of laminated paper taped up on the gate of the Unitarian church read SOUP KITCHEN TODAY. VOLUNTEERS ALWAYS NEEDED.

Without thinking too hard about it, Amy parted the gates and went inside.

The smell was stronger in the common room of the church, and it seemed to be coming from somewhere in the back. There was a small team of elderly ladies ferrying foldable furniture around the room like an army of ants, unfolding tables and chairs with brisk speed. Just watching them, Amy's sad laziness began to slip off her. They didn't look up from their tasks to acknowledge her presence until she announced herself.

'Oh, you're new. Are you from the CSA?' the elder of the two ladies said.

'No, I'm just ... I just saw the sign.'

'Okay. In that case, you don't have to fill out a form for your hours, you can just go straight back to the kitchen. Find Chrissie, she'll tell you what to do. Are those comfortable?' She was pointing down at Amy's sad taupe interview shoes.

'Um, no, not really.'

'Oh.' The old lady shrugged. 'Well, next time you'll wear comfortable shoes.'

Then she was in the kitchen, which was tiny and full of people, some of whom were obscured by a cloud of steam or maybe smoke coming from near the stove. A tall man with the look of someone who'd been in bands was reaching up to unlatch a window. Amy had never known this church existed; she'd walked past it hundreds of times in her life but never really thought about it at all. The windows in the kitchen looked a hundred years old, at least. The musician was having trouble. 'Maybe it's painted shut?' Amy volunteered.

A fiftyish woman with a nice figure and a long blond ponytail was the only one who noticed Amy. 'Oh, another one from the CSA? Okay, honey, I'll get your form for your hours later. We have a little crisis here.'

'I'm not from the CSA. I just ... sorry, up front they said to ask for Chrissie?'

'You see anyone else here who might be named Chrissie?'

Amy scanned the room. The musician had managed to open the window, and the smoke was beginning to dissipate. A broad-faced youngish woman with stick-straight hair and freckles, a woman who looked to be about her mother's age and was covered in tattoos, and the big blonde, who had that inimitable John Waters-movie Maryland accent.

'Nope?'

Chrissie smiled. 'Just get an apron and a cutting board. There's a box of onions over there to the left of . . . ugh, are those cold cuts? Just ignore those, those shouldn't be there. Anyway, they give us these onions – about one in three is okay. Cut them open and see, then cut the good ones into, I don't know, I guess little pieces?'

'Little like . . . chop them? Slice them? Dice them?'

But Chrissie's attention was already elsewhere.

For the rest of the afternoon Amy mostly listened to the banter of the more experienced soup kitchen volunteers. She tried to talk, too, but stopped after the first couple of times she tried to say something and was plainly ignored. She cut open a mountain of brown-hearted onions and produced a smaller mountain of chopped onions, and after that she sautéed them, per Chrissie's instructions. Her feet were on fire, if she stopped to think about it, but mostly she had no time to think about it. The smell that had almost gagged her when she first walked in – hot, greasy food, questionable fridge, unemptied garbage – was barely noticeable now; it was up in her nose and in her hair and all her clothes. The little window was the only ventilation in the room. When everyone was quiet and she thought there would be more of a chance that they'd listen to her, she asked whether they had to pass some kind of inspection to serve food. The musician smirked. 'It's a house of worship. We get an exemption. We could be slaughtering our own chickens for some Santería ritual back here.'

'It smells like a slaughterhouse already, so why not?' said the tattooed woman who tended the soup. They all laughed, and for a warm moment Amy felt accepted, but then they went right back to ignoring her.

Eventually it dawned on Amy that this coldness was only because so many people showed up and cooked and served, all of them initially high on their own virtue and the idea of themselves as the kind of people who came back to do this week after week, but then none of them ever did. So why bother to get to know them? And probably Amy was just another of these dilettante volunteers. She was thrilled when six o'clock rolled around and she was officially released from her obligation to be there any longer: the meal was complete, and serving would soon begin. Then one of the elderly table arrangers, whom she'd met when she first walked in, came back to the kitchen just as she was removing her apron and announced that they were short a serving volunteer. Amy heard herself saying she'd do it, and they handed her gloves and positioned her at the back of the long room of tables with a big aluminum tray of roasted chicken pieces in front of her. The tables were now full of people. Amy tried not to stare at them. She could smell them. They smelled much, much worse than the kitchen.

She used tongs to dole out the slippery chicken. The people she served were mostly men, some of them mean; they glared at Amy and didn't say thank you. Some were either so drunk or so tremulous from lack of booze that they seemed almost certain to drop their overloaded Styrofoam plates on their way back to the tables, but none of them did, or none that Amy saw. Some of them looked perfectly ordinary, just slightly more deeply suntanned than your average person typically was in March. But even when people had clean clothes and haircuts, their fingernails betrayed them. Every single person who came to get chicken from Amy had callused, filthy hands, nails like thick pieces of horn, and jet-black cuticles. Some of the women tried to conceal the dirt with nail polish applied over layers of caked-on grime, which was worse than just the dirt by itself. They reached out their hands toward Amy, and Amy looked at their hands and into their faces and tried not to flinch. A lot of people thanked her, sincerely and profusely. They came back for seconds, thirds, fourths, which was allowed, but only after everyone had been fed and only with a new Styrofoam plate each time.

On her way out, she asked one of the old ladies whether the soup kitchen happened every day, and she was disappointed to learn that it happened only once a week. She wanted to feel that way every day. She wondered if it counted as being good if you did the good thing for purely selfish reasons. Probably not, but who cared. What was important was what you did, not how you felt.

43

Bev didn't want to get too dressed up to meet with the dean; the point was to demand better financial aid as a condition of her return to the program, so she didn't want to look like she had any money. Flicking through her closet, she picked a dryer-fried tunic and black leggings, plus the pretty new clogs she'd bought with her employee discount at the boutique. The dean was a dude; there was almost no chance he'd register them as expensive. Pulling the tunic over her head and then down over her giant stomach was a task. Once again, standing in profile in the mirror and feeling alternating bouts of horror and wonder at what was happening to her, she marveled at her unwieldy body.

She was already running slightly late and would be later if she spent any more time staring at herself, so she finished dressing and bolted the rest of her coffee before hustling to the C train. She could still move fast. A meaningful throat-clearing was necessary to get a seat this time, but soon she had a nice, solid perch on the hard plastic. She planted her feet wide, like a man, and took out the folder of forms she had to review before the meeting. You had to look busy all the time on the train or people fucked with you, she'd discovered. Busybodies asked when you were due, religious old men blessed you – all kinds of strangers wanted to touch you. But she had gotten to the point where she could shut it down with a cold stare. Already, motherhood had sharpened her defenses.

The dean's office was in the university's renovated Thirteenth Street building, where everything was so new that it smelled like paint and wet concrete. As she was no longer a student, the front desk guard made her stand there while he scrutinized her driver's license, called up to the dean, then issued her a sticker that gave her access. It hardly seemed like New York City's third-best private university would be number one on any terrorist's to-do list, but she supposed she was happy for the guards that they had jobs.

It was midsemester, and no one else was waiting to see the dean. He ushered her straight into his office, a small, unwindowed space that he'd tried to render cozy via a desk lamp and a wall of African masks. He hadn't unpacked his books yet, and the empty shelves behind his desk made him seem more like what he was: a middle manager for a smallish corporation, to whom Bev was something between an employee and a liability.

The dean steepled his hands and smiled. She smiled back from her chair on the opposite side of the desk and waited for him to speak. He was her father's age and wore little round glasses. She could see his gaze darting down to her stomach and then correcting itself, zooming back up to the safe zone above her collarbones. Finally, no one had spoken for so long that she began to want to put him out of his misery.

'So I want to come back next semester and complete my master's, but my financial situation makes it really difficult for me to do so. I was out of school for long enough that I started having to pay the interest on my loans. I am really committed to finishing my degree, and I hope I've been a worthwhile addition to the program here. I have some letters here from my teachers . . . they're all very eager to have me back in class. I've applied for a teaching fellowship and all the available scholarships, but even if I got them all, I'd still be taking out loans for the remaining seventeen thousand. And the stipend the fellowship provides is less than I make at my retail job, so it doesn't make a lot of sense for me to take hours away from that job to do a lower-paying one . . . I'm sorry if this is rude, but I'm wondering how anyone does this. And I'm hoping you can help me. I mean, like I said, I do want to finish.'

The dean chose his words carefully. 'We also want that for you. You're a great asset to the program. But we're not . . . in a position of being able to offer additional financial aid at this point. The university in general has not chosen to make that a priority.'

'I know. They've decided to knock down giant buildings and build new ones instead. I bet you wish the money that went into designing this fancy building was in your paycheck instead – no offense.' She felt reckless and powerful, physically big and with nothing to lose. She could say whatever she wanted.

'None taken. I don't . . . Beverly, you understand that I'm just speaking theoretically here, right?'

'Um, sure.'

The little round glasses seemed not to have a nosepiece; they were perpetually in danger of slipping down the dean's nose.

'Well, I am a great fan of our program, of course, and feel that it is among the finest of its kind. But it's hardly the only one. In fact, there are several M.F.A. programs in creative writing that give full scholarships to every student they admit. Maybe you should consider applying to one of them.'

'But none of the work I've done here would transfer. None of the credits, I mean. I'd have to start over from the beginning.'

'Well, that's true.'

'And none of those programs are in New York City, which is where I live. Where my life is. Where all my friends live.' Bev suddenly thought of Amy, whom she hadn't heard from since the day Amy asked for money. Bev had heard a rumor from a mutual friend that Amy really did move back in with her parents.

'It's two years.' The dean pressed his hands together and slowly moved them from side to side, a gesture almost of wiping them clean.

'And would you recommend me, personally? You'd write me a letter of recommendation?'

He looked up at the corner of the room then, and Bev had the bizarre thought that he feared that the room was bugged. Maybe the room *was* bugged. He lowered his voice significantly. 'I would feel like it was the least I could do. I think what we're doing here is just as disgusting as you think it is – bilking kids who dream of being writers out of tens of thousands of dollars, with only the vague promise that they might be able to get jobs as writing instructors at the end of it. I mean, for rich kids it's one thing. But with someone like you, it's obscene.' He straightened up again. 'Speaking theoretically, that is.'

'I wish you'd mentioned that when I was first admitted.'

He shrugged. 'Would you have listened?'

'I'm listening now.'

44

Amy had found a job working at the Ben & Jerry's in Georgetown, a job she would have considered beneath her in high school. She was hired as a manager, thanks to a recommendation from Chrissie at the soup kitchen, who'd lied when they called to check her references and said she'd been supervising meal preparation there for years. She had far more responsibilities at Ben & Jerry's than she'd had at Yidster, a shocking number of which involved math. That was heinous, but other aspects of the job were almost fun, such as how the mostly teenage employees actually seemed, to some extent, to respect her. Maybe it was just that she was older than they were, but for whatever reason, they didn't sass her and seemed scared enough of her not to try to get away with bullshit sick days or clocking out early. She was nice to them, but not too nice. One of them, Alicia, was pregnant, and every time Amy saw her, she was uncomfortably reminded of Bev. But Bev wasn't pregnant anymore: she'd had her baby. Sally had called Amy during Bev's labor, but Amy had avoided answering her phone. After that, calling Bev had become progressively less possible with each passing day, until it ceased to be thinkable at all.

At first she thought she'd live with her parents and save money until she could afford to move back to New York, but as her paychecks accumulated and her debt began to slowly subside, she began to think that she might as well accept that she was living in the D.C. area and try to have an actual life there, which entailed finding a place on her own. Looking for apartments was at least not as harrowing as it was in New York. She just went to the rental office of one of the high-rises in downtown Silver Spring after comparing prices and amenities online, and she filled out an application, listing her job as 'manager, food service,' her salary, and her mother as her most recent landlord. Her application was accepted that same day, and she moved into a studio the following afternoon with help from her dad and Mike F. from the soup kitchen, who helped carry the futon she was borrowing from her parents' basement until she could afford to buy an Ikea bed of her own. She hadn't made the payments on the storage locker where her New York furniture was languishing, and she suspected it had all been thrown out or sold; it was mostly worn-out anyway. There had been a painting of Sam's in there, and she hoped that whoever bought it, probably for a discount price, was aware of the deal they'd gotten.

There wasn't a lot to unpack; too soon, she was done pulling her clothes from the suitcase, hanging them in the little closet, and figuring out where to put her folding chair in relation to the card table, where she figured she'd watch TV on her laptop. There was a view of what could charitably be called the Silver Spring skyline from floor-to-ceiling windows on one side, and she positioned the chair so that she could stare out toward the Metro station across the street below and watch the trains come and go. She thought about the first night she'd spent in her lovely brownstone apartment, how Bev had intuited that she'd been feeling lonely and had come over with sushi and wine. She couldn't even stand to think about how much she missed Bev. She would kill for some sushi, too.

She had just counted the fifteenth train when she heard a slow, strange creak, then a deafening crash.

The futon frame she'd assembled somewhat hastily, without consulting the instructions, had collapsed, sending nuts and bolts and shards of plywood flying. Amy sighed and resigned herself to spending the next few hours figuring out what had gone wrong, but as she went to turn the frame over and figure out how to fix it, she saw something that made her blood run cold: a tabby-striped tail sticking out from underneath the frame at an awkward angle.

She screamed, of course, then realized that the walls were thin in her cheap building and that this was not the way she wanted to meet her neighbors, and she limited herself to cursing loudly. 'Fucking, fuck, fuck, *fuck*! *Shit! Augh!*' Had she squashed Waffles? She could not, would not deal with the aftermath if she had. Except, what if he was still alive and just horribly maimed and in pain, or even possibly could be saved? She tried to make herself calm down. 'Waffles? Buddy?' she called tentatively, approaching the edge of the futon. She heard a muffled meow.

Waffles, the last remaining thing she valued from her old life – and, more important, her companion, her last loyal friend. She could not be responsible for his death. Steeling herself to face the worst, she reached under the collapsed frame and touched soft fur. 'It's gonna be okay, buddy,' she made herself say, even though she was crying, silent tears coursing down her face.

She felt him wriggle under her hand, and then he seemed to suddenly get free from whatever had trapped him. Waffles bolted out from under the frame and ran into the bathroom. Amy ran into the bathroom too, to find a seemingly undamaged Waffles sitting on the tile, tail fluffed up to full alarm position and licking himself violently but otherwise apparently unscathed.

'Um, you're kidding. You're fine, really?'

Waffles looked up at her, seeming slightly annoyed by her presence. He lowered his face to his groin and licked the base of his bristling tail.

'No internal bleeding? If you die later because I didn't take you to the vet now, I'm going to be annoyed,' she told him, hearing the tremble in her voice. She was talking to her cat. Well, who even cared. She bent to pet him and inspect him for obvious injury, which he grudgingly allowed her to do. 'Oh, Waffles. I'm so sorry, Waffles.'

She sat there petting him for a long time, then went back to her laptop, where she started writing Bev an email.

45

In order to start writing, Amy had to imagine Bev reading her email. She held an image of Bev in her mind, but it was hard to figure out what Bev could be doing in this fantasy. Okay: she thought of Bev balancing the sleeping baby on her hip as she sat in front of her computer. The details of the baby were vague. All babies look similar anyway, she figured, features indistinct, not yet shaped or warped by the experiences that create personality. Maybe it's been a long day and Bev is just getting home from work, having picked the baby up at Sally's, and the baby's asleep and now she's in her silent apartment, feeling tired and satisfied but lonely. Amy tried to imagine Bev feeling happy to receive an email from her. Finally the image was vivid enough, and she could begin.

Dear Bev,

I wish I had been there for the birth. I didn't think you would want me there. But now I feel like I should have come regardless. So, sorry about that, and about everything else.

I want to say that I always imagined that I would be at your side for the birth of your children, but that would be a lie: I never imagined that you would have a child. I must have thought we would always stay essentially the same as we were when we met. I didn't imagine any other futures might be possible for us. Well, that's a lie too. I imagined all kinds of possibilities for myself, but I didn't do the same for you. And those rosy futures I imagined for myself were bullshit, anyway, which should have been obvious, because I did know that I wasn't doing anything to make them real. And I was counting on you to be the same way, which was what made it so hard when it turned out you were going to be a mother. You were right: I was jealous! And I feel horrible about feeling jealous, especially because I know it wasn't easy, and at first at least it wasn't what you wanted. That part was hard to understand. I thought I was just trying to help you realize what was best for you. That was bullshit, too, though: the whole time, I was only thinking about what was best for me.

I think about you all the time, and I want to call you. There's all this little stuff that happens that I think you would be the only person to appreciate, and I don't know what to do with those thoughts, those jokes, those feelings. I should write them down, I guess. In case we ever become friends again, I can hand you a notebook with every stupid joke I thought of during the time when we were apart. But it's hard to imagine us being together. I worry that even if you can forgive me for abandoning you when you most needed a best friend, I won't be able to fit into your new life.

On the day that your baby was born, Sally called me and left a message, asking if I wanted to be there for the birth. I was really grateful to her for doing that. But I didn't know whether you'd want me there, even though she seemed to think that maybe you would. I didn't want to risk making something that was already going to be hard for you even harder. Then she called me later to say that there were complications and that they were moving you to the hospital instead of letting you have the baby at home, and she sounded so scared. Until right then it had never occurred to me that anything bad could happen to you or the baby. This sounds deranged, but I'm just going to tell you: in that moment I thought that if you died, or if the baby died, it would be my fault. I know that makes no sense. I don't mean my fault for not talking you out of the pregnancy, I mean my fault for not being there, not spending every second willing everything to be okay, as if, if I'd been in the same room as you, I could have protected you just via how much I cared.

The reason I didn't get in touch sooner is that I was so ashamed of myself for not being there in that moment, and I was scared of how it would feel if you picked up the phone and sounded disappointed to hear my voice. Which in and of itself is selfish. I'm going to stop making excuses. I'm sorry.

She looked at what she'd written, hated it, and decided to hit 'send' anyway. Then she went back into the bathroom and petted Waffles some more. She almost didn't hear her phone when it made its tinny text sound.

It was Bev. 'YT?' the text said. It meant, of course, 'You there?' But they usually used it to see whether the other person was on Gchat. Amy's heart leaped, then sank as she worried that Bev hadn't intended the text – had sent it accidentally or to someone else. But she wrote back anyway: 'Yes!!!!'

'Hi.'

The message was intended for her; somehow, she knew.

Amy wrote back: 'Hi. :'('

There was a pause. Those three horrible dots. But they disappeared, and then in their place there was a '<3.'

'<3' Amy replied.

Acknowledgments

Thank you to Keith Gessen, whose all-encompassing support made the writing of this book possible, and to Ruth Curry for being not only my best friend but the best friend possible. Thanks to Writing Club (Bennett Madison, Anya Yurchyshyn, and Lukas Volger) for help, encouragement, and cheese. Thanks to Cookbook Club (Sadie Stein, Lukas Volger, and Ruth Curry) for emotional and physical nourishment. Thanks to Book Club (Nozlee Samadzadeh, Zan Romanoff, Logan Sachon, and Miranda Popkey) for befriending me, and for introducing me to Miranda. Thanks to Miranda also for her dogged, sensitive, and brilliant editing.

I worked on this book in a lot of different friends' and relatives' and even some strangers' homes. Thanks to Rachel Cox and Greg McKenna, Sarah Cox, and Jennifer Kabat; also, apologies for stealing various aspects of your decor and putting them in this book. Thanks to Sari Botton for her extensive yenta-ing and her expertise in all things Rosendale.

Thanks also to the Gessen family – Alexander, Tatiana, Philip, Daniel, and Pushkin – for many writing residencies.

Thanks to bosses and mentors past and present: Will Schwalbe, Choire Sicha, Alex Balk, Alison West, Deborah Wolk, David Jacobs, and Natalie Podrazik. Thanks to everyone at the Greenpoint Reformed Church Soup Kitchen and Food Pantry, especially Christine Zounek, whose spirit lives on. Huge thanks to our cherished Emily Books customers and subscribers. Your enthusiasm for offbeat books by women and other weirdos makes me feel hopeful about the future of reading, writing, and publishing.

Thanks to everyone at FSG, especially publicity guru Gregory Wazowicz and genius copy editor Maxine Bartow. Thank you, beautiful and brilliant Mel Flashman, and everyone at Trident Media Group, especially Sarah Bush, Sylvie Rosokoff, and Michael Ferrante. And thank you, Rowan Cope at Virago/Little, Brown UK.

I could not have written this or any book without the love and support of my parents, Rob and Kate Gould; my brother, Ben Gould; and the rest of the Deshler-Gould clan, especially my grandparents Walter and Ila Deshler and my grandmother Doris Gould. I love you all very much.

Shout-out to Raffles (RIP): You were a great cat.

virago

To buy any of our books and to find out more about Virago Press and Virago Modern Classics, our authors and titles, as well as events and book club forum, visit our websites

www.virago.co.uk
www.littlebrown.co.uk

and follow us on Twitter

@ViragoBooks

To order any Virago titles p & p free in the UK, please contact our mail order supplier on:

+ 44 (0)1832 737525

Customers not based in the UK should contact the same number for appropriate postage and packing costs.